LIFE CLASSES

Life Classes

Susan Sebastian

First published in 1998 by
HEADLINE BOOK PUBLISHING

A HEADLINE LIAISON paperback

10 9 8 7 6 5 4 3 2 1

ISBN 0 7472 5813 9

Typeset by Avon Dataset Ltd, Bidford-on-Avon, Warks

Printed and bound in Great Britain by
Mackays of Chatham plc, Chatham, Kent

HEADLINE BOOK PUBLISHING
A division of Hodder Headline PLC
338 Euston Road
London NW1 3BH

Life Classes

One

Amy Harrison fumed at the traffic, though it was really with her lover, Reuben, she was angry. With an effort, she dismissed the beguiling face that came into her mind. As in life, Reuben's smile threatened to deflect her anger. Sometimes, when she argued with him, she had to turn away so as not to be seduced into kissing him. Damn the man! Amy forced the clutch down hard to prevent the car from stalling. She had not wanted him to leave. But he had gone, nevertheless, and by now his plane was heading for Italy. And here she was, stuck in the Saturday morning traffic.

Why had she agreed to drive him to the airport? Her annoyance now included herself too. She really hadn't wanted him to take this year's course in Italy. Far from it. For weeks she had been dreading his departure. Yet here she was, likely to be late for her first art class, having actually been coaxed into taking him to Stansted. And why had he missed the early morning train he had planned to catch? Because they had made love. Amy's body surged as she recalled his arousing touch, his hands on her breasts, the feel of him inside her. She squirmed on her seat. Their passionate love-making had only served to make her more aroused. They made love often – usually several times a day, and now she had no easy fulfilment to look forward to later. Amy knew that her driving was erratic because of her preoccupation. She told herself it would be sensible to stop, have a coffee – and, yes, she deserved it – a cigarette. Her anger abated a little as she took the opportunity to turn off. She decided that it would be better to get home in time to shower before the class, rather than break her journey.

It hadn't been very sensible to make love this morning, she thought crossly, attempting unsuccessfully to repress her lascivious memories. But then Reuben never was sensible, and Amy could never resist him. He was very sensual, and an excellent lover. However, this last session had only served to remind Amy what she would be missing. At the airport, Reuben had cheerily kissed her goodbye, and assured her that he would not mind what she did whilst he was away. That gave him carte-blanche to pursue his own desires, no doubt! Who was he to give her permission as if he owned her? By now, Amy's feeling of pure rage had been dissipated into a more complex distillation of passion, loneliness and arousal. Thinking of Reuben always aroused Amy, but then, she grinned dirtily to herself, her sexuality was easily stimulated. That was how Reuben got round her, she thought, slamming on the accelerator. He was aware of how attracted she was to him, and that she could not resist his physical presence. Again came the mixture of irritation and attraction.

Well, now she would be able to resist him, wouldn't she? She would have to manage without him, and his expert caresses. Her body seethed in longing for his intimate touch. He would be in Italy for a whole year, studying Art History. Her anger, and the prospect of physical deprivation spiked at Amy once more. Then, with pride, she suppressed thoughts of Reuben. He had said, in a reasonable tone (Reuben was always reasonable when it suited him), that she could easily visit him in Florence, Venice or Rome. But the mere thought of Reuben having a wonderful time in these magical Italian cities while she was facing an English winter enraged her even more. A tiny voice inside reminded her that she did not have to stay; she could leave her assistant in charge of her boutique. However, though this was possible, Amy preferred to be in charge of things – both in her work, and in her private life. That applied also to the way she tried to control the people she knew, and it was frustrating not to be justified in talking Reuben out of going to Italy. It was a wonderful opportunity and she knew he could scarcely give up his future to stay at home and satisfy his voracious lover. Though that idea seemed attractive to Amy right now. She narrowed her green eyes devilishly.

Then, getting weary of arguing with herself, she told herself she was a free agent and today was a new start. She was going to art classes – Life Classes. She quickly repressed the thought that her choice of course had anything to do with Reuben's art course, and that one element of it was a study week in Florence. She had always been interested in art. In fact, she had met Reuben at an exhibition at the Royal Academy. Amy smiled at the memory. They had both been standing for a long time in front of a painting by Poussin. Amy had been engrossed, but, as she turned to leave, she had become aware of the young man beside her. By now, Reuben was also regarding her with interest. They had begun to talk of Poussin, arguing on moot points as if they were old friends. Then they had withdrawn from the picture to let others in. Sitting on the nearby seats, they had begun to talk about themselves. Amy had immediately liked this handsome young man, with his red-gold curls, and laughing dark brown eyes. The attraction had been mutual. Always sure of her physical response to certain men, Amy knew that they would sleep together. She had soon made up her mind what she wanted. They had had lunch in the restaurant downstairs, and then they had walked through London to the National Gallery. After spending the evening in a pub, they had ended up at his flat, making love. Amy's body was restless in memory of this first wild passion. Their chance meeting had given her a perfect partner: a man as indefatigable and energetic as she and the relationship had remained passionate. Now he had left her, Amy felt bereft.

As yet another memory of their frenzied love-making infiltrated her overheated brain, she was filled with a surge of jealousy at exactly what Reuben would get up to in Italy with all those sultry Italian women – not to mention the liberated Art History students. She was convinced they would find his unusual combination of golden hair and dark eyes as irresistible as she did. Not to mention his lithe, muscular body, and his charming smile . . .

3

Amy squeezed her thighs together, stimulating her sex as her body pined for her lover. She pictured him, lying naked on her bed, his thick, easily-erect penis lazily in his hand as he eyed her seductively. Amy suppressed a surge of sexual longing. This was crazy. Her vagina throbbed spasmodically now, and her breasts swelled, ready for his touch. Anger flared again at Reuben leaving her like this. Then, she tried to be rational. They had made love. He had brought her – as usual – gloriously to orgasm. Several times. He had had to leave. He would be back in a year. In the meantime, she would visit him in Italy. And in the meantime, they were each free to do as they wished. That made sense – neither of them were likely to do without sex for a whole year. Such freedom could be fun. And Amy had never had difficulty finding lovers . . . She was a determined and liberated young woman. She usually achieved what she desired. Reuben may have been a match for her, but now she would have to find another! However, her green eyes flamed and her long auburn hair flew as she got out of the car, and slammed shut the door.

Amy entered her small terraced cottage. There was always the art class. She was filled with sudden laughter. It would probably be filled with elderly artists *manqué*, middle-aged queens, and adolescents. She stripped off her clothes and underwear, still filled with dynamic energy, and wondered what this Jacob Laurence would be like. Old and married, probably. Somewhat calmed by her amusement, and beginning to think that she could continue to exist without Reuben, Amy prepared for the class.

Before showering, she lay on her bed. She thought of Reuben as she lay, idly fingering her enlarged clitoris and running her hand over her naked breasts. Her body still smelt of his spunk. The animal scent inflamed her lust. Hungry for some release as ever, Amy concentrated on her own body. Soon, her finger was between the warm folds of her vulva and then into her moist vagina. With her other hand she squeezed her breast. Her mind was fed with recent images of Reuben attending to her primal needs, and she longed for his hands to be on her, and his swollen member entering her – filling her. Thoughts of him, and what he did so expertly to her, released tendrils of delicious sensitivity, which came from her womb and filled her body with sensuality. Her muscular passage pulsated around her seeking fingers.

She turned onto her belly, and positioned her knuckles under her clitoris. She began to undulate her body against them, controlling the increased surge of sexuality which began to possess her. She imagined raising her bottom, so that Reuben could push his erect penis into her gaping vagina. She imagined him coming back suddenly, discovering her thus engaged, and, filled with lust, taking her roughly. Her body recalled the feel of his cock, sliding into her hole. She paused in her self-pleasuring as the first waves of her orgasm spread through her body, throbbing and burning, then she began to stimulate herself again. As ever, this solo-sex merely served to raise her pitch of sexual awareness, and she sighed, knowing that her state would be discernible to any hot-blooded male she should happen to meet later. She imagined simply grabbing one, and getting him to satisfy her. She laughed at this idea. It was very appealing.

Jacob Laurence stood at the door of Louis' studio watching his friend paint. The piano strains of Debussy's *Images* filled the large room. He had really just popped down to tell Louis that he was leaving. But Louis was taken up with his painting and soon Jacob had also become engrossed. Louis had been up for most of the previous night, immersed in his work. At times like this the time flew, and Louis lost all sense of it. Louis' model, Sarah, was not there at present, and Louis was concentrating on painting the luscious folds of the brown velvet cloth she had been lying on. Jacob realised that Louis was completely unaware of his presence as, repeatedly and with great patience, he dipped his brush into the thick well of paint and lavished it on the canvas. Frequently, he glanced up at the drapery. It was as if he was taking its material form into his brain and then transferring it, via the paint he had mixed to its exact colour, onto the painted sofa.

Jacob smiled at the portrait of Sarah. Louis had posed her as Francois Boucher's *Mademoiselle O'Murphy*. And like Louis XIV's mistress, Sarah lay naked on her front with her rounded bottom exposed and her legs spread wide. Her right leg was raised, higher than the other, propped on cushions, whilst the knee of her left leg rested a little below the seat of the sofa, on its padded frame. Her upper body was also lifted, pressed against the soft ivory and pink satins and silks under her. This position urged her crotch against the gathered cloth beneath it. Her right arm was propped up on the high arm of the old settee, whilst the other elbow rested where the lower end of the arm joined the seat. Her fingers met, languidly, under her chin. Her left arm bent to achieve this. Thus her upper arm hid her breasts – just. Sarah's ample bosom was a little more exposed than Miss O'Murphy's. And, unlike the original model's tight coiffure, Sarah's silky brown hair hung loose against her neck, though it was tucked behind her ear so that Louis could paint her delicate profile.

The large painting was so life-like that Jacob's fingers itched to trace the warm-seeming flesh. He felt his body respond to Louis' representation of the young woman. This response was deepened by his knowledge of Sarah herself. She was warm and vibrant, sensual and friendly. He knew that there had been opportunities when he could have made love to her. Perhaps Sarah would have been glad of his warmth. But Jacob had thought that this would have seemed like sacrilege to Louis.

Like the original 'boudoir picture', painted in 1752, a copy of which was pinned to Louis' easel, this painting was extremely intimate and erotic. Sarah's figure was voluptuous, and her skin soft and supple. She lay on rumpled garments of deep cream and rose pink, which were raised under her breasts and arms. One corner of the cushion which supported her right leg was tucked under her pubis. The viewer was invited to imagine looking between those parted thighs, and at her full breasts. But Louis had actually looked, thought Jacob. The artist had given back what he had chosen, and withheld the rest in his memory. Sarah's pose was entirely lascivious. The viewer – now Jacob –

wanted to lay himself down, naked between her fleshy thighs and feel for her warm breasts, to urge his stiffened penis into the cleft between her buttocks. Jacob closed his eyes as this irrational surge of longing overcame him. He told himself that he was recalling the model herself. Sarah was very sexy. Not only was her generous body enticing, but her voice was husky, and her hazel eyes warm and imbued with sexual knowledge.

Jacob had to admit though that Louis had successfully conveyed all this. Her hair looked so real that he was tempted to reach out and tangle his fingers in its rich chestnut mass. The colours were wonderful, the warm brown-red of the velvets complemented the richness of her hair. The satins enhanced the warm hue of her skin. She was so lifelike, so warm and tempting that Jacob could imagine turning her over to expose her breasts. They would be full and creamy with red nipples.

The materials on which she lay, velvet, silk and satin were as sensual as her creamy flesh. The lush velvet of the settee, and the matching cloth on which the model rested her left foot, were what Louis now painted. He had almost finished the little stool on the floor, this a redder velvet, and the lighter brown-red of the carpet and wall. He had perfected the intricate polished wooden frame of the settee. But he had not yet finished the subtle lights of the warm skin tones, nor the rich brown of the hair which so enhanced the velvet. This portrait was a *tour de force*, a challenge for Louis, and Jacob knew only too well that he had spent very many hours over it. Louis still painted in a classical way, using oils. Many of his paintings harkened back to the Old Masters. Jacob himself liked this. Too many modern portraits were flat and empty: such was his personal opinion. And Louis had certainly found his market.

The portrait was very good. The painted woman looked just like Sarah, though more wanton than he, Jacob, had ever seen her. It was tantalising and full of sexual promise and because it was modern, and he knew the girl, it seemed even more accessible than 'Miss O'Murphy'. He wondered whether the decadent king used to lie in his chamber and fondle himself as he looked at the portrait of his lover. Perhaps he made her pose thus, so that he could satisfy himself with her, later to be aroused by the memory of taking her, as he gazed at her painting.

Jacob realised that his own prick was filled spontaneously with life. He would have to suppress this urge as he taught his new class. To be so easily aroused was a nuisance sometimes. He was not surprised to see Louis' dark eyes were heavy-lidded and lustful as he turned lazily towards Jacob, his sensual mouth a little parted. Jacob shook his head at his libidinous friend. Most of Louis' models succumbed – either to his rampant sensuality or because of a narcissistic awareness of his appreciation of them. The artist's scrutiny and the model's acquiescence was somehow more intimate, certainly more lasting, than making love. Jacob imagined Louis existing in a lascivious haze which enveloped his victims. Louis usually managed to suppress his libido until he had finished his painting. Quite an achievement. But then his art was vital to him, and, Jacob believed, his immersion in this was almost as enjoyable to him as sex itself. The sensuality of the portrait was a chemistry between Louis' fertile brain and the compliance of his liberal model. Louis recognised and drew out what was within her. It was a gift he had with all of his models, and very many, Jacob knew well, had been impressed by his ability and, because of this, had lain for him hour after hour – for days. Once, almost entirely for love of art, or Louis. Now the successful artist could afford to pay his models well.

Jacob tried to assess how near to completion the portrait was. He imagined having Sarah himself. Right now – that would be a relief! Sarah's sexuality was in her eyes and character as well as in her delicious body. He met Louis' eyes, expressing his appreciation, both of Louis' skill and of the model's qualities. He envied Louis the certainty of his sexual fulfilment. He had seen Sarah looking at Louis. There was no doubt she wanted him. Hours of lying naked in his presence whilst the artist stared avidly at her body, concentrating his skill on capturing her on canvas must arouse any woman. Especially when the artist was so attractive. Women seemed to find Louis, with his wild black curls and black eyes, extremely desirable. Probably, it was all that suppressed lust, thought Jacob. It was an enjoyable form of foreplay. He knew that Louis must realise how he was affected by this painting.

'So, is she coming for a final sitting – laying – tonight?' he asked Louis.

Louis' eyes expressed fleeting annoyance at Jacob's jocular tone.

'There's more than one session left,' he explained patiently.

Jacob lifted an eyebrow, suddenly wanting to laugh at his friend's intensity.

'I'll bet,' he commented flippantly, knowing that his attitude would rile Louis. However, he himself was subtly frustrated by his friend's skilful evocation of his licentious model. He was fretful at this inconvenient arousal. Louis' attention returned to his work. He was free to inhabit his sensual world. Jacob had to go and teach.

'See you later, Louis,' Jacob repeated from the door of his friend's studio.

He watched as Louis looked up from his painting and at Jacob. It seemed to take him several seconds to refocus. Then, he grinned.

'Ah, the Life Class?' he queried.

Jacob nodded, surprised that Louis actually knew that it was Saturday.

'I'll have to tell them about the trip. Give them time to think. You've had enough. Can I tell them there'll be a real live painter accompanying us?'

Louis shrugged and twisted his mouth in distaste.

'Florence, Louis,' Jacob reminded him.

'In January?' Louis grimaced.

'You know you'd go to Italy at any time.'

This was probably true, though Jacob had to admit that Louis would probably be happy to remain in his studio for most of the time. As long as he was provided with models, that was. And sex. Although, with a supreme effort of will, Louis was able to sublimate his sexuality to art for a long time, he was always very randy after completing a painting. As if making up for lost time, and thwarted desire whilst he painted, once he had completed a canvas, Louis spent perhaps weeks engaged in whatever sexual liaison came his way. Luckily for Louis, he seemed to have the ability to charm his patient subjects into having sex with him, as well as providing him with food and drink. That was if he allowed them to come near him at all. He could be arrogant and moody and Jacob was sure he himself wouldn't put up with his friend's vicissitudes. Though he had even caught his decadent friend regarding him speculatively, when particularly desperate. He had put him off with an imperative shake of his head. Still, he expected Louis would have another go, when temporarily devoid of a partner. Whore that he was.

'So – yes?' he insisted.

Louis shrugged dismissively, which Jacob took to mean an answer in the affirmative.

'Who's the model?' Louis asked as Jacob was leaving.

Jacob smiled. He asked with the intense interest of a vampire (and it was as such he laughingly described himself). Louis' sexuality seemed caught up in the pictures he loved as well as those he painted. Jacob decided that he would have to get his friend to accompany them on their trips to London galleries. At least then the students would be inspired by Louis' passion. And probably by Louis himself, Jacob thought ruefully. Louis was a brilliant painter. Of that there was no doubt. And that was what Jacob reminded himself of when Louis was annoyingly temperamental or demanding.

'Simon,' answered Jacob.

Louis nodded. Obviously he approved. Jacob smiled and shook his head as he left. Actually, Simon was a good model to begin with, and they would have him for two or three weeks. He was quite young and easy to get on with. None of the models were shy, but Simon seemed particularly unselfconscious, with a natural pride in his young, unblemished body. As he drove from his Victorian Villa in Dedham, Jacob recalled Louis' painting of Simon. It was very revealing. It now hung in the Lavenham Gallery. He laughed to himself as he wondered how Louis would have reacted had it been a new model today.

Someone he had not yet possessed on canvas. Or in bed. Would he have jealously insisted on coming along first, at least to look – make some sketches? Jacob shook his head at his incorrigible friend. He would need a new model soon. For a time, as he drove, he entertained a whimsical idea of supplying Louis with victims for his delight, rather than as models. In a way, he took their life from them. Though most of them were pleased with their representation on canvas.

He wondered what the class would be like this year. There were fifteen, though a few usually dropped out. He knew that Marie-Anne, who had attended last year, and Sam and Robbie, likewise, had signed up again, but the rest would be new to him. This trio was amusing and light-hearted, and would help break the ice. Jacob's approach nowadays was to give the students merely a brief introduction. Many of them had done some drawing anyway before embarking on a Life Class. It was a good idea to give them plenty of time to draw their first model. That way they would feel they had got over the first hurdle – those of them that were shy, anyway. It also gave him an opportunity to go round to each, individually, to assess their work and to talk to them. In ensuing lectures, he would introduce them to anatomy, technique and something of the history of nude painting, with accompanying slides. That was where the trip to Florence came in. There, they would have the opportunity of studying important Renaissance sculptures and paintings. This particular course was aimed at learning to draw in a classical way, with reference to famous works of art.

Amy relaxed a little under the shower, meaning to wash away all traces of Reuben as she slithered her palms all over her smooth body, but instead recalling him, and re-awakening her greedy body all too vividly. She smoothed the soap over her breasts and belly, enjoying the smooth feeling as she massaged roughly. Then she rubbed the foam over her back and buttocks, and between her legs. She turned round and round under the powerful jet. But its pounding on her body, and the recent memory of Reuben's masterful attentions merely served to turn

11

her on even more. Damn the man, Amy repeated, closing her eyes and resting against the tiled wall as she took her swollen clitoris between finger and thumb and pinched it tightly. She was not sure whether her intent was to stop her longing, or – as was the case – to release herself into an immediate throbbing. Her vagina pulsated strongly and she was overwhelmed with a luscious sexual feeling.

As Amy rubbed her slim body vigorously with her towel, she realised that her brief session of self-pleasuring had indeed rendered her prey to her own wild passion. She sighed, peered at her misty reflection in the steamy mirror and shook her long hair over her face. Then, ever resilient, she laughed and went to dress in her little black dress. Reuben would be touching down at Florence airport, just as she began her first Life Class.

She was quite looking forward to the challenge of this and had planned it as a new interest for when Reuben left. She had been quite good at drawing when she was younger, although there had not been much time for that lately. Anyway, it seemed to her, Reuben thought he had the monopoly on artistic sensibility. Artists were like that. Perhaps she had given in to him a bit. But she had always been able to appreciate fine art. She dragged a brush through her thick loosely curling hair, leant forward to shake it and then threw her head back to allow it to cascade down her back.

She dabbed a little crimson lipstick on her full mouth, closed her lips together to spread it evenly and then scrutinised herself in the cheval mirror in her bedroom. She met her own gaze steadily and smiled at her slim, shapely image. Her tiny dress hugged her gently rounded breasts and hips, her derriere showed, curvaceous and enticing, and her legs went on for ever, slender and firm. She pouted at herself in mock seduction, then shook her head ruefully, her damp curls caressing her face. Her wet hair was an even richer, more sensual, colour. A pity her lascivious state would be wasted, she thought to herself. She ran downstairs to find her shoulder bag, and filled it with pad (containing nude sketches of the obliging Reuben), pencils, charcoals and putty rubber and went out into sunny mid-day.

Reuben had reminded her that Clarissa Laurence, the elderly aunt of Jacob Laurence, the teacher, was a very successful local artist. She had specialised in delicate watercolours of landscapes, children, and still lifes. Amy wondered whether the class would take her mind off sex for a time. She grinned to herself. Probably not. Already, she was wondering what the male members of the group would be like. She did not doubt that Reuben would indulge himself as he fancied in Florence. He had probably started already, she thought, building up in her mind a scenario at the airport – or, even earlier, on the plane, in which Reuben beguiled some dark and provocative Italian woman. There was no reason why she should not be as free. At least then she could match him, when he phoned, with lascivious stories. And, if opportunities should not come her way, then she would just have to invent them for now. She would not let Reuben know that she was deprived. This liberated feeling was exhilarating, though she could not easily shrug off the envy that returned each time she thought of Reuben with some sexy Italian. Swine! At least she would not let him know that he was missed. Amy decided that it was easier to catch the bus, which passed the Adult Education Centre, than to park. She had had enough of traffic for one day.

Eleanor Morrissey waited with trepidation in the studio of the Adult Education Centre. She had arrived far too early. In fact, she had been here so long that she had begun to think that she would go home again. She looked around the large room. A few people had just appeared. They seemed to know each other and had chosen desks on the other side of the room. Probably the best places. No doubt she herself was in the worst position possible – too near the model. Her apprehension rose almost to engulf her. Life classes. Naked people. She lowered her head to hide her flush, pretending to search in her bag and telling herself not to be ridiculous. She was going to Art School next year, and this was an ideal opportunity. Life classes at the local centre. Everyone had said it was too good to miss.

Eleanor sighed. She wondered whether to go out to the

Ladies' again, but then felt too self-conscious. The room was filling up. Eleanor surveyed the newcomers clandestinely. They were certainly a mixed bunch, of all ages and types. Two middle-aged men and a plump American woman were laughing together over the other side of the room. The woman came over to introduce herself with a friendly smile and a firm handshake. She was called Marie-Anne and wore lots of costume jewellery and coloured scarves. Marie-Anne indicated her jesting friends, Sam and Robbie, who were obviously not worried about the impending ordeal. Eleanor smiled and nodded to them. They soon went off to accost other newcomers. A little shaky, after their unexpected intrusion into her private thoughts, Eleanor got out her drawing-pad, and immediately felt better, stronger. She wondered why she hadn't done this before. Eleanor always felt in charge with a pencil in her hand. With this she could trap anyone on the page. Make them do as she wished. Hostile people were made to look ludicrous; friendly people sweet and affable. Sometimes she felt that this secret power then gave her the confidence to smile at people. They almost always smiled back.

But then Eleanor did not yet realise the power of her own attraction, her big black eyes staring out of a pale face with unfailing interest as she assessed and sized up victims for her page. She was very appealing with her delicate bone-structure, creamy skin, cheeks rouged occasionally with self-conscious-ness, and her passionate red mouth. People looked at her now, as they entered, drawn by her youth and freshness. Some gave her a second look, drawn, as strangers sometimes were, by her compelling quality of inner spiritual life. Though not all could define what had attracted them.

But Eleanor was frowning now, wondering how it would be to gaze upon a naked man – or woman – and try to forget that they were so. Just to capture the lines of their bodies. She wondered whether it would be a man. She was a little appre-hensive. It was not that she had not seen a man naked. She had a brother. And she had had a lover. Though she had not lingered too long over her perusal of his body. They had both been too intent on the sexual act itself. Getting that accomplished.

14

Eleanor pushed that complex memory from her mind. She would concentrate on her art for now. Men were a bit of a mystery to her. Thinking of them made life too complicated.

The room was almost full. Eleanor watched a self-possessed young woman linger at the door, looking around the room as if assessing its occupants in her calm perusal. Eleanor envied her her confidence. Everyone was looking up at her. And no wonder. She was tall and slim with masses of long auburn curls which shone in the sunlight from the window to her side. She looked more like an actress than an art student in her tiny, figure-hugging dress. Eleanor thought that she looked wonderful. And that she paused deliberately for effect.

Amy looked around the studio speculatively. Its occupants were varied and no doubt interesting, though she had to admit that there was no-one who immediately grabbed her attention. She was a little disappointed in this, but then pulled herself together. People smiled at her and she returned their friendly gestures as she made her way to the last remaining empty desk. She was aware, as she walked, of the sensual movement of her body under its scanty dress and smiled inside to think that several of the men were doubtless following her course avidly.

She sat down next to a very pretty girl with black hair and black eyes. She nodded and smiled, then said,

'Hi – I'm Amy.'

'Eleanor – Elli,' responded the young girl, a little shyly.

Very sweet, thought Amy, taking out her equipment. Her attention was caught as a man – probably in his late twenties – entered. Amy smiled, her eyes widening in appreciation, her unruly body responding dramatically. This was better! The young man took off his long grey coat and placed it carefully on an unused desk by the wall. He was lovely, with mahogany-dark curls framing his angular face. Amy was captivated by the unusual colour of his intelligent eyes: an intriguing shade of dark grey, she thought. His small beard and moustache lent distinction to his sensitive-seeming face. He was tall and slim, though he moved with agile grace, and was obviously very fit and strong. Amy imagined the muscles beneath his loose clothing. His shoulders were broad enough and his hips narrow. He was dressed in a dark blue satiny shirt and thick cream trousers and carried a large battered leather bag over his shoulder. With a reflex glance, Amy eyed his crotch, wondering how well-endowed he would be. He was certainly well concealed, however, she had no doubt that he was a sensual man, and had already picked up on his invisible chemistry. Just as Amy was thinking how interesting it would be to have such a student in the class, she realised with a stab of excitement, as he went to the centre of the room, that this was Jacob Laurence, and her whole concept of the impending course somersaulted pleasantly. How delightful it would be, to come here each week to respond to this attractive man. There would be ample opportunity to get to know him . . .

Jacob Laurence was now at the desk in the centre of the room, smiling at them and arranging his papers. Amy was taking the opportunity to drink in his strong, supple body, her breasts glowed as she imagined his touch and her pants suddenly wetted with her secret liquor. This amused her. She told herself that she was so easily stimulated because she had, of late, been used to making love often. However, there was no denying that Jacob Laurence was very sexy. She watched the subtle movements of his body as he prepared to address his class. She was sure his bottom would be firm and neat, good to touch.

'Hi, everyone,' Jacob said in his lilting Irish brogue. 'Welcome, to those of you who are new and welcome back to those from last year.' Jacob nodded towards Marie-Anne in her colourful garb, and Robbie and Sam, who sat next to her. These latter two were an entertaining double-act, and had already begun their usual banter. Jacob smiled at them, and then addressed the others: 'You will realise of course that I am Jacob Laurence. I'm here to help you with your drawings of the models we have this year. Most of them will come along for two or three weeks to begin with. That will give you an opportunity for some concentrated sketching. Oh, first I have to take the register. I don't know how many of you know each other. I know a few do.' Jacob smiled. 'I'm sure it won't be long before we're all on good terms. Okay. I *will* get to know you, but this week I'll call out your names and then I'll do the list for drinks. If I don't get it in early, you won't get one.' He smiled round at them before pursuing his tasks. The class fell to quiet chattering.

Amy continued to gaze at Jacob as he performed these small duties. He really was most attractive. Well, Reuben had insisted they were free to do as they wished . . . She wondered whether the handsome Jacob Laurence was as free as she was. He was surely too good-looking to be unattached. But already his perceptive eyes responded to her obvious interest. She told herself that if Reuben was unfortunate enough not to have met anyone suitable on the plane, or at the airport, he would certainly bewitch someone in Florence. She occupied herself by continuing to imagine what Jacob Laurence would be like lying naked here on the dusty wooden floor with the sunbeam washing over his lithe body. She was sure that he was well aware of her direct glances. He met her eyes once or twice knowingly, and she deliberately allowed her slow gaze to drift down his strong body to his crotch. He did not flinch. Instead, there was a flicker of a smile over his handsome face. Amy smiled secretly, assured. Here was a man who was not fazed by a liberated woman. Mmmm . . . She continued to watch him, happily.

Beside her, the young Eleanor was also regarding Jacob with admiration, tempered with shyness. Jacob smiled reassuringly at her and she flushed.

'Okay now,' Jacob continued, 'Well, of course some of you will have been to Life Classes before, some to general drawing classes, others will be complete novices. It doesn't matter. We will, in the duration of the course, discuss different approaches, from that of classical Greece, right up to more modern ideas. We'll consider anatomy – an important aspect of life drawing, and take a look at some of the famous paintings of nudes. I'll bring in slides. Those of you going on the trip to Florence will of course have the chance to see, and perhaps copy, some of the sculptures and paintings we'll discuss. You'll find some useful books on the list I'll give you. On this first occasion, I would like you to draw exactly how you wish, but when you draw, begin to consider the body in terms of volume and space. Consider the clear lines of the body. But don't forget to observe the shadows which fall upon the body, and are formed by different parts of the body – if you can sketch these in, you will give your drawing a feeling of being three-dimensional. Of mass. Later— ' he indicated with laughter, the model of a skeleton in the corner of the room, ' —you will become more aware of the bones beneath the flesh . . . Now, I think you should all have a go. Your first model is male.

'Today, it's Simon.' Jacob gestured to a young man dressed in a dark green robe who had just emerged from behind the screen. Simon smiled and nodded to them. 'While you're drawing Simon,' he grinned, 'I'll come around and look at your work. Then, there'll be a break, and I'll discuss a few points with you, of approach and so forth. So, use what you will this first time – pencil, charcoal, chalk . . . Okay.'

The atmosphere was a little tense and hushed as the students prepared their materials, and Simon went over to the wooden chair in the centre and, first taking off his emerald robe, sat on it. He sat with his legs outstretched casually, his arms resting on the arms of the chair. Though he had smiled at them at first, now his expression became composed and serious. He gazed calmly into the middle distance, seeming to settle into a kind of reverie as he rendered his material being up to them. Amy glanced around the room. Jacob Laurence was engrossed for the moment in some paper work, bending over his desk. Her eyes caressed his neat behind. It was difficult not to think of him, though she tried to concentrate on the naked youth before her.

Most of the students were already immersed in their drawing. They had chosen a variety of instruments. Many had selected a pencil of preferred quality; hard or soft, thick or thin; some, charcoal, and one or two, chalk. There was an atmosphere of absolute quiet and concentration. All eyes were focused on Simon, with his streaked blond and dark hair, as he reclined casually on his chair. Eleanor was drawing in an engrossed manner. Amy sighed and turned to the model herself. She felt rather irreverent as she eyed his firm, muscular body speculatively. She instructed her wayward mind to concentrate on Simon's body in an artistic sense, to see him in terms of shapes of space, as Jacob had advised. However, she was most aware of how appealing he was. She wondered whether all their models would look so good without their clothes. This evening, she could have done with it being an elderly woman. Not young enough to tempt Jacob Laurence.

She turned back to watch Jacob, and smiled to herself. He really was very desirable. Her gaze lingered on his lean, supple body. Then, as he began to go from desk to desk, glancing at people's work, stopping to chat with a plump bespectacled woman who sat between two middle-aged men; friends, they all seemed as they whispered together. Amy decided she had better produce something. She allowed herself to be taken up by the reverential atmosphere of the studio. In this she thought that people recalled the influence of classical Greece and its worship of the – male – naked body as an object of perfection. Well, it could be, she had to admit. She conjured up images of Greek and Renaissance models, and sensual paintings of the neo-classical age. She thought of Ingres' evocative 'male torso', with its erotic undertones. She became lost in a kind of languid reverie, enjoying her mental immersion in this most seductive world of masculine nudity.

She had spent some of the past week doing sketches of Reuben. She flipped back the pages of her sketch-pad to look at these. Not bad, she thought. She smiled to recall how each session had been foreshortened by Reuben enticing her over to him. Amy felt herself become even more aroused as she mentally re-lived their torrid sessions of love-making. She smiled at Jacob as he glanced in her direction: she was sure Jacob Laurence would be an ardent lover . . .

Despite her instructions to herself, Eleanor was painfully aware of the young man's sexuality. Simon. Her heart thudded painfully as she attempted to control her shaking hand. She told herself that she was good at drawing. This was her sanctuary. She reminded herself that she was too sensitive. Everything affected her like this. It was not just because there was a naked young man in front of her. She would be alright. She glanced at the clock and wondered what time the tea break was. She concentrated on various sections of the young man's body, dividing him into circles and spheres. She assessed the relationship and size of each to the others. She drew boldly, her confidence gaining. The room was silent, with the students concentrating on capturing the young man as effectively as they could. This knowledge helped Eleanor to concentrate.

She was aware that Jacob Laurence passed her, glancing at her work, though he did not pause to discuss it with her as he had some of the others. She was relieved really. She looked at Simon. His fair hair fell over one side of his face. It was almost straight, and thick, cut neatly over his ear. She spent a few moments drawing the fair and dark strands. She followed the strong planes of his lean face, and denoted these with a few confident strokes. She shaded in the hollows beneath his sharp cheek-bones. She checked her dimensions, and drew in various points of his athletic body. His legs were long and strong. His arms muscular. She followed the lines of his pectoral muscles, sketched in the nipples on the smooth chest. His eyes were very blue.

She took a deep breath, looked at the area she had been avoiding, and made herself stare unflinchingly at his penis. This was ridiculous. It was just another part of his body she had to draw. She didn't even have to draw it, if she chose not to, she could just do a bit of shading. It was quite long, bigger than her ex-boyfriend's, but thinner. She wondered what it would be like erect. It rested between his legs, against his testicles. With her heartbeat resounding in her ears, she made herself complete her sketch. The tip of her tongue was between her teeth and lips as she concentrated.

Jacob smiled to himself as he passed her, then spoke quietly to Simon, who grinned and nodded, then put on his robe. Eleanor sighed with relief, and closed her pad. Someone brought the tray of drinks in. There would no doubt be a different pose after break. Eleanor had no doubt that everyone else did not even consider the man's – Simon's – sexuality. They would not be embarrassed. She went out to the Ladies to cool down her flushed face before she had her Coke. Simon smiled at her as she passed him. Eleanor blushed even more deeply. He was probably not very much older than her, she realised.

Amy watched Eleanor go before she grabbed a coffee and went to talk to Jacob. Several people had the same idea, so it would be some time before she could speak to him. She was however aware of his friendly smile at her as he discussed points with the older members of the class. His eyes were amazing – very grey, with a deeper outline. They were the kind one wanted to stare into – marvelling at their colour. The group of friends – Marie-Anne, the plump woman, and her two male friends, Sam and Rob – had the confidence of old students and were encouraging to the newcomers. They also obviously got on very well with their friendly lecturer. They introduced themselves to Amy, explaining that they had been to Jacob Laurence's Life Classes the previous year, and could not speak highly enough of his patience and instruction. They were now attending this as well as his advanced course, so as to get as much practice as possible in drawing and painting the nude. Amy thought that they came as much for the social side, and the fun they obviously had together. She laughed at their amusing comments as she flicked her eyes frequently towards Jacob, seeing the interested way in which he responded to queries and she noted the reflex admiration with which he glanced at the young Eleanor.

Jacob responded to the usual banter of the group around him as he drank his coffee. He sensed that most of the students were relieved to have achieved this first drawing. He had an opportunity to look across to Amy Harrison, standing casually at the edge of the small group, having been introduced to the trio. He smiled to himself. Their eyes had locked several times during the past hour or so. His gaze lingered, captured by her bewitching green eyes and his smile lingered; she was very attractive. Jacob was still easily aroused. Her close-fitting dress caressed her perfect body, clinging to her bottom and her breasts; her hair framed her small, finely-sculptured face, and then fell, in glorious cork-screw curls, to caress her bare shoulders. It gleamed in the sun-light coming through the long window. It was only a matter of time before they spoke, scarcely needing this to affirm their liking for each other and to confirm their strong attraction.

As the small group around him dispersed, she came over to him. He smiled at her. He watched her appreciatively as she approached, giving him time to take in her lovely form. Jacob thought what a wonderful painting she would make, in her tight black dress, with her slim figure and luscious hair. Her lush curls were reminiscent of Pre-Raphealite models, hanging down to her slender waist. And she knew she was attractive . . . He had no doubt that Louis would be interested in her. He pictured Amy naked. He knew, with that deep auburn-coloured hair, that her skin would be pure white, her body much whiter than her exposed arms. He thought of her, standing naked in the studio with her hair cascading over her pert breasts. He glanced at them, gently moulded by the soft material of her black dress. He would enjoy ministering to her whilst Louis painted. Perhaps he would commission and keep the picture himself or perhaps he would even have a go at painting her. He smiled secretly. In his sexually receptive state, he had immediately realised that here was a very powerful and self-assured young woman. He met her eyes and smiled once more, filled with pleasure just to be close to her. He did not think he would have to wait long before he could get her, naked.

'How are you doing – Amy?'

'Fine,' Amy nodded.

Eleanor doodled on her pad, sipped at her coke and watched covertly as Amy chatted to Jacob Laurence. They looked very good together. Amy, with her womanly figure revealed in that tiny little dress. What confidence she must have to wear it, it hid nothing. Eleanor looked at her with admiration. The soft cloth clung possessively to her body, reaching only a little under her bottom, though it remained there, jealously covering her neat little behind. Her slim legs were very long and her breasts were clearly outlined by the fit of her dress. Jacob was taller than her. He smiled as she spoke to him. He obviously liked her. He could scarcely take his eyes off her. Eleanor smiled to herself as she sketched them quickly. She blushed as she found herself imagining them in bed together. She quickly turned the page, on which she had drawn them both naked.

'Do you teach during the day?' Amy asked Jacob as she sipped at her coffee.

Jacob nodded, his warm eyes glinting as he took the opportunity to drink in this lovely young woman. He felt his penis unfurl as she moved – as if by accident – closer to him. He was aware of her subtle perfume, and the swell of her breasts under the soft material of her dress. The image of Louis' naked model arose once more in his mind and he silently cursed his friend for rendering him thus receptive. He wondered if Sarah had arrived for her 'sitting' and just what Louis was doing right now. Jacob would be amazed if he was actually painting . . .

'All kinds of classes?' Amy persisted.

'A variety, yes.'

'I've seen quite a few of your aunt's paintings,' Amy lied. 'I'd love to see some more.'

Jacob looked at her in a slightly different light. People were returning to their desks.

'My great-aunt,' he corrected her, foreseeing an easy opportunity to get her to meet Louis, and, he thought to himself, to get her home with him. 'Would you like to see some of her work?' he asked.

She smiled. 'I'm free this afternoon,' she told him, thinking wickedly of Reuben, and excited by the ease of this prospective conquest. Perhaps she would be even quicker than him. Ha!

'Okay,' Jacob nodded and smiled. 'You can meet Louis.'

'Louis?'

'Louis Joseph. My friend. He's an artist.'

'Oh.' Amy shrugged as she returned to her desk, more interested in being alone with this handsome lecturer.

'Haven't you heard of Louis Joseph?' asked Marie-Anne,

from her seat, a few desks away from Amy. Her voice was full of enthusiasm. Amy fully expected her to launch into a tirade of praise for his talent. Instead the woman grinned wickedly and merely said, 'He's very, *very* sexy.' Sam and Robbie exchanged ribald comments. Amy glanced at Jacob, wondering whether he was as oblivious as he seemed to these lewd remarks about his friend. It seemed strange to her that Marie-Anne should sing Louis Joseph's praises when his friend was so obviously very sexy too, and he was here.

Jacob was posing Simon in the typical 'contrapossto' stance of a Greek statue. They fell silent and began to try to capture this classical pose. The agreement which Amy and Jacob had speedily, and silently, reached was further affirmed as they could not help but glance repeatedly at each other, smiling. They would enjoy the necessary civilities before – very soon – savouring and nurturing the sexual chemistry between them.

At the end of the class, Eleanor was filled with relief. It hadn't been too bad, after all. She felt that the worst was over. She could enjoy the rest and benefit from the ensuing lessons. Jacob Laurence had liked what she had done, and she herself had felt reasonably pleased. She realised that when she felt less nervous, her work would improve. Simon had spoken briefly to her. She thought he was nice, but could only allow herself to think of him as a model. Otherwise it would be too embarrassing. She felt quite light-hearted as she left the old building. She would walk through the park and look round the shops, before going to the library and ordering the books on the list Jacob had given them – books on technique and art history, and books on the treasures of Florence. Eleanor felt a flutter of excitement at the prospect of visiting that unique city. For her it was a dream come true. As she passed the car-park, she saw Amy getting into Jacob Laurence's old Rover. She felt her cheeks redden as an unfamiliar feeling of envy filled her. Jacob Laurence was much more handsome than she had imagined he would be. She envied Amy as she was driven away.

Two

Louis let Sarah in and followed her back to his studio. He offered her a drink, but she shook her head, her hazel eyes full of laughter as she began to undress. Louis leaned against the wall and watched, his arms folded across his chest, and one leg crossed over the other. His sultry black eyes gazed unflinchingly at her. As though he possessed the right to her nakedness. Not for the first time, Sarah wondered whether all artists were so lascivious as they watched their models undress. Of course she knew that many artists had affairs with their models, and some artists painted their mistresses. Raphael, for example, had featured his beautiful mistress in many of his famous works.

She undressed slowly, already turned on. She had reached the stage where she only had to think of Louis, and she was wet and ready. Her fantasies were centred around him. She didn't particularly want to be under his power, but it seemed inevitable, given the circumstances. Posing for this picture took up most of her time. When she masturbated, she imagined his hands all over her. Just as his eyes were, as he stared at her for hours.

Most models, she knew, would undress briskly behind a screen. The whole transaction would be businesslike. After all, she had been persuaded to pose for him for the money. Louis paid well, and she needed to supplement her income from selling the jewellery she made. She would miss this, now he had nearly completed the painting, though she would have the sessions for Jacob, at his Life Classes, and she was to be paid for accompanying the group to Italy, to model for them there. However, Sarah was not shy and she had always simply taken off her clothes in front of Louis. At first, she had thought he was totally unaware of her, intent on preparing his brushes, or mixing paints. Before she got to know Louis and Jacob well, she had assumed they were gay, but this assumption had soon been dismissed. Now it seemed crazy that she had ever imagined so, as the men were very powerfully heterosexual. Or, so she thought, from their response to her. Though she knew from Simon, through whom she had met Louis, that Louis could be more flexible . . . It was difficult to believe, from the way he looked at her, that he would really prefer a man. Nevertheless, from the beginning, she had found herself feeling a little more self-conscious than she had expected to be. This was because Louis Joseph was a very attractive man. He was beautiful, in fact. More beautiful than any of the women he had painted. She looked at him now as he stood, silently regarding her as she stripped slowly. His large, dark eyes watched keenly. There was little that he had not seen. His thick black curls fell over his brow, one or two over his eyes. He did not smile. He had an intensity that was disturbing, but it was also very exciting. He seemed to burn with cold fire. She had no doubt that he was extremely passionate. The sparks from his controlled libido seared her. It was as though she was his unwilling victim. But she could scarcely complain of lying for hours in the exclusive company of a handsome and gifted artist, having her body recorded for posterity. And being paid.

As her visits had progressed, Sarah had become increasingly aware of Louis watching her as she undressed, and she had begun to take more care in doing so. Stripping slowly. Giving herself up to him, layer by layer, until at last she took up the pose as he had directed. And there she lay, more aroused each time, in her erotic and exposed position, feeling the cool satin under her, the cool air between her parted legs. And very aware of Louis' keen eyes upon her, travelling over every centimetre of her exposed body.

When Sarah slipped on her robe, and stood, shivering, some-times (if Jacob was at home), drinking tea, she was filled with a strange sensation. Of awe – certainly – at his ability, but also with a feeling that he knew her, and possessed her in a way that

26

she did not recognise. This was somehow intensely sexual, and a little disturbing. As if he reached deeply into her integral being. His paintings reminded Sarah of famous ones she had seen in galleries. They had the same kind of richness and depth. This was because Louis still used oils, eschewing the modern use of plastics. He could afford to do this. Few young artists could – even they preferred to.

Increasingly, as Sarah lay there, she had to prevent herself from moving to appease her intense longing. Earlier and earlier in the sessions, she found herself sexually aroused. At first, it had been after lying there for a time, in that languorous yet expectant pose, under the critical scrutiny of the artist. Sarah felt that in the original, the mistress was ready – any second now – for the king to come upon her, cover her with kisses, caress her intimately, and then penetrate her. There was a frisson in the thought of being fucked by a king, Sarah had thought. Or indeed, an artist. Louis Joseph. As time went on, and Sarah encouraged herself into a trance-like state, she became increasingly aware of the thought of Louis, unseen, eyeing her intently. Always at a distance. Sarah wondered if he would ever come close to view her more keenly. But he was always over there, safely behind his easel. She had tried to see if he was aroused, tried to imagine that he could not be. Then, from the sensual expression of his face, when she saw him, she knew that he was. Very much so. His expressive eyes, the fullness of his passionate mouth, gave him away.

But Louis was an enigma to Sarah. She had expected – longed for – him to touch her, to make love to her, but he remained, steadfastly aloof. Perhaps it was his art that turned him on. Maybe that was why he painted so many nudes. For Louis did not show her any warmth and saw her only as an object. He was scarcely even friendly, merely polite, and she was relieved when Jacob was around. Jacob was altogether different. He talked and showed concern that she may be cold, or hungry or thirsty. Louis did not seem able to consider such mundane concerns. Sarah noticed that he himself did not eat or drink whilst he was working, even when she had asked for a break. He merely continued to paint, somewhat petulantly, as if annoyed that his concentration had been broken. Jacob even took her home, sometimes, and talked to her on the way. He seemed to understand her state after a session with Louis. Sarah told herself that she was merely vulnerable after lying still for so long, often cold. Emotional after being naked under the eyes of a beautiful, but icy, man.

However, she was turned on. At this stage, she was aroused even before she was fully undressed. She wondered if the cold Louis noticed that her nipples were erect. But then Louis noticed everything: he was merely immune. In retaliation for his coldness, Sarah feigned a haughtiness which she hoped belied her state of sexual arousal. Louis, who must recognise her state, was probably pleased that it enhanced her suitability. He probably thought that she conspired with him to make the painting authentic. Sarah sometimes envied the king's mistress. But then, the artist, Boucher, could have been as cold as Louis Joseph. And kings, like artists, were self-engrossed and fickle.

Sarah took up her familiar pose on the couch. She now had to concentrate on not pressing her quim down on the rumpled satin beneath her. (Though, in truth, she scarcely needed the stimulus of material touch to reach climax.) It tickled at her exposed clitoris. Her sex was parted, though hidden from the artist. Waves of lust swept through her naked body. She wondered whether Louis noticed the occasional small stain. Already, her body was suffused with desire. She had lain here for so many times now, in a position of sexual expectation and readiness that she considered that, in all fairness, she deserved a good fuck.

Sarah spent many hours in bed pleasuring herself and fantasies of Louis now filled her life. Yet she had never even kissed him. He had never touched her, and scarcely spoke to her, but he drove her wild with the need to possess him. She lay on the bed and tried to imagine him stripped naked. And there he stood, calmly matching his palette to the colours of her skin whilst she tried to suppress her orgasm. Her body glowed under his cool perusal. Her vagina burned. This time, she would not even have to move, to come.

Sarah imagined being left alone whilst he popped out – say to go to the toilet, the thought of him handling his prick thus casually sent stabs of lust up her vagina – whilst he was gone, she would rapidly jerk her body against the cushion, and allow her orgasm release. Would he return to watch her, or would he ignore her? She envisaged him leaning casually against the door, regarding her with cold interest. Waiting for her to finish so he could continue to paint. Perhaps he *was* gay? There were enough portraits of naked men around. Perhaps he preferred Simon? Sarah thought of Louis and Jacob here. Even that turned her on. After all, they lived in this vast house alone together. But then, Sarah was aware of how Jacob looked at her. And, she was sure Louis wanted her, though he would not admit it. She grinned secretly to herself.

She pictured going to the bathroom, with her gown around her, and meeting Jacob en route. She would only have to open her robe to him and, she was sure, he would reach out for her. What a delicious relief. He would fondle her full, aching breasts and kiss her. He would take out his rigid cock and fill her. She imagined the tip of a full cock rubbed against her clitoris. Sarah felt her body become dangerously alive. Every nerve was filled with sensuality. Sexual energy, gathered at her vulva and streamed out to flood through her limbs and body. She liked Jacob; she merely wanted Louis. But Jacob was at the Life Class. She wondered whether Louis would become annoyed at the subtle change in her skin colour, for she was becoming very very hot. He would notice the telling flush of her throat and cheeks. He would have to re-mix his colours. Would he be angry? Sarah felt the hot juice come from her vagina. She willed Louis to come to her. She wanted him to lie between her legs, (as Louis XIV no doubt had with his mistress) and take her, after all these days of tantalising readiness.

But Louis could not do that. It would be like a violation. Of his art. It would be like rape. Louis was all too sensitive to her state. It distracted him, made him feel wild. All the supreme effort he had put into controlling himself – in making himself concentrate, and be detached, – now threatened to break up. He felt anger. Rage at himself. At his failing control. Over and over, an image of himself going to Sarah, taking out his cock and ramming it between her parted thighs, letting it go into that delicious place, filled him. Soon, it was all he could think of. His cock remained rigid inside his jeans, and Louis' face became set, his jaw-line firm and his eyes flickered with cold fire. He knew that he was in danger of ruining his painting. His face was set, his mind rigid. If Sarah would get off the settee, then he would be released: he could go and take her in his arms. If he could move. But he could not. Though he told himself that he could easily make some excuse – or none – and go from the room. Sarah would probably be relieved. But he could not go. He could not leave her, and he had made himself continue with his work. He was as trapped as she was in this web he had spun around them.

He looked at her through languid, hooded eyes. His mind was filled with sex, with need. That was all he could think of. He was angry with Sarah. She had broken his concentration. He wanted to sink his teeth into her neck and make her cry out in pain. He began to lose the sense of value of his painting. Sensibly, he put down his brush. He could go, now. It was easy. But, it was not. He was breathless, riveted to Sarah as she began to move, almost imperceptibly. But Louis was filled with desire for her as her body became slightly rigid and the waves of her subtle orgasm possessed her. She was beautiful. He was aware of the delicate change in her, in the pigment of her skin and the tension of her body. Louis bit his lip and closed his eyes. If the painting was complete, perhaps he could go and take her there. But, in his madness he knew that if he did, now, he would crazily destroy his own work.

Louis wrenched himself from the room and went up to the bathroom on the next floor. Once he had begun to move, though half his mind was still with his painting, he began to feel powerful anger, and this further fired his lust. He went into the dark room and with a violent movement unzipped his jeans. The pressure on his cock was released. He leaned back against the wall, determined not to touch it. But his need was too great. He pushed on the soft material, still containing him, and moaned, sinking down against the wall.

Even if he allowed himself a few rapid jerks, he would achieve nothing, and Louis' willpower was strong. He wanted Sarah. He felt so wild that he could easily have torn down there and taken her. But he had to force himself to be more civilised. Even if he knew that was what she wanted too. After all, he was an artist, a lover of order, a civilised man. Not a wild, unfettered beast responding to the chaos of his primeval urge . . . Louis smiled languorously at this. All his wildness welled inside him. He was aware of the sensuality of his heavy eyes, the fullness of his lips; his body, charged with sexuality.

He ran his palms over his chest and belly and into his pants. He threw his head back as he grasped his swollen cock, feeling it rear in his firm hold. Already, he was panting, ready, swooning. If Sarah should take it into her head to come up here. She was already naked. Perhaps she would don the gown. Louis licked at his luscious-feeling lips as he imagined reaching out for her swollen breasts and caressing them. He knew them so well. He pulled the loose skin slowly down his penis to its base, squeezing very tightly. Already a pearl of liquid gathered. He could almost feel the tight warmth of her vagina as his huge cock was taken slowly in. Louis was beautiful. Louis was sensual. If Sarah just came up to see him now. Not cold and distant. But hot and ready for her.

Sarah had risen, slipped on the cool satin robe and gone out to the conservatory. Her spontaneous orgasm had only deepened her need. She felt she would go crazy. She was smoking one of Louis' cigarettes. It didn't calm her, but the action allowed her to give an imitation of composure for when Louis would return. She was confused as to what to do – should she leave? Would he still want to complete the damned painting today? All she could know, positively, was that she wanted him to take her,

31

ravish her, possess her – with energy and for a long time. Anywhere. She didn't care. Even here on the cold floor. Then perhaps she could be free of him.

Louis had managed to zip up his flies, though his cock had been reluctant to be shoved away again. It propelled him now, simplifying the situation, urging him just to go and take her. Stop intellectualising, and act. Cut out all the necessary pre-amble. As he returned, it fretted Louis. He didn't like talking much. Especially when he was painting. And now, his thoughts were muddled by his desire. It was with a kind of pain that he returned. He saw the empty settee with relief, closely followed by dread – perhaps she had left?

He saw her in the conservatory, surrounded by the strange plants that belonged to Jacob's aunt. He leaned against the door and looked at her, crossing his arms, one leg over the other. Posed like an Elizabethan galliard, he was the epitome of elegant control. Inside, he raved. His penis grew even larger under the harsh denim, so close to the object of its intent. He feigned casualness. When she turned, became aware of him, he would ask her if she wanted a drink. Better make it alcoholic, he did not have the patience to make coffee right now.

Sarah was aware of Louis' return immediately. She knew that he stood, watching her, always watching her, never touching her. Only with his mind. That had driven her crazy. She took her time in turning. When she did, she was cut to the heart by the burning in his black eyes, by his controlled stillness. Intimation of his savage state came at her. Assured now of his need, she had pity on him. And, anyway, she wanted him. Sarah did not waste words on the taciturn Louis. She merely parted her gown and opened her legs and watched with supreme pleasure as his dark eyes flooded with desire, his red mouth parted and a sensual flush hit his throat and cheeks.

She could see for sure now the generous bulge beneath his jeans. She smiled seductively and caressed her breast languidly. She knew that he wanted to take her, just as she wanted him to. But Louis did not push her off the chair and ravish her, though

32

she would not have complained. Louis came to her and lifted her. He carried her back into the house. Neither did he throw her to the couch or floor. Instead, he took her upstairs to his room on the first floor. Without even kissing her, he placed her gently on his bed. The room was huge, as was Louis' bed. There was a piano in the corner, and pictures all over the walls.

Louis drew the curtains and turned on various small lights, softening the light of the room. Sarah looked around at the sketches of naked men and women covering the walls, even the ceiling. Some were antique, copied from Michelangelo and Raphael, Titian and Rubens. Others were of his friends and models. Male and female. A large number were of Jacob, especially when he was younger. She looked at the drawings of Jacob. Naked, and in many classical poses. She looked at Louis. Looked up at his strong, fit body as he looked down at her. He sat on the bed beside her, and cupped her chin with his left palm. He smiled gently at her. She returned this. She was surprised at his sudden warmth, and suddenly realised that his seeming coldness was perhaps as a result of his suppressed sexuality. It was to do with the fact that he had to paint her. He indicated that she should take off her robe, and she obliged. Then Louis let his eyes wander all over her naked form. As if he had never seen her before. Or as if he had seen her body many times, and treasured it. Sarah felt glorious under his invisible touch. Moved by the tenderness in his beautiful eyes.

Sarah thought that she should have known that he would be an artist to the end. As he looked at her, Sarah felt that she was being very softly caressed. Her body purred to a different, gentler life under his perusal. She relaxed. It was as if he was painting her body with a warm soothing liquid. As if he was giving back to her something of what he had drunk in – with his soul. Sarah felt that Louis did not need to touch her. If he allowed his eyes to dwell on her breast it would swell, or focus on her clitoris it would throb. It was as though his hours of avid attention had enabled him to possess her entirely. She scarcely needed foreplay.

Instinctively, her thighs parted a little, inviting him in. Louis smiled at her again, a smile so radiant it was like that of an angel. It was as if he gloried – exulted – in the sight of her body displayed here for him. He feasted upon her, his gaze returning now to her thighs, now her gently rounded stomach, now her jutting breasts. And everywhere he looked, Sarah now felt that her flesh was seared. Soon, she thought, he would turn her over and look keenly at the view he knew so well. Sarah wondered whether he had been longing to fuck her as much as she had him. She began to writhe gently on his bed. She wanted to see him naked. She wanted him to touch her. She was suddenly afraid lest he should decide that this prolonged perusal would suffice.

She reached up and took hold of his T-shirt, signalling with her eyes that she desired him to strip. At her touch, Louis seized her wrist and held it tightly. As his face descended to meet hers, Sarah's guts burned at the change of expression in his eyes. Louis' mouth neared hers, but he did not merely kiss her, impatient as he was. He parted his red mouth and with the tip of his protruding tongue he licked the inner flesh of her lower lip. His potent tongue seemed to burn her. She relaxed into this for a little, still feeling his tight grip on her wrist. Then she slipped out her own tongue and met the tip of his with hers.

Louis' tongue was inside her mouth, just as she desired his naked prick to be within her vagina. She lifted her abdomen, to urge him to penetrate her. His mouth was on hers, and he was on the bed beside her. Very close. Louis, in black, with his black hair and black eyes. Sarah could feel his sheathed body next to her naked flesh. It was like madness, not to have him naked. She wanted to feel his flesh. But it was also exciting to submit, giving him increased dominion over her. A natural conclusion to her lying for him. Louis' clothed leg was over her bare one, pinning her down. He moved his mouth from her mouth to her throat, and his kissing and sucking was filled with hunger. He released her wrist. Sarah's hands clutched his tight buttocks, but she could not yet reach his hidden cock, though she smiled to feel its bulge, hot against her thigh.

Louis touched the taut flesh of her breast very lightly. A

feathering. But Louis knew his power and the state of his prey as Sarah leapt further into life, his touch sending assurance through her. Licking at her throat, Louis looked up at her through his dark eyes, a savage gleam in them, and a cruel smile. Sarah felt a surge of fear at his satanic look. But her arousal was even more acute. Louis trailed his hot tongue down her throat to her breast and clamped his mouth on her nipple. Sarah cried out in anguished pleasure. Louis took her other nipple between his finger and thumb and began to squeeze it in concert with his hard sucking.

Sarah saw that his eyes were closed as he concentrated on this pleasure. She writhed under his attentions, thrusting her breasts eagerly at him as he licked and rolled her erect nipple with his tongue. And, with his long fingers, he tweaked and squeezed her other nipple. Sarah felt this nurtured pleasure spread through her body. She writhed her pubis against his leg and whimpered in pleasure as Louis continued to work on her teats. They grew fuller and firmer. Her pleasure was infinite and she never wanted him to stop. She thrust her breasts repeatedly towards him, urging him to squeeze them more tightly: to take her. She felt that her enjoyment could not be bettered.

Then Louis slipped his other hand between her thighs and Sarah sobbed in acute pleasure, melting, as his fingers touched her at last. Sarah clung to him as they took her clitoris between them and squeezed on it, and his tongue returned to her mouth, echoing his movements as he expertly fingered her tight bud. His fingers moved to her hot, wet passage and the other hand to caress her breast as he inserted his fingers and slid them up and down her rhythmically, gradually increasing his movements until he jerked rapidly into her. Sarah continued to whimper, lost in his pleasuring.

'Louis . . .' she whispered into his ear, longing for the feel of his big throbbing cock inside her.

Panting, Louis lay upon her. His body was getting hotter and hotter. She could feel his heat. He pressed down on her sex; the roughness of the swollen denim both stimulated and frustrated her.

'Louis—' She had her hand under his crotch, and could feel the unbearable straining within.

He unfastened his trousers and with a groan released his swollen cock. Sarah wanted him to strip: to feel his warm, naked body against hers, his chest against her breasts. To feel him, as exposed as she was. But she knew that Louis planned to take her as he was, merely releasing his prick to insert it. Sarah was desperate for him, whatever, and there was a certain excitement in him being clothed whilst she was naked. Feeling the coarseness of his denim, and his zip against her tender body. She gave in to him. She ran her hands up from his abdomen over his strong back and to his shoulders. She opened her legs, dropped her knees, feeling the tip of his penis against her sex. Louis groaned deeply once more, holding his cock for a moment and rubbing it vigorously against her clitoris and then suddenly thrusting it deeply into her vagina. Sarah thrilled to feel him shudder and groan with pleasure as he entered her. He raised himself and rammed his prick deeply home. Sarah cried out in deep satisfaction as Louis filled her. There was a sense of completion. Immediately, they were taken into a wild rhythm as Sarah raised her legs around his bottom and urged her body against his. It was the culmination of all of their slow time together, when she had lain for him, giving herself up to him, and he had penetrated every inch of her body with his eyes.

Already, she was throbbing at the reality of him, so big within her. She gloried as Louis began to fuck her with the savagery she desired. Supporting himself with his hands on the bed, he raised his body and rammed repeatedly into her, making her body judder with the force of his masculinity. Sarah began to cry out as her repeated orgasms washed over her, losing a little as Louis continued to thrust into her, his speed increasing rapidly. Sarah thought that she had lost the opportunity to capture and savour each one, but as Louis' body became rigid and his penis continued to pump sporadically inside her, Sarah pressed her clitoris hard against him and cried out as the overwhelming waves of sensation spread over her. Flooding her. Her vagina beat in time to Louis' strongly pulsating cock.

Louis remained for a few moments and then went from her. Sarah didn't care. He was probably going to agonise over his painting. She was grateful that he didn't demand her immediate presence in his studio. She felt a sweet lassitude overtake her, and she snuggled down to sleep in his bed, with the animal scent of him all around her. She was confident that he would return, later. Or, she could go and entice him back.

Louis looked at his work through narrowed, savage eyes. Then, in a reflex safety action, he went to prowl around the garden, smoking fiercely, prey to the gold of the sinking sun and the scent of honeysuckle and roses. He went back into the house, and stood once more before Sarah's portrait.

'You're not going to hack it to pieces?' asked Jacob, as he came in, quickly assessing the situation and the artist's mood.

Louis glanced at him irritably. Jacob wondered where Sarah was and whether she had energy for Louis' likely passion tonight.

'Come and have a drink,' he invited. 'I'll tell you about the group. Some of them are quite talented and all of them keen.'

Louis followed Jacob to the kitchen. Jacob selected a bottle of claret from the rack and held it up to Louis. Louis nodded absently. Jacob poured a glass for him. Louis drained it in one go. Jacob wondered whether in his dark and glowering state, Louis imagined he tasted blood. Most men felt sated after sex, but if Louis was still in the middle of a painting it seemed rather to rile him. Jacob was thankful that he did not find sex so complex and grateful not to be one of Louis' lovers.

Jacob could not quite understand him. He had obviously had sex, yet he was discontented. When he himself had made love, he always felt happy and fulfilled. Jacob thought that Louis' frustration was connected with his unfinished painting. It was most unusual for him to indulge himself before it was completed. Not the best time for Jacob to introduce him to a new prospective model. Ah, well . . .

'I've brought someone back . . .' he began, not meeting Louis' eyes, but sensing his distaste as his body tensed. Though Jacob

37

was gathering things to take through to the lounge, he delayed as Louis swept past him. He decided that Amy could cope.

Amy felt her stomach tighten, her entire body flood with intense excitement as Louis entered the room. She tried not to stare. She was filled with sex. He was exquisite. Beautiful. The most beautiful man she had ever seen. Amy wanted him. She was immediately aroused by his presence. She could feel the waves of powerful sexuality come from him. She would let him have her now, without even speaking to him. She knew that he would be very powerful: that his sexual capacity matched her own. Instinctively, she parted her thighs beneath her little black dress. Louis seemed to scoff silently and look away. But he could not help but look back at her. Amy felt that he had touched her breasts as his dark eyes caressed them. Her mouth parted as his eyes narrowed at her.

She took in his tousled jet curls, his pouting lips, his glowering dark eyes. His mouth was very red, as if he had just been kissed. He frowned as if annoyed with her. Amy allowed her predatory gaze to travel over his lithe body. She felt that he was discomfited by her unusual confidence. Perhaps he was used to women wilting under his look. He turned away, to pour himself a drink and she was given a view of his taut buttocks. She already knew that he had an erection and smiled to herself. Jacob came from the kitchen, smiling, breaking the intensity of the moment.

'Louis – this is Amy, a student from the Life Class. Amy – Louis, my friend . . .' Jacob gestured to Louis, and smiled.

Amy was at once aware of the intimacy between the men.

'Amy wanted to see Clarissa's paintings,' Jacob said.

Louis raised an eyebrow at Amy and half smiled scornfully at her as if seeing through her ploy. They stared challengingly at each other as Jacob handed Amy a glass of the red wine. Amy felt hot waves of attraction and hostility raised in her as she glared back at Louis, who drank copiously from his glass. It was as if, without a word, they were immediately engaged in some kind of duel. She smiled ironically at Louis. When Sarah entered the room, dressed only in her robe, and stood close to

Louis, he embraced her and met Amy's eyes in a kind of triumph. Amy was filled with acute jealousy, wanting to tear at this woman who now stood so close to Louis. Nevertheless, she smiled at Sarah, and smirked superciliously at Louis.

'Sarah's my model— ?' Louis drawled, waiting for Amy to supply her own name, acting as if he could not be bothered to retain it in his mind.

Amy did not comply. She merely looked at him in distaste, meeting his magnificent eyes. Even as he referred to Sarah, it was as though she was some possession of his he was showing off to this newcomer. The woman was certainly lovely, made more so by her libidinous state. Sarah pressed herself against Louis, and Amy realised with certainty that they had just made love, and would do so again. Soon. She knew that Sarah wanted him: it was all she could think of. Amy suppressed a surge of envy as Louis kissed the top of Sarah's head. Amy could feel the hunger in Louis' body, see it in his hooded eyes. He smiled at her.

'So – shall we look at your aunt's paintings?' Amy asked Jacob in a business-like tone, as if she were immune to the animal magnetism which had obviously stripped the other woman of her pride.

Louis appeared to sneer at her as Jacob agreed. However, his superiority was short-lived as he realised that Jacob was taking her to his studio. He left the room, wanting to prevent this. He was enraged at Jacob, and bewildered by his uncharacteristic insensitivity. No doubt his friend was still playing the teacher. Doubtless Amy had asked to see his paintings, and Jacob was obviously under her spell. The idiot! He wanted to stop, Jacob, but did not relish the satisfaction that would give Amy. Jacob had never taken anyone else to his studio without asking him. Louis stood in an agony of restlessness. Sarah rescued him as she came out to the hall, and held out her hand to him, obviously expecting them to return to his bedroom.

Louis' cock reared angrily. He dismissed the possibility that the newcomer, with her supple feminine body and flaming hair, had anything to do with this. He was not affected by her wonderful green eyes and the intuitive intelligence contained therein. He could see at a glance that she was predatory. Powerful. She would not dictate his needs to him. He would be in control. The woman probably expected to get all she desired. She filled his mind with her vivid colours as he went upstairs with Sarah.

Sarah was astounded by Louis' wildness as he took her. He acted as though they had not recently coupled. After her initial shock, she was gratified at his capacity, little realising that the reason for his rapid re-arousal was at that moment standing before her portrait, admiring her nakedness.

Louis lifted her, penetrating her deeply and shafting her with urgency. Sarah cried out in anguish as he withdrew, but he did so merely to get her to pose, doggy-fashion, thus allowing him, still clothed, to hold onto her ample, shaking breasts as he fucked her. He slammed his body against her bottom as his rigid cock slid along her wet muscle. He tore at her breasts as he laboured. Sarah was amazed at the length and violence of his possession, though her body delighted in his mastery. Louis held onto her waist as his ramming became more urgent and vigorous. Sarah felt her body pulled back and forth as Louis glided along her, moving her to his own rhythm with his hands. He pulled her close to him as he was suddenly rigid, groaning as if in pain, and pumping his hot liquid out.

Sarah collapsed onto her stomach, seeking her own contained release. Louis lay beside her, his cheeks flushed, his mouth parted and his eyes almost closed. Sarah was torn between anger at his selfishness and admiration of his loveliness. She saw the dark glints of Louis' eyes as he watched her.

Amy had stood before Sarah's portrait in astonished admiration. Holding her cool glass of wine to her hot cheek, she gave herself up to a feeling of awe at Louis' prodigious talent. She looked at Jacob, who smiled in pride, as though showing off a protégé. She returned his smile. All illogical anger she had felt at the dark stranger was pushed to the back of her mind as she basked in his talent. Sarah was certainly shown here in all her glory.

She suppressed her own unexpected waves of sexual awareness as she surveyed the naked girl. She supposed it was because she was so aroused. She imagined herself lying naked for Louis, offering him her naked sensuality. She made a decision that Louis would paint her. She was confident of her own attractiveness, and knew that a painting of her would be very good, executed by this talented artist. However, she was also annoyed at her need, and the influence he was already having over her. Naturally, he was used to having what he required. No hot-blooded woman could resist his powerful mixture of extraordinary good looks, extreme sexual libido, and the opportunity to have her body rendered for posterity by his expert hand, whilst he looked at her, and no other woman, all day. The model possessed the artist as entirely as he possessed her. Amy decided that she would be his next model. Though, already, she knew, she had riled him with her aggression and assumed disdain, while she was enraged by his supreme egotism. (She could not know of the searing uncertainty which possessed him entirely sometimes, and which he constantly suppressed.) She was certain that he expected her to accede when he proposed to paint her, and decided to refuse and laugh at the disbelief in his eyes. She was sure that Louis Joseph was not accustomed to being refused anything he demanded.

In a haze, she followed Jacob around the large studio as he showed her some of Louis' other paintings. The large canvasses were of male and female nudes. All of them were extremely good. Louis had captured the personality of his sitters. Amy was aware that he was an intelligent and perceptive man and she wondered what complex game she had embarked upon with him. He was powerful and charismatic. He attracted people to him, and possessed them in his mind – as demonstrated in his paintings. Amy had no doubt that he possessed whom he chose physically, too. A flicker of fear edged into her brain, but she told herself that she was as powerful as any man.

Part of her longed to succumb to his artistic and sexual prowess, but Amy refused to submit. She was too proud and successful and used her sexual attractiveness to play games to get who she wanted. She realised that Louis had recognised a kindred spirit in her – hence his hostility. She laughed to herself as she imagined his fury at her being let loose in his studio. She detached herself from these complexities and concentrated on surveying his canvasses once more.

'He has quite a few paintings permanently on exhibition in various galleries,' Jacob explained. 'There's another exhibition of all his work in March next year. Here at the Art Centre. That's why there are more pictures than usual, here. Some of these have been sold, but lent back to Louis – for his exhibition. There's an excellent one of Simon – our model today. He'll get that back from Lavenham soon.'

Amy nodded.

Coming at last to a painting of Jacob, Amy smiled. There was no mistaking the simmering sensuality of the subject. She wanted to laugh at Louis' perceptiveness. The naked, and younger, Jacob in the languid and sensual attitude of Cephalus, awakened by Aurora. Amy gazed at the portrait, enjoying Jacob's painted nakedness. It was unique, to be allowed to peruse Jacob's body like this, before having sex with him. Jacob smiled.

'I spent a lot of time modelling for Louis, when we were younger,' he informed her.

Amy wondered at their relationship. Many artists allowed themselves to partake of all sensual pleasures. Suddenly, she had no doubt that Louis would screw whoever he could. She glanced at Jacob speculatively, and asked:

'Does he sleep with *all* of his models?'

Jacob grinned.

'Most of them,' he agreed non-commitally. 'He seems to get them under his spell.'

Not me, thought Amy with determination.

'My aunt said he was the very devil,' Jacob told her.

As Amy was about to agree, Jacob continued, with a twinkle in his warm eyes, 'She adored him. She said he was the most talented artist she had met.'

Amy nodded.

'She left me the house, and she left Louis her baby grand

piano, and sufficient funds to continue painting. She had made some money from her painting, but her second husband had been an excellent businessman and left a tidy sum. I was her only relative. We were close. She introduced me to art. When I was young, she took me to galleries, exhibitions. And I spent hours painting with her. Pity I didn't have Louis' natural ability.' He smiled.

Amy touched his arm in sympathy. He obviously still missed his aunt, who, she recalled, had died only last year.

'You're not jealous – of his success?' Amy asked.

'No, I'm not jealous of Louis.' Jacob's tone, and the warmth in his eyes, expressed his affection.

'Does Louis live here?' she asked.

'Yes. Mostly. We get on okay. He spends hours cloistered in his studio. He exhausts himself, then spends hours sleeping or slobbing around. In between that, we get on well.'

'Mmmm . . .' mused Amy. 'Does he paint other subjects?' she asked.

'Yes . . .' laughed Jacob. 'You must go and see his exhibition. Come on. I'll show you Clarissa's paintings. There is quite a collection here, though of course, the majority are in galleries. You will have seen some?'

Amy nodded vaguely, wishing she had read up a little on Clarissa Laurence. Still, she could not have known how attractive and desirable Jacob Laurence would be, and how intriguing his friend. They climbed the stairs to the first floor and Amy wondered behind which closed door Louis was now doubtless fucking Sarah. She suppressed a ridiculous surge of jealousy and desire. They passed one door and Jacob opened the next. The walls were lined with charming oils and water-colours in heavy ornate frames.

Jacob stood back and watched Amy as she went to look closely at the tiny paintings in this room, devoted to its previous owner. Her hair hung down her back, capturing the light of the setting sun through the window. Jacob looked idly through the glass at the deep red in the western sky. Then he looked back at Amy, his gaze caressing her pleasantly rounded bottom. Her skirt was so very short, but it did not rise to reveal her as she leant to peruse the paintings. He imagined the delightful place between her thighs. His responsive cock reacted dramatically to this vision. Jacob lit a cigarette and drew deeply on it, trying to control his craziness as he watched her. His cock stiffened further. Her dress was made of some clingy material which hugged her form closely. He itched to caress her; to lift her little dress and smooth his palm over her bottom; to edge his hand between her thighs and go into the welcoming feel of her warm sex. He wanted to make love to her. He felt sure that he had not misinterpreted her eloquent glances. He was certain that Amy was a liberated and experienced woman, with a high libido. He smiled wickedly to himself.

Amy wandered around the room, taken by the paintings. There were minute and delicate water-colour studies of children on a beach; family groups; meticulously painted bowls of chrysanthemums, and bowls of fruit. there was even, to her delight, a small painting of Jacob and Louis as children. Louis with masses of curls and sultry eyes; Jacob smiling charmingly. They sat, close together, on the beach. So, they had always been friends. Fascinating. She turned to Jacob and smiled. Caught unaware, his naked longing for her was revealed. He smiled, caught out. He shrugged, splayed his arms. His eyes met hers levelly.

Amy went to him and stood before him. Placing his palms on her hips, Jacob leaned his face towards her and kissed her tenderly. He was immediately fired by the strength of Amy's passion. He cupped her breast gently, feeling it become firm at his touch. He caressed it and then held it more strongly, squeezing her erect nipple. He moved his hands to her bottom, sighing with relief, and pulled her against him, knowing that she was at once aware of his erection against her pubis. He opened his mouth as she urged her hot tongue between his lips and delighted in the thrust of her nipples against his chest. He found her tremendously exciting, she was soft, and delicate, yet at the same time confident and forceful. He felt her hands caressing his back and reaching his buttocks. He tensed them as he pushed towards her, rubbing her pubis with his hidden phallus. As he felt her fingers going deeply into the cleft between his muscular hemispheres, he put his hand under her short dress to touch, with delight, the mound of her sex. At last.

He smiled inwardly. It was hot and damp. He pressed against her clitoris, under the fine gossamer of her silken panties. Amy moaned, her kiss becoming fiercer. Jacob slipped his fingers under the elastic to touch her hot, moist flesh. He fingered her labia. He felt Amy press more firmly between his buttocks, feeling for his sensitised perineum as she began to push against him. Jacob traced her fleshy lips, gasping as Amy reached for his testicles and began to fondle them. His need increased as he felt her open herself to him as he found the entrance to her vagina.

Supporting her with his other hand, he inserted, first one, then several fingers deeply into her, feeling them gripped spasmodically by her vagina. He felt her hold on his balls tighten as she began to grind on him. He pulled up her dress and held onto her bottom as she moved. Amy now held his head between her hands and kissed him deeply as she moved more quickly against his expert and deft caress. Jacob slipped his fingers up and down her as she slid along his insertion, pressing rhythmically against her enlarged clitoris as she slithered against him. He could tell that her orgasm was close and held her tightly as she came, moaning with excitement.

When he met her eyes he was moved by the increased lust in them. Fleetingly, something in them recalled Louis to him. But then it was gone. He knew that, though she had found some release, her need was increased. She pressed her body against his and then slithered down to kneel before him. She looked up at him. Her red hair fell wildly around her small face. Jacob's heart raced at the vamp-like look in her green eyes. He lifted the silken hair and let it fall as he stood still, allowing her to unfasten his trousers and release his rigid cock.

His lips parted and his breath came rapidly as she reached out her long red tongue to lick along its glorious length. He held onto her head, closing his eyes in anguished delight as she continued to lick him from head to base. He thrilled as she found the thick vein on his penis and concentrated on this. Her hand crept between his legs, fingering the sensitive place between anus and testicles, and then caressing his balls with a touch so delicate that it was exquisite. He felt her palm stroking and squeezing his abdomen. He thought of her breasts, longing to touch them again, but rooted by her attentions.

He gasped loudly as, very slowly, Amy took his thick penis into her mouth. He gloried in the muscular warmth, and the scratching of her teeth against him. Her tongue examined its length minutely with its tip. He felt her open her throat to let him go more deeply. The stimulation of his cock was extreme. A delicious feeling spread through his veins and he was in a crimson heaven as the door opened and he smiled lasciviously at Louis, who lingered at this beguiling sight; leaving with difficulty.

Gradually, Amy increased her rate of sucking. She held onto Jacob's pumping buttocks as he forced his prick along her throat, holding them apart as she sucked more strongly, feeling his skin slide along his rod. Patiently, she administered to him as Jacob gave himself to her. Jacob felt the pressure increase on his cock. He felt his buttocks widely stretched. He looked down to see Amy's now naked thrusting breasts and his spunk burst from his balls in a tremendous gush. Amy swallowed some of his seed, but retained some in her mouth as she rose to kiss him. Now, he was soft and loving and she gave him back some of his fluid as she kissed him deeply. Jacob fondled her breasts and returned her kiss. He was filled with delicious languor and contentment.

Amy adjusted her clothes. She was still aroused, but knew that they would make love later. Jacob was a generous and sensitive partner. It would be pleasant perhaps to go out for dinner first, spend some time talking to him, and basking in the prospect of going to bed with him for the night. She released him and smiled at him. He returned her smile happily, and kissed her forehead gently.

Louis reached out for Sarah, who slipped into the room and went gratefully into his arms. He thought of Jacob's ecstatic expression as Amy sucked his cock. His own prick rose at the thought of this. He knew that Amy would be able to give great pleasure. For her own end, no doubt, he added cynically to himself. He wondered what impossible demands she would put on poor Jacob later. He suppressed any arousal he felt at this challenge, and its promise of sexual endeavour and accomplishment. He realised that Sarah was cleaving to him, and he reached down to take her clitoris between his fingers. He fingered her idly and then released her and, licking down her body, he came to her sex. He mouthed and sucked until she came but his mind was elsewhere as he took her to heaven.

Amy looked again at the dark, beautiful man sprawling on the hearth. The log-fire flickered in its grate before him and he held the semi-naked Sarah between his legs. He looked calmer now, although he did not smile. His eyes were very clear, and very dark. Sarah half dozed against him as he fondled her lazily. The firelight painted them in its passionate glow. Amy told herself that the throbbing in her sex was because she had been touched by Jacob, and would have more sex with him tonight. It was nothing to do with Louis' lascivious expression, or the way he casually and possessively caressed Sarah's breasts, languidly slipping his elegant hands down into her gown. Sarah was content; she smiled dreamily at Amy, her hazel eyes expressing her pleasure at Louis' intimate touch.

Louis did not ignore Amy, but neither did he smile nor speak. He merely looked her over acutely, as if mentally stripping her to assess her suitability as a model, and then returned to his drink. Had Amy been less self-possessed and assured of her own attractiveness, then she may have withered under his terrible scrutiny. As it was, though she was still intrigued by him (mostly by his talent, she had convinced herself), she was determined not to fall under his spell. If she was ever gripped by desire for him, she would not show it. She would suppress it before she would allow herself to become as befuddled as Sarah.

Louis' eyes lit with dark amusement as he increased his attention to Sarah's generous breasts. Amy thought that it was as if he thought he could read her mind, and was goading her with this intimate caress: as if he thought she wanted it! And though secretly Amy could not prevent herself from imagining Louis' fingers on her swelling breasts, she smiled at him with pity to dispel his egotistical assumption. However, no passionate female could be immune to Louis Joseph. He was an extremely attractive, very desirable male, whose sexuality radiated from him – no doubt trapping everyone in its sphere. Sarah continued to smile softly from her cradled position. Amy realised that the woman had been watching her for some time.

She met Jacob's eyes in bemusement at Louis as he handed her another glass of wine. She realised that Louis was regarding her challengingly as his palm slipped down Sarah's belly. Sarah did not care that he revealed her to them. Anger with Louis flared in Amy's eyes as she turned away. However, the dark image of him remained with her. She could not help but look back, sideways along her eyes. Now he was fingering Sarah's sex. He would exhaust the poor woman. Amy's vagina pulsed erratically. She avoided looking directly at Louis, but his dark eyes continued to regard her, as if in some sort of challenge.

'Louis is coming to Florence with the art group, when we go, in January.' Jacob told her as if unaware of Louis' provocative actions. Perhaps he saw Sarah only as the unreal model naked on canvas. He went over to the stereo, to choose some music.

'I'm sure he'll make himself very useful,' responded Amy curtly, refusing to fall under Louis' spell, at least publicly.

Louis smiled darkly at her. Then he moved to lie beside Sarah, pulling her close to him, kissing her hair, and urging her pubis against his own. Amy's body throbbed in longing. She drained her glass rapidly.

'So,' she addressed Jacob, trying hard to ignore Louis' sinuous body, undulating gently against Sarah's as he began to kiss her passionately. Amy would not put it past him to fuck Sarah in front of them. She stood up, though part of her wanted to watch Louis in masochistic fascination. He was sinking his teeth into the soft flesh of Sarah's neck. He looked across at

Amy, laughter in his eyes. Amy looked quickly away, though only to look back immediately, bewitched, as Louis closed his eyes and sucked with vampiric hunger beneath Sarah's jugular. His hands were on Sarah's bottom, urging her closer to his crotch. 'Right,' Amy said, turning to Jacob, who had just selected, and put on Van Morrison, 'Shall we go for a walk, and then out for dinner?'

'Sure . . .' Jacob smiled. 'Now?'

Amy nodded, steadfastly ignoring Louis and Sarah.

Jacob and Amy went to the 'Duke of Marlborough' for a drink and then to the 'Sun' for a meal. It was a most enjoyable evening. Jacob was charming and entertaining. The proprietors knew him well, and obviously liked him. Amy tried hard not to think of Louis, but this was difficult as, naturally, Jacob mentioned him often; Louis was so much a part of his life. When they returned, Louis and Sarah were not in evidence. It was late. They went up to Jacob's room, where Jacob gently lifted her to lie on top of him, and Amy made love to him slowly, pressing her clitoris as she wished, against his pubic bone, basking in the feel of Jacob's hands, on her breasts and bottom, making the session last as long as she desired. She gazed down on her handsome and generous lover, thinking back to when she had first contemplated him, only yesterday. She felt very happy.

Amy encountered a weary-looking Sarah in the kitchen the next morning. They eyed each other warily, with suspicion, then smiled: they were, after all, engaged in identical pursuits in this masculine household. Amy looked in the cupboard for coffee.

'There's a machine,' Sarah told her, coming over, 'and beans to grind if you want. I got to know where everything was being Louis' model. He's not exactly domestic, if you know what I mean.'

'I don't suppose he is . . .' Amy agreed. 'So, Jacob must be well-organised? It's a beautiful house . . .' she observed.

'Yes, it is,' Sarah agreed, eyeing up this vivacious young woman, who would surely be Louis' next model. She felt a little sad that her own role as such was almost complete, but mostly relief that it was all over. Now she had had Louis, she felt free. All her tension and longing was past. She did not want to be involved with him on a regular basis: he was too exhausting for her, both physically and mentally. This woman seemed more his type. If their relationship could be promoted, that would leave Jacob free for her. Both she and Jacob had recognised the fire between Louis and Amy. But, for some inexplicable reason, they chose to be hostile to each other. Sarah could not be bothered with such complex game-playing, though she fully understood Amy's attraction and pride. She watched her as she fiddled around with various items in the kitchen. She was extremely pretty. Sarah's body was languorous and aching, after Louis' ministrations. It seemed very appealing to her, to go and lie in bed, naked, with Amy, away from Louis. She sighed silently – it was a pity she did not know her better. Right now, she knew that the woman was jealous of her night with Louis. He certainly scorched anyone who came within his orbit. Sarah did not want to lie for the portrait today, she felt weary. But Louis would insist, and she couldn't blame him. It was almost finished. Anyway, he would pay her today.

'I think I'll make instant,' Amy decided. 'Do you want some, Sarah?'

'Yes, thanks.' Sarah smiled, idly leafing through the Sunday papers.

Amy prepared two mugs of coffee and took them through on a tray with cream and brown sugar.

'So what's it like then?' she asked Sarah, pouring cream into her coffee.

'What?' Sarah looked up at her, for a moment thinking that Amy was wondering about sex with Louis.

'Posing for Louis.'

'Oh,' Sarah smiled, crinkling her eyes, reading her mind accurately. 'You have to be very patient, and it helps if you don't need to eat or drink, or go to the loo.'

The women laughed together. Amy looked up as Louis came into the room. Her stomach churned in response to his vivid life. His black eyes held hers for a moment, then Louis simply

50

nodded at her and Sarah (as if he had not made love to the woman all night), and went into the kitchen. Sarah regarded Amy's acute appraisal of Louis as the woman half-closed her striking green eyes and watched his every move, followed every line of his body. Her face eloquently betrayed her keen interest.

Sarah followed Louis to the kitchen, and Amy watched avidly as Sarah stood behind him, placing her arms under his and beginning to caress his chest and belly. Amy's vagina contracted spasmodically. She thought that Louis would disengage himself if he could, but he allowed Sarah to continue to caress him. His eyes met Amy's. Sarah's hands crept slowly down, over his belly. Amy saw Louis' eyes become hooded, and his mouth sensual. Already his breathing had become faster. Amy's body was flooded with sexuality. Louis continued to meet her gaze. Sarah had now reached his crotch and was pressing on his growing member, stimulating him to a full erection. Amy could tell that Louis' entire body was fired with lust. She felt very excited at witnessing this personal act. At seeing Louis in Sarah's power. She met Sarah's eyes and saw, with shock, Sarah's expression. It was as though she was offering Louis to Amy. And, had she the nerve, Amy could have gone and touched him. Sarah seemed to urge her, silently, with eloquent eyes, now kissing Louis' head. She slipped her hand down the waistband of Louis' loose black trousers and smiled wickedly at Amy as she fingered his hot stiffened penis. Amy's body seemed to pound with the rapid beating of her heart. Louis was still looking at her. Amy was sure that he wanted to turn to Sarah, to kiss her. But though he did not prevent Sarah and obviously responded naturally to her advances, it was as though he sensed her deeper motives. To an extent, narcissistically, or perhaps merely to goad Amy, he participated. Sarah withdrew her hand, and put it to his mouth, still holding him from behind, pressing her body against his. Louis kissed her hand and moved away from her.

'Are you going to make us some breakfast, Lou?' Sarah asked jokingly, returning to Amy, smiling at her, meeting her look and smiling at what she had done.

Amy was so turned on that she could scarcely think. Her

primitive self suggested that she should go to Louis and continue what Sarah had started. Louis himself must be extremely aroused, though he chose to ignore his state.

'Pure orange?' he offered, in response to Sarah's request.

'Oh, go and wake Jake up, Amy . . .' Sarah laughed.

'He's awake,' Louis said, as Sarah shook her head at him, 'I'm just going to take him some coffee.'

Amy imagined for a moment, the men sitting on Jacob's bed and discussing them. She had a wild image of Jacob reaching out to appease Louis. The women watched Louis in silence as he prepared filter coffee.

'You can help yourself – to anything,' he said graciously as he went off.

'Cheers, Lou . . .' Sarah sighed. 'Still – you can't have everything,' Sarah said to Amy. 'After all – he is an artist . . . and – he's a bloody good fuck,' Sarah lowered her voice at this last observation.

Amy shrugged, feigning indifference, though this was difficult as her body was shot through with excitement at her words, especially after watching her arouse the randy artist. Sarah herself seemed immune – for now. Amy thrilled at the capacity of a man who could leave a woman feeling so thoroughly satisfied. Though she could not imagine not concluding any encounter she had begun with any man. But then, she was, she had learnt early, exceptionally highly sexed. And so, it seemed, was Louis Joseph.

'Oh, come on – I've seen you looking at him.' Sarah laughed. 'You should have seen yourself just now. You looked as if you could have raped him on the spot.'

Amy's sex responded dramatically to this lovely idea, her vagina immediately emitting the necessary lubricant. 'He's very attractive . . .' she heard herself admitting. 'No one could deny that.'

Sarah laughed at her. 'Jacob is more my type,' she then confessed, regarding Amy steadily.

'He's very sweet,' Amy agreed.

'No one could call Louis sweet,' Sarah said.

Amy recalled the way he had looked at her whilst kissing Sarah, and her body responded with an echo of darkness.

'Although, he *can* be very tender, but I reckon once he's got you he's an animal,' Sarah continued.

Amy smiled dirtily at her. She suspected that the woman was goading her now.

'So, are you going to be modelling for the art class?'

Sarah nodded. 'Simon's okay, isn't he?' she asked.

'He's got a good body, ideal for drawing. He's very patient and obliging.' Amy smiled.

'I think that Louis would agree . . .' said Sarah significantly.

'Mmmm – I see. What about Louis and Jake?'

Sarah shook her head imperatively.

'Jake's strictly for the women, but I expect Louis would fuck anyone.'

'Hmm . . . You can't be sure, about them, though?' Amy rather relished the idea of the two men together.

'I must admit, I'd thought of it, especially when Louis seemed so distant. Turns you on, does it? The idea of male gay sex?' she asked, looking at Amy directly.

Amy shrugged, then, meeting the other woman's twinkling eyes, grinned broadly. Sarah joined in.

'I know what you mean. I don't like to think of it wasted, though. Men get excited at the thought of two women together . . .' she said.

'Right,' agreed Amy.

'What about you?' challenged Sarah, her tone changing suddenly.

'What do you mean?' asked Amy, though she knew that Sarah was asking her whether she had had sex with a woman. She began to reinterpret Sarah's motives in handling Louis, in seeming to offer him as a gift. She narrowed her eyes at this woman. Her stomach felt tremulous as she met Sarah's hazel gaze once more, and shook her head. Sarah continued to regard her with interest.

They remained silent as Louis returned. Amy fell to watching him once more. He had such a dramatic effect on her that everything he did seemed imbued with sexuality. No doubt he sensed this, and played on it. Or, maybe he always looked that sexy? Perhaps Jacob had encouraged him to provide them with food, as he went again to the kitchen and began to offer them things.

'Croissants?' he suggested generously, as if this was absolutely his last offer on the domestic front.

'What do you eat when you're on your own, Louis?' Sarah asked.

Louis shrugged, abandoning the kitchen, drinking coffee, looking vaguely out of the window and into the garden.

'Nothing, probably,' Sarah said to Amy. 'He'd probably starve if Jake didn't cook for him.'

'Are you going to let me finish the painting, Sarah?' Louis asked, ignoring her jibe.

He seemed to have resumed his cold manner towards her. Sarah had thought he would be warmer, having made love to her for much of the night. Still, she was not going to let him get under her skin.

'When I've had a bath and eaten. I'm starving, Louis . . .' she complained.

Louis gave her an apple from the bowl on the Welsh dresser by him. Sarah shook her head and smiled at Amy, then she bit into the red apple.

'Shall I make something?' Amy asked Sarah, having sympathy for the woman who now had to spend the day posing for the arrogant artist.

Louis was still drinking coffee, and now smoking a cigarette. If he was tired, Amy marvelled, as she took the opportunity to fill her eyes with his firm strong body, clad in the silky, expensive, loose black trousers and a wine-red shirt, it did not show. Hours of making love must have refreshed and invigorated him. His face was clear, his eyes pellucid, his hair still damp from his shower. She breathed in the clean, masculine, slightly musky smell of him. Sarah nudged her, widening her eyes in her recognition of Amy's incipient lust.

'Go and get Jake . . .' she joked, pushing Amy.

Jacob made them breakfast without complaint – croissants and cold meats, hard-boiled eggs pâté and rolls, marmalade and honey. Louis actually sat with them, read The *Observer*, and ate hungrily. Jacob smiled at him, feeling that his friend had regained his equilibrium – for now. Sarah looked very lovable, in her pink robe, still flushed from her bath. He would miss having her constantly around. They exchanged a friendly smile. A smile which lingered . . .

Before she left, Amy stood behind Louis, watching him painting for a while. She looked at Sarah as she lay in her familiar pose, at least, for now, a little more composed than she had been. Sarah looked across to her and smiled conspiratorially.

'Do you have to leave?' asked Jacob.

Amy nodded. 'I've got to go to my shop – sort some things out. Having Saturdays off means I have to work Sunday. Lizzie – my assistant – is excellent, but – you know,' she shrugged. She wondered whether Sarah and Louis would make love. Perhaps she could arrange to meet Jacob later, or tomorrow. She could invite him to her flat for dinner. 'I suppose I'd better go,' she sighed.

Jacob nodded.

'I'll take you then – or take you home?'

'Okay, thanks . . .'

Unseen by Amy, Louis turned to watch her go. Sarah shook her head at him.

It was a good thing she hadn't fallen in love with Louis.

Three

On the following Saturday, Eleanor got to the Life Class too early, because she had not wanted to refuse her brother's offer of a lift. She had planned to do some shopping in town, first, but then, because it had started to rain heavily, she had decided to go straight to the centre instead. It was pleasant, to wander around the huge studio. To get the feel of it. Always, when she was alone, she felt receptive and relaxed, able to appreciate the atmosphere of a place. The Adult Education Centre was based around a large Victorian house, and the studio had once been a huge first-floor drawing room. Eleanor scrutinised the ornate plaster ceiling rose and picture-rail, then went over to the window to look down at the car-park in the erstwhile garden to see whether anyone else had arrived. There were still several large trees, left amongst the cars. She could see Jacob's old maroon Rover.

As she looked at the cars, she recalled how, last week, Amy had gone off with their handsome lecturer. She became lost in imagining how they had spent their afternoon. She was sure that they had made love; they had obviously been very attracted to one another. She soon became lost in a sensual reverie. After a time, Eleanor became aware that someone had entered the room. She turned to see Simon watching her. He was already clad only in his green robe. As he smiled at her in obvious appreciation, Eleanor felt herself flushing. She knew that she ought to say something friendly to Simon, who was scarcely older than she. But all she could think of was Simon, naked on the wooden chair. Her blush deepened.

To Simon, Eleanor looked enchanting as she stared across

the room at him through her wide dark eyes. She was wearing a deep blue cotton dress; her leather art-case was still over her shoulder. She clung to it, as if for comfort. He felt that she would be more at ease behind an easel. Like Louis. He walked slowly across the empty room to stand beside her. She was as dark as Louis, he thought.

He was very close to her. She could smell the masculine scent of him, clean and fragrant with the subtle aroma of his aftershave. She felt her senses quicken. She could feel the heat from his body. She smiled up at him, and Simon returned her smile. For a moment, Eleanor was sure that Simon was going to kiss her. He was so very close. It would be so easy. Though this was unexpected, she thought she would not mind. She would like it, in fact. It would only take a simple movement to slip her hand under his silken gown, and to feel his warm skin. She was shocked at her thoughts. She saw Simon's eyes close slightly, his lips part as he moved imperceptibly towards her. She wondered what it would be like, to take the initiative and touch him. Such a thing had never occurred to her before.

Jacob, entering the room, broke the spell even as he stood to appreciate the two young people, Eleanor in her long blue dress, Simon in his green robe. They were a vivid contrast, Simon, fair, with his blond hair close to Eleanor's dark looks. They turned to him and smiled. Eleanor, subtly aroused by Simon's animal proximity was now aware also of Jacob's magnetism. With an effort, she drew away from Simon and went to sit at her place of the previous week. Simon went easily to Jacob, who was unpacking his bag. Now safely ensconced behind her desk, and with her sketch-pad before her, Eleanor watched them.

As Jacob smiled up at Simon, Eleanor felt that Simon knew Jacob Laurence very well. She felt that in their initial silence, the men exchanged some tacit comment on her.

'Louis said not to forget his party,' Jacob said to Simon quietly.

'As if . . .' Simon responded, scoffing at the joke between them. 'So he's finally conceded?'

'Under duress!' Jacob smiled ruefully.

Simon smiled. 'Do you reckon I could bring someone?'

'If he could stand the competition.'

'*She* . . .' Simon's gaze drifted across to where Eleanor was seemingly immersed in her drawing.

Jacob raised his eyebrows, shrugged and grinned. As the other students began to arrive, Simon disappeared until Jacob should call for him to pose.

Eleanor concentrated on expanding her rapid line-drawing of the two men chatting, whilst they were still clear in her mind. Glancing up at Jacob, she saw Amy enter and witnessed the lingering knowledgeable smile that passed between them. Amy smiled broadly at Eleanor, seeming to envelop the younger woman in her secret.

'This week, before you begin to draw Simon, I'd like us to consider the representation of the nude in history,' Jacob began. 'I've brought some slides to show you. Could you turn off the lights, Marie-Anne? Cheers. I thought it would be useful if, whilst I show you some of the classical poses taken, Simon could take up some of these, and you can just have a think about the way he looks to you, and the way such a pose has been represented in art. Naturally, later in the course, we'll study more modern ways the nude has been represented. However, considering the trip to Florence, it may be interesting for you to see how the Renaissance artists achieved their results. The term "Renaissance" means "rebirth" – a return to the values of Classical Greece, after the strictures of Mediaeval times.

'This week, I'll concentrate specifically on representation of the male, and later, we'll look at the female nude. First, statues from ancient Egypt . . .' Jacob began to operate the projector, and they were enveloped, in the darkened room, with the focus of the bright screen to concentrate their attention. Jacob showed them the earliest statues, seemingly stiff in their execution, as were 'kouroi' from ancient Greece. He then moved on to the Classical Age, introducing to them, through his slides, the concept of 'contrapposto'. When he came to Graeco-Roman statues, he asked Simon to take up identical positions.

Eleanor, existing deliciously in this sensual world, was

fascinated, both by the ancient statues, and by Simon's lithe body as he moved easily from pose to pose in the dim light.

'Don't worry if you can't see Simon too well. When we turn on the lights, I'll get him to repeat the poses, and I want you to examine him carefully, perhaps beginning to think of the placing of his weight, his muscles and sinews. His centre of gravity. We'll also have a look at some diagrams later, to give you an introduction to anatomy. As I said last week this is a vital consideration in drawing from life. It will help you if you study this in some depth, become familiar with the inter-relationship between bones, muscles, sinews, tendons—'

'Some personal examination?' asked the risqué Robbie.

'If you like,' grinned Jacob, unabashed. 'You may find it helps your art.'

'Mmmm . . .' retaliated Robbie, apparently, by his tone, choosing to interpret his advice as being sexual.

'Apollo was of course the ideal for the Greeks. Though nowadays we may have a different opinion of the "Apollo Belvedere", it's interesting to note Winckelmann's comment, and I quote, he perceived this particular statue as "the highest ideal of art among all the works of antiquity", and he urged, "Enter, O reader, with your spirit into this kingdom of beauty incarnate, and there seek to create for yourself the image of divine nature." We may now consider the "Apollo Belvedere" to be inferior to other works, which Winckelmann had not seen, but his advice, pertaining these, holds true.'

Eleanor let these words sink into her soul, though she was dimly aware of the background murmur and laughter at Robbie's comments. She saw that Simon was smiling, as though entering into this challenge: to represent ideal beauty for them. Jacob continued to flash before them wonderful images of Classical and Renaissance statues of sensual naked men.

'And so— ' continued Jacob, disregarding the buzz of chatter, though his voice rose a little in order to find ascendance, ' —The figure of Apollo, the most beautiful of the Greek gods, remained the ideal, and very many statues, though under other names, originate from him. As you may know, to ancient Greeks, the ideal was represented by the *male* nude. Men exercised naked, and generally wore only a short cloak in daily life, while women were cloistered in domesticity, and were covered. To the Greeks, the romantic ideal in love was that of one man for another.'

Amy smiled significantly at Jacob, thinking of his friendship with Louis, and what Sarah had told her of Louis' own interest in their attractive model, but Jacob did not respond. He continued,

'You may know that in Renaissance times, friendship between men was highly valued.'

He smiled at his audience and indicated for the lights to be turned on. He then got Simon to take up similar poses to the ones they had seen, explaining to them the various changes in his centre of gravity, as his weight was shifted, depending on where he placed his leg, and whether his body was twisted.

'As you'll recognise – this stance is the typical "contrapposto" pose, so familiar from classical statues. As you have just seen, before the classical age, the statue is firmly on two legs. The emotional content of this symmetrical pose is limited.

'Here, the point of gravity remains in the middle of the body, but the weight now rests upon one leg, and this leg is held obliquely. The pelvis sinks down on the side of the free leg, which is therefore bent at the knee. The torso is inclined slightly out of the vertical. The head is inclined sideways in the opposite direction.

'I know that Simon posed for you briefly last week in this position, but now have another go – taking into account the sense of balance. I'm sure you've all been studying the books . . .' he grinned at them as he went to check his slides.

It was more difficult for Eleanor to concentrate on drawing the naked Simon this week. She kept recalling his closeness to her, his lovely smile and the potent fact that she *had* wanted him to kiss her. She had also had plenty of time to gaze on his nakedness, and mingling, in her mind, its loveliness with the representations of the ancient statues she had looked at so often in books. Seeing his naked penis, she could not help but imagine reaching out to touch it. She felt that he was aware of her wayward thoughts as she drew him in this pose of the Greek gods, standing in imitation of ancient Greek statues. The beautiful Apollo! Simon's testicles hung low and heavy, his penis seemed full. Eleanor wondered how he would react should he begin to become erect. As she gazed at his full member, it seemed to her that it was just about to become fuller. Perhaps he had to think of other things to deflect sexual response. She realised that she was unconsciously depicting her rude thoughts on her paper, instead of concentrating on the classical approach. She quickly covered the drawing as Jacob came round to peruse their work. Jacob smiled.

At the end of the afternoon, Eleanor had planned to make a quick getaway so as to avoid any embarrassing meeting with Simon. However, Jacob had naturally discussed their work with them after they had finished their session with Simon, who therefore had plenty of time to get dressed. And then, as people asked various questions, they had begun to examine the plastic skeleton and had looked at diagrams of muscles and tendons. Simon was waiting for her at the door. As she was first out, at least there was no one to witness their meeting. She averted her eyes from his friendly smile, and made as if to hurry past. Simon grasped her arm. Eleanor was all too aware of the electricity that shot through her body at his touch. She smiled shyly up at him.

The rain had cleared and the autumnal sun had emerged. It was now quite warm.

'Would you have lunch with me, in town?' Simon smiled.

It was impossible to resist him. Eleanor returned his smile. He looked very cheeky.

'I was going to do some shopping.'

'That's fine.' Simon shrugged. 'Then we'll have lunch?'

'Okay.'

They went together towards the town centre, beginning to get to know each other as they chatted, asking each other about their lives, families and plans for the future. Simon was very keen on cars and motorbikes and was studying to be a garage mechanic. He had a job at his uncle's garage in Ardleigh.

Eleanor liked Simon, and tried to forget the originality of their meeting: that she had gazed for hours now on his naked body.

Amy lingered, and when everyone else had at last gone, she went over to Jacob, whose intelligent eyes met hers in understanding. They embraced and kissed, their passion immediately all-consuming. Amy gasped to feel Jacob's hands deftly exploring her yielding body. They fell back against the door, pushing it closed. They could hear sounds in the building; a banjo group sent jarring notes echoing through the corridors. They laughed. Jacob's hands were inside Amy's dress, caressing her warm breasts, cupping her small bottom, delving inside her knickers to feel the moist fleshy heat of her sex.

'Yes . . .' Amy murmured, kissing Jacob's neck, feeling his hair against her face, holding him close, manipulating his erect member.

'There's a lesson in here now,' Jacob told her, his voice husky.

Amy pulled his stiff penis towards her sex and, looking up at him seductively, began to pull on it. It was delightful to have him in her power. Someone tried the door and there were voices outside. Jacob groaned. Amy knew that he wanted to fuck her. People were gathering outside, trying the door. Amy pressed his sex against hers. Jacob held her and kissed her as she began to writhe and moan. She came so easily. Then he pushed her away, though the voracious Amy would have continued, wanting him inside her.

'I'll lose my job,' he laughed, forcing his unwilling cock into his pants. 'Come on . . .' He zipped up his trousers, and opened the door, saying in a low tone, 'We'll go back to my place, yes?'

'Is Louis there?' Amy asked, thinking it might be preferable to go to her house, which was in any case, closer. Louis had not seemed at all keen on her presence in Dedham during the past week, when she had stayed with Jacob a couple of times. She was consumed by the burning between her legs. Jacob seemed pretty desperate too.

He shook his head, in answer to her question. 'He's gone to London.'

As they crossed the car-park together, Amy took his hand, still needing to be close to him, and he did not take it away.

'I said I'd pick up some stuff for Louis . . .' he recalled, frowning, a little impatient.

'At Trinity Arts?' asked Amy.

Jacob nodded.

'Okay. It'll save . . .' She caressed him deftly, laughing as he moaned longingly in response.

It was lovely to walk with him through the crowds, knowing she had just turned him on. He was still aroused; and she wanted to make love to him and soon would. She thought too of the dark, arrogant artist with his demands on Jacob. Thoughts of Louis excited her further, though anger at his supercilious attitude towards her possessed her too. These combined emotions showed in her body as she walked, and many men turned to look at her. She knew that Jacob was aware of this.

'Shall I see you next week?' Eleanor said to Simon as her bus arrived. She had enjoyed her afternoon with him. He was good fun to be with. They had visited the library, laughingly tried on clothes in various shops, had lunch and a few drinks and generally got to know each other quite well. Their physical attraction for each other was definitely there; bubbling below the surface.

'Eleanor . . .'

'Yes?'

Was he, after all, going to invite her back with him? Eleanor wanted to spend more time with him, but was too shy to invite him back to her parents' house.

'Will you come to Louis' party on Friday?'

'Yes . . .' said Eleanor, wishing that it was tonight, wondering who Louis was, not really caring.

As others pushed past to board the bus, Simon quickly wrote down his phone number and pushed it at her.

'Phone me?'

'Yes!' Eleanor laughed as the bus pulled away, wondering why he had not asked her earlier. She waved to him through the window, smiling as he ran by the bus.

At home, alone in her room, Eleanor took off her clothes and lay on her bed. She ran her palms all over her tingling body, and then pressed on her sex, pleasuring herself, thinking with happiness of Simon. Giving in to the undercurrents of sex which had grown steadily all afternoon. This was the first time she had concentrated her wild energy on a particular man, whose body she knew so well, though she had not yet touched him. At last, hearing her brother Robin arrive home, she dressed in her robe and sat at her desk by the window, looking over their garden, and adorning her pictures of Simon.

The fact that Jacob and Amy had to wait to indulge their need for each other merely fed their passion. They glanced at each other repeatedly as they drove along the county roads to Dedham. Each look affirmed their mutual longing. Jacob laughed as Amy reached to caress his swollen crotch. As soon as they got into the lounge, they grabbed at each other, laughing and kissing and stripping, until they were naked, and on the settee, and Jacob was kissing Amy all over, only able to resist for a little time the overwhelming need to thrust his stiff and aching cock into her. He groaned in abandon, as if he had waited too long, and, after all, Amy *had* come, in the art-room. He closed his eyes in absolute pleasure, conscious only of her delicious body, and the feel of his prick held tightly by her muscular warmth. After a few minutes of necessary rapid thrusting, gliding along her tight muscle (in which he knew Amy revelled as much as he; she responded to his every nuance), Jacob opened his eyes and smiled at her. She was lovely.

'Hi . . .'

'Hi . . .' she replied, receiving his kiss and feeling renewed gushes of pleasure as he rocked his pubic bone against her clitoris. She gazed affectionately up at her handsome lover.

Then, suddenly, he moved her to lie on top of him and Amy took control, gazing with intense pleasure into his grey eyes, and at his reddened mouth, partly hidden by his moustache, and slowly ground her sex against his. They took it very slowly, nurturing the spasms of immense pleasure which invaded their genitals. Jacob was patient and generous. A sweet lover. Amy took air in through her mouth, an expression of ecstasy, and threw back her head, her breasts tingling with sexual electricity as Jacob reached to grip her nipples and pull on them. She felt his rigid cock filling her as she worked her clitoris against his sharp bone, grinding and lingering.

She felt his hands on her bottom, caressing her slowly, letting his fingers slip between her cheeks as he raised her fevered pitch still higher. Amy's powerful orgasm began, and Jacob kissed her as he felt her throbbing all around him, as patient as he could be, until he allowed himself release, and Amy's ecstasy was increased by the added stimulation of his pulsing cock as Jacob began to moan expressively, and ramming upwards into her, coming with sudden violent abandonment.

They did not see Louis, standing at the open door, watching them through dark, hooded eyes. He was riveted to Amy's undulating white abdomen, the glory of her red curls, cascading over them both, her perfect rounded breasts with their crimson nipples, manipulated so expertly by his friend. He saw Jacob's bliss, mirrored in his face as he let himself go, now taking back control as he thrust into Amy, agile and fit as he manipulated her soft yielding white flesh. His friend was possessed by sexual energy. Louis watched Amy grind provocatively against Jacob, sucking the breath from his strong fit body as she kissed him deeply. Louis was acutely aroused as they groaned and panted and climbed inexorably to their all-engrossing climax. His cock was stiff. He caressed Amy with his greedy eyes, aching to pull her away from Jacob and take her.

Jacob noticed him and smiled dreamily, his familiar face expressing his satisfaction, his lovely grey eyes pellucid as they met Louis' affectionately. Louis did not smile. He was more inclined to hit Jacob. He went from the door as Amy looked round. He drank whisky in the kitchen, but it did not douse his burning. He went and stared at his portrait of Sarah, as though he would bring her to life. Somehow it was difficult to talk to her now. Perhaps that was because his mind was filled with that witch of a woman. Jacob's lover! He went to the kitchen, to pour more whisky. He felt filled with anger at Jacob.

Jacob came to make coffee for Amy.

'Are you okay, Louis?'

His voice was filled with such damned concern. Louis moved away from him fretfully.

'I'm just fine and dandy, Jake,' he drawled sarcastically.

Jacob laughed.

'You shouldn't drink so much. You've got to finish "Sarah".'

'If only . . .' Louis said sarcastically, then added, 'Don't go on at me, Jacob.' His voice expressed his extreme irritability. 'I suppose she's staying for dinner?'

'Amy? I thought we might go for a drink.'

'Hhhh . . .'

'You're jealous . . .' Jacob expressed his realisation without thinking.

'Don't be stupid!' Louis scoffed, as if such an extreme and irrational emotion would be the last thing he could be expected to experience.

'I was *sure* you'd want to paint her. She'd be marvellous, wouldn't she? With her colouring, and . . .'

'I hadn't really noticed,' Louis answered airily, attempting to convey extreme lack of interest in Amy. Jacob sounded just too enthusiastic, he thought. Louis had skilfully avoided all conversation about Amy all week. He had not told Jacob how she was incandescent in his mind. But then Jacob would not have to be told. Louis continued, 'Anyway, I've got plenty to do. The exhibition, and . . .'

'And?'

Jacob could not believe that Louis even expected him to be unaware of his interest in Amy. She had visited him during the week, and the atmosphere between them was like live electricity. He decided to ignore his friend's attempts to dissemble.

'So, why aren't you in London?'

'I've been, Jake . . .' Louis sounded bored.

'Where did you go? You weren't long.'

'I just saw Jonathan about the exhibition.'

'You didn't go to one single gallery?' asked Jacob in disbelief. 'What about the Géricault exhibition?'

Louis shook his head. It occurred to Jacob that Louis had come back on purpose to see Amy. Things must be serious if Louis had not felt he could take another look at his beloved Gericault. He shook his head, wondering how tempestuous his evening would be between these two fiery and elemental creatures.

'So. How was Jonathan?'

'Fine.'

'I'm surprised he and Lisa didn't invite you to stay?' he goaded.

Louis did not respond. Obviously they had.

'Are you coming out to dinner with us, then?'

Louis shot him a dark look.

'I wouldn't want you to starve.'

Louis looked away. Amy came to see where her coffee was. Jacob shook his head, sighing inwardly at the silent animosity between them.

'Hi, Louis,' said Amy coolly, as if he was some insignificant creature she scarcely deemed to notice, and was surprised even to see.

Louis cast her a look of hostility and went out to his studio.

'I thought we could all go out to the "Sun",' Jacob ventured, thinking he must be crazy.

'Okay.' Amy nodded.

However, Amy and Louis did not argue. Louis was withdrawn and quiet during the meal. Jacob was used to his moods, and disregarded them as far as possible, merely continuing to expect Louis to accede to his suggestions. Louis generally did. He was surprised that the tension between him and Amy did not find release with bickering. Perhaps they considered themselves above this.

Amy had plenty of opportunity to regard this handsome, sexy man, to drink in his potent aura. She scarcely spoke to him, not wanting to be drawn further into their silent game at Louis' provocation. Jacob was friendly and chatty and they enjoyed the meal, for even if Louis did not eat much, he was not immune to his friend's warmth, and occasionally responded. He watched Amy as avidly as she did him. Each thought that their piercing glances were invisible to the other. Jacob wondered what would happen if he left them together. They would probably refuse to respond to the fire between them. He could not understand why Louis did not simply ask Amy to pose for him. He needed a new project, but he never thought ahead, always consumed by his current work. Perhaps, thought Jacob, he was too interested in screwing Amy to concentrate on painting her. And, if he had given Louis a thought, later, he may well have appreciated the anguish Louis suffered, alone in his studio, whilst Jacob made love to Amy.

Amy could not help but think of the dark artist. She was drawn to him, with a passion that was so intense that sometimes she felt dizzy with it. He seemed to have got into her soul, and she felt close to him, even though they weren't able to have a successful conversation. She was intrigued by the powerful sexuality and dynamic mental energy which exuded from him. She was attracted by his knowledge and ability. She wanted to pose naked for him, to lie in his presence and display her body to him. That he did not ask her riled her. She did not understand that it was because she had had such a dramatic effect on him that he fought her.

Louis could not sleep. He could not even go up to his room, thinking of Amy, with Jacob. He was very aroused, but too much so to go through all the difficult civilities of getting someone to fuck him. He thought of Sarah, but, although he knew she was still attracted to him, it would be too complicated to get her now. It would necessitate a lot of words, anyway, she had some kind of affinity with Amy. They had obviously got on well. He sensed that Sarah wanted Amy for herself. He thought, with longing, of Simon. Things with him were always straight-forward. But, even when he had summoned up the capacity necessary in his distracted state to phone him, Simon was out.

Louis wanted to take off all his clothes and go out into the rain. He fingered his erect cock, but masturbation would not appease his terrible longing.

The next morning, Sunday, Amy drove him crazy by coming down in Jacob's gown to make breakfast. Louis watched her hungrily from the breakfast-room. He felt like a wild animal, trapped by his own nature, maddened through hunger, lack of sleep and the need for sex. Most of all the need for sex. He watched Amy avariciously, seeing the undulating lines of her body beneath the fine satin robe, which smelt of Jacob. He clenched his hands against the compulsion to rip it from her and sink his teeth into her white flesh. He closed his eyes as he imagined the feel of her smooth full white breasts. He would suck on them until she screamed.

'What?' he snapped at her as she repeated some phrase to him.

'I said,' began Amy with exaggerated patience against his petulance, 'do you want breakfast?'

She seemed to Louis to be fully aware of his consuming need to fuck her; his cock rigid beneath his jeans. He shook his black curls at her, his eyes cynical. She seemed to smirk at him. Well, it was alright for her – and Jake. Impulsively, Louis went up to Jacob's room, perhaps to speak to his friend now that Amy had left him alone for a minute. Perhaps to belt him across the face and rid him of his satisfied smile. He lingered at the door, tightening his eyes against Jacob's contented nakedness. Louis would not mind who he fucked.

'Louis? Didn't you go to bed?'

'What do you think?'

'Oh, Louis . . .'

Louis ran his eyes briefly over Jacob's relaxed, warm-seeming body, seeing his detumerscent penis, generous against his thigh.

He turned away, looking only sideways at Jacob as he addressed him haughtily, crossing his arms over his chest.

'I'm going to see Simon.'

Jacob laughed.

'It's that bad, is it?'

'Fuck off, Jake . . .'

'Have a bath,' Jacob advised.

'Or a cold shower?' Louis asked.

'You ought to eat,' said Amy, albeit coldly, coming past him with a tray.

'Ttt . . .'

Louis resented their sensible advice. He grabbed his long black coat and car keys and slammed the door as he went out into the cold morning. Jacob listened in concern as he drove rapidly away.

Louis did not really want to leave. However, he drove on to where Simon lived in Ardleigh, in a house he shared with some friends. That he was using the young man was buried deeply at the bottom of his mind, but Simon was really very sweet.

'Louis! So early on a Sunday?' Simon smiled at him, and stepped back to gesture him in.

'Who's here?' asked Louis, suddenly fretful at the thought of people.

'Actually, no one. Pete and Dave are away, and Ken's at his girlfriend's.'

Louis raised his eyebrow as he came inside. He took off his coat and slung it over the settee. He stood before the fire-place, and lit a cigarette. He did not look at Simon. Simon smiled, sympathetically, at his back, as Louis held onto the mantelpiece, bent his head and looked into the empty hearth. He understood that Louis had come here on impulse, and now he was nervous. He was tired and looked pale. He looked up at his reflection in the mirror above the fireplace and met Simon's eyes. Simon smiled again, but Louis looked quickly away. It was possible the unpredictable Louis would change his mind and go home. Simon did not want that.

Simon went and stood before him, filled, as ever, by affection for him. And more – he was always affected by Louis' chemistry, or whatever it was. Sex. Simon was not one for soul-searching or guilt-trips. As Louis raised his eyes, Simon was struck by the intensity in them, causing a reflex gathering of adrenaline in his guts, and a quickening of his penis. He didn't want any of

Louis' complexity, so he kissed him, feeling the responsive surge of sexuality rising in Louis as he tossed away his cigarette and returned Simon's kiss with passion.

'Come on – come to bed, Louis,' Simon took his hand.

Simon was excited by Louis' dark decadence. This had somehow had its genesis in Louis' painting of him, and his early exposure to this passionate and liberal man. He felt he was caught up in Louis' wild energy as he tore at his body, as if in punishment for Louis' own desperate need. And when Louis fucked him, he felt him, huge and pumping, inside him, and as if his body would explode with his force. But he gloried in this, in the man's possessive caresses as he felt at his body, stimulated his testicles beyond endurance, and catered to the unbearable excitement of his cock. And Louis sucked on his flesh as though he would have the life out of him. Though later, Simon always felt that he had been given some feral gift. Simon cried out as the spunk shot forth from him, and he felt Louis' body shuddering at his own orgasm as he emptied his prick dramatically.

Louis lay beside the young man, tracing the familiar lines of his body slowly, his eyes following appreciatively.

'Do you feel better, Louis?' Simon asked.

Louis smiled gently up at him, and nodded, but Simon saw that the hunger remained in his eyes, and recognised in that instant, that probably Louis was only as gay as he was. He was liberal, and sexual, but, right now, Louis needed a woman. Simon knew this because his mind had been full of Eleanor. He reached out for Louis' re-tumescent prick, but Louis shook his head slowly, indicating that Simon did not need to feel obliged to attend to him. He continued to stroke Simon's body, moulding it as if it was plastic, and Simon tried to conceive the creative urge that made Louis respond to him sometimes as though he was glorying in his body purely for its beauty. This was separate from his greedy lust. Simon did not mind, he liked Louis a lot and Simon gloried in the simplicity of his own philosophy. He was not open to Louis' complexities.

Louis lay back at last, and Simon covered him. He went to

make him some food, but, when he returned, Louis was deeply asleep.

When Louis returned home, fed and bathed, Amy was leaving, and she narrowed her eyes at his changed state, as though trying to conceive where he had satisfied his animal lust and human needs. He smiled archly at her, hiding well the reflex reaction of his body to her vibrant sexuality.

'You know I didn't want this damned party!' said Louis truculently.

Jacob did not rise to his aggression. He realised that Louis was nervous and tired. The portrait of Sarah had taken him longer to finish than he had anticipated, probably because, in his mind, he had sullied its execution by screwing the model too early. This had complicated his pure relationship with her and now he had felt it would be too complicated to ask her back too often. And Sarah, freed (perhaps temporarily) from his thrall, had regained her independence, and had not fancied much more posing. Still, he had not abandoned his portrait nor destroyed it. And it was true, he didn't really need Sarah. He had worked very hard to complete it by this weekend, so that the party would still be a celebration of its completion as well as of his twenty-seventh birthday. Jacob dreaded to think what would have happened if he had not finished it. They would have had to cancel the party, and waste all the food. The caterers had finished. Louis had had a bath, and looked wonderful, despite his fatigue. It was a pity he had not had another day to re-acclimatise himself. His anxiety was due partly to apprehension of all the people who would soon arrive, and partly because he had not yet really emerged from the exclusive world of his painting. He kept returning to it, haunting it, regarding it critically and with disdain. Their guests were old friends, Jacob's colleagues, Louis' contacts, and a few people from the Life Class. Louis knew Robbie, and Sam and Marie-Anne. The latter, Jacob was aware, had always had an eye on the gifted artist. Perhaps Louis could confound them all and paint her. Her body was voluptuous and generously curvaceous. She was at least easy-going, and amusing in her own way. Sarah and Simon were to be there, and Eleanor – if Simon had managed to persuade her. And Amy. So Eleanor would be the only person Louis did not yet know.

'Here.' Jacob handed Louis a glass of Graves as he went back to his studio.

He watched Louis in affection as his friend prowled around the painting of the naked woman as though it was a hostile adversary, with designs on his sanity.

'It's fine. It's wonderful. It's the best thing you've ever done!' Jacob laughed, tousling the dark curls.

Louis shook him off moodily.

'You always say that!' he accused Jacob, flashing his magnificent eyes at him.

'It always is,' responded Jacob. He shook with silent laughter as he escaped from the room, wondering which lucky female would arrive first, to help deflect Louis' rampant energy. The doorbell rang. Naturally, Louis remained petulantly in his studio as his guests began to arrive. Jacob would not put it past him to refuse to come out all evening. Still, the phlegmatic Jacob refused to let Louis get under his skin. He had had a lifetime of dealing with him. Their friends were tolerant of his temperamental nature for the most part but when they were not, things could become a bit wild. Newcomers were usually sufficiently beguiled by his talent to think him justified, or at least forgivable. A temperamental artist.

Jacob smiled to see Simon; Louis would be glad to see him. He smiled at little Eleanor. A faint doubt struck at the back of his mind. Would Louis take Simon from Eleanor? He welcomed the pair in, taking the bottles from them. Simon clenched a parcel to him. Jacob sensed, rather than heard, Louis come from his studio. He stood at his door, down the hall, regarding his guests through his dark eyes.

'Interesting . . .' thought Jacob, seeing the subtle change over Louis' face as he looked speculatively at Eleanor, and then glanced, almost jealously, at Simon. 'Complicated . . .' he added, to himself, sighing as though his fears would be verified.

'This is Louis,' Simon told Eleanor, taking her hand, and leading her down the hall, smiling proudly. He was very fond of Louis, and bruited his talent to all.

Jacob saw Louis' eyes narrow as he followed them. As usual, Simon kissed Louis, giving him the present. They were very close after all. Louis embraced him briefly. Jacob saw that Eleanor was a little taken aback by this display of affection. She was very young, Jacob thought. He wondered how she would deal with the reality of their liberal relationship. He himself had been a little surprised at Simon's obviously natural interest in this young woman. He saw that Louis was very taken with Eleanor, that he was drinking in the delicate lines of her elfin face, letting his eyes sweep over her wispy black hair, appreciating that the skull it clung to was perfect. Louis' eyes were lustful, his pouting mouth sensual, but Jacob knew that his lust was for art rather than sex, and he was very needy at present.

'Say hello to Elli . . .' Simon cajoled, playfully.

Louis took Eleanor's hand and raised it slowly to his lips. Jacob wondered if he imagined beginning to seduce her right now as he began to kiss along her slender arm, and then take her masterfully to him. He was very drawn. She would have no defence, and Simon would merely be shoved away. But Louis merely kissed her small hand softly and then met her eyes and raised his glass to her. Flushed, Eleanor glanced at Simon, who was too besotted with her, and with his idol, to take in the subtleties of this romancing. Jacob realised that Eleanor was already falling under Louis' rich enchantment.

Louis met Jacob's eyes, opening his wide, and Jacob shook his head, smiling, thinking that this was just the intellectual equivalent of him raising his clenched fist. He sighed again. The bell rang again, and it was Amy. Louis still lingered in the hall, though Simon and Eleanor had gone into the lounge. Jacob kissed Amy, and led her in, seeing her eyes light instinctively as she noticed the artist, and then fill with supposed hostility. Louis' own eyes drifted slowly over her lovely body, lingering on her breasts and crotch, then moving lazily upwards to meet hers with a cold smirk, before he turned away.

Jacob put his arm round Amy, feeling her tremble with anger. Luckily, just then Marie-Anne arrived with her twin entourage in tow.

'Hi there!' said Marie-Anne, in her friendly, transatlantic accent. She planted a fleeting kiss on Jacob's cheek, and then bustled in, keen to locate Louis, with whom she had assumed a motherly relationship.

Sam and Robbie greeted them affectionately, taking the opportunity to kiss Amy, who laughed at them. Jacob gestured them towards the lounge, where they went in search of drinks. Marie-Anne had stopped off there and was admiring the colourful display of food. Jacob thought that that would suffice for a while, in terms of playing host.

He led Amy to the kitchen, aware that she was suppressing her anger at Louis. He was Jacob's friend, after all. Old Dire Straits music came from the lounge as they passed, Robbie liked to organise the music and had found the CDs. Jacob was surprised, now he thought about it, that Louis had not got in first with Debussy or Ravel. Or John Williams. Still, he had been preoccupied with his portrait. Laughter also issued forth, which was a good sign. Robbie and Sam always made great efforts to be friendly with everyone. They were good at parties. No doubt they'd dig out vintage Stones' albums, and have everyone dancing, before too long.

Alone in the kitchen, Jacob smiled at Amy, and then laughed, pulled her close and kissed her.

'Don't let him get to you, he's a swine,' he whispered, hugging her tightly.

'I don't know what you mean,' Amy replied coolly, releasing herself and looking at the bottles on the pine cupboard, picking them up in turn and replacing them a little distractedly. Jacob poured her a drink, and went to answer the door again. He was kept busy at this task for some time, especially when their old friends from college, including Lisa and Jonathan, who were arranging Louis' exhibition, arrived. He took them through to Louis' studio. Jonathan immediately became engrossed in looking through Louis' paintings. At last Sam took over opening the door, and then Jacob made sure that the glasses were replenished. Next time he saw Amy, she was ensconced comfortably on the sofa in the lounge with Sarah. He hoped Sarah was not dissuading Amy from posing.

'I've got this bracelet for Louis,' Sarah told Jacob as he refilled her glass,

'It's lovely . . .' Jacob felt the delicate weight of the silver chain in his hand as he looked at the unusual design. *Celtic dragons*, he thought. 'He's in his studio – probably showing off your portrait to people. Why don't you give it to him?' He trickled the chain through his fingers back into Sarah's palm.

'Did you make it?' asked Amy admiringly, wondering whether perhaps she could sell such items in her boutique.

'Yes, making jewellery's my main interest – not modelling for Louis.'

'Are you going to give it to Louis?' Amy asked, as Jacob's attention was taken up with Sam and Robbie, who were asking him about the CD collection.

Sarah crinkled her nose and looked at Amy. Amy thought of her fondling the artist seductively last week.

'I suppose so. I mean, yes, I want him to have it – I made it for him – but, no, I don't want to get involved with him tonight, if you know what I mean? I fancy some simplicity. He's in a funny mood. Anyway, I feel a bit guilty about abandoning the last few sittings, especially as he had paid me in advance. Though he didn't complain.'

'I thought you were besotted with him?'

'Did you? Louis gets you that way – an aftermath of the portrait. Perhaps I was – for a while – but, to be honest,' she moved closer to Amy, glancing at Jacob's back as she whispered, 'I really do fancy Jake . . .'

Amy nodded, disregarding a sudden stab of jealousy.

'He's very sweet . . .'

'Well, sweeter than Louis,' Sarah agreed. 'Though Louis certainly has something. I just don't want it at the moment. Now it's all over, I need a break from him.'

'Right. So – can you give me any advice?'

Sarah grinned. 'I knew you had it for him.'

'He's an arrogant bastard.'

Sarah agreed.

Nevertheless, they both looked silently up at Louis when he entered, looking stunning in black.

'Jake—?'

'Ah – Simon – take these coats to the cloakroom.' Jacob thrust a pile of coats and jackets at him. The doorbell rang again. Mick Jagger, singing 'Dancing with Mr. D', came loudly from the lounge.

'Sure. Jake – can we – use your room?'

Jacob glanced at Eleanor hovering shyly in the background. He patted Simon's arm and nodded. Simon gave the coats back to Jacob. The two went upstairs. When he got back to the lounge, determined to have a drink, and a morsel to eat – he was famished – Jacob was relieved to see Louis in the midst of a group of their old friends from Art School. He was smiling and drinking wine, regaling them with witty tales and generally looking as though he was actually enjoying his party. Though no doubt he would deny this at some later date. Jacob felt a small knot of tension that he had not really acknowledged dissolve from the pit of his stomach. He glanced over to where Amy and Sarah were still gossiping away. They had obviously had a few glasses of champagne, and were getting on like a house on fire. Perhaps he would be sleeping alone, he thought philosophically as he recognised their intimacy. Right now all he wanted was a drink.

As if telepathic, Louis turned and handed him a crystal stemmed goblet of champagne. Jacob drank it as if it was lemonade and his friends laughed. Louis poured more into his glass and then his own, and over the floor, and Jacob's clothes and into his own mouth and then into Jacob's. They all laughed uproariously. *Bacchus*, Jacob thought, wild and ecstatic. And he was Apollo, calm and measured and in control. That was the way it had to be. Louis put his arm companionably around

Jacob's neck, and blew onto his neck. He was very drunk. Lisa handed Jacob a piece of spinach quiche, and he ate ravenously.

'Poor Jake – you've been so busy!' Lisa kissed him on the cheek.

'This is all wonderful,' her lover (on and off for many years) Jonathan told him, widening his arms expansively.

'Yes – wonderful . . .' Louis repeated, drawling extravagantly, a hint of sarcasm in his tone. He was still very close to Jacob, licking at, and kissing, his earlobe now.

Jacob made to push him away, but Louis stuck like glue. Jacob drained his glass, ready to break away and refill it, but Lisa did it for him, obligingly. Jacob cast her a look, which said sarcastically 'Thanks a lot!' Lisa laughed. Louis was even closer to him. Louis was at a loose end, full of energy, full of sex, now he had relaxed. He had no painting to drain him, and his next possible conquests, Eleanor and Amy, were occupied. Even Simon, ironically. Sarah was becoming very pally with his 'enemy', and seemingly was temporarily free of his enchantment. Their immediate friends were in pairs, though not all would refuse Louis at his most adamant. 'Shit!', thought Jacob, realising Louis' lascivious and public intent. He thought, in retrospect, that Louis had settled too well. And no doubt burning in his mind were images of Amy and Eleanor. Eleanor could wait, but he must all the time be aware of Amy. Amy! Amy was whispering to Sarah now, and Sarah laughed.

How long had he been in here, aware of Amy's supposed obliviousness to him. Hurt by this and by Sarah's complicity? How naive he was. Jacob knew that – handled correctly – either or both women would be upstairs with Louis like a shot. But Louis was too engrossed in self-pity to see this. And too drunk! He felt Louis' erection against his leg, and moved away decisively. He dismissed his own reflex reaction as animal lust. He did not think of it. He would not. And when Louis moved back, touching his crotch fleetingly, laughingly, with recognition, he whispered clearly into his friend's ear:

'Go and have a wank, Louis.'

'Come with me, Jake . . .' Louis invited, unperturbed, and

then kissed him passionately on the mouth, taking him unawares, despite Jacob's instinct.

Jacob was amazed to find that his entire body flooded with dark, excited passion, as Louis held him very close. For a long moment the room spun, and when Louis released him, all sound was distant. He knew that his own eyes were as smouldering as Louis' as they looked at each other. His face was flushed and his cock was visibly erect. He wanted to shake his head at Louis but he could not. He bit his lower lip, tasting blood, and continued to see the seriousness in Louis' black eyes. At last, Louis moved away. Louis was gone. The sound of Mick Jagger sailed loudly through the room, and once more people danced all around him. Jacob swallowed hard. He felt weak, and sick, as though with a surfeit of emotion. He realised that he was not alone, but in the midst of his oldest friends. He smiled, dizzy, wanting to be alone. To have a cigarette in his darkened garden. To look calmly up at the stars. He did not want to see Louis. How could this be?

'He loves you, Jake.' Lisa was saying tenderly, rubbing his arm as if she understood.

Jacob shook his head and excused himself, shaking people off as they passed him, he went upstairs and was relieved to find the bathroom free. He doused his face with cold water and slowly began to recover his *sang-froid*. He leant against the wall and closed his eyes, remaining thus for a long time. Then he shook his head at his reflection and smiled to himself. He did not want to lose Louis' friendship. He did not want to live in this house without Louis. But he did not want sex with Louis. Nor with any man. Of this he was certain. It was the champagne, the evening. Louis! He wanted Amy, or Sarah. He wanted Amy or Sarah badly – now! He could hear Debussy's *Claire de Lune*. Louis was playing Clarissa's baby grand in his room. Jacob opened Louis' door. Louis was smoking and drinking and playing like an angel. He had a bottle of champagne by his side. He smiled beatifically at Jacob, composed and directed now, in his music. Louis was simple really. Jacob was lonely. Filled with longing for a woman, Amy, or Sarah, or . . .

'You shouldn't leave your guests for too long . . .' he said quietly to Louis, who nodded, sober now.

'Come and play, Jake . . . ? Just for a few minutes,' he added as Jacob though drawn, was about to demur pleading hospitality. 'It is my birthday . . .'

Jacob nodded, drained Louis' glass and went to pick up his clarinet, already assembled, from where it lay next to Louis.

He answered Louis' smile, and they began to play. Jacob felt infinite relief, safe, once more in their familiar world.

Simon and Eleanor locked out the party, though the throbbing rock and roll music reverberated even through this solid house, coming from the room below Jacob's. Eleanor was tremulous; shy, but certain. They stood before the huge ornately plastered marble fireplace. They faced each other, and their eyes met. Then they kissed tenderly, slowly exploring their clothed bodies. Though it was not, it was as if for the first time as they gently undressed each other slowly and marvelled at one anothers' bodies. Eleanor had had only one lover, and, so far, Simon was as familiar with men's bodies as with women's. Simon took Eleanor's hand and led her to Jacob's bed by the window. They lay on the bed, and embraced each other.

Simon smiled as he regarded Eleanor's nakedness, touching her tenderly, causing her to relax with his gentle touches, and be able fully to experience her growing sensuality. Slowly, he cupped her breast and caressed the roundness of her bottom and Eleanor felt her body longing for his caresses, the secret juices came from her, ready for him. Simon's fingers began to feel for her vulva. Eleanor welcomed his easy touch – her last experience of sexual intercourse had been hurried and unsatisfactory and had not seemed to bear relationship to her private solo-sex. It was nice to have someone else's fingers where hers often were. Simon did not seem to mind if she directed him, indicating where he should concentrate. It seemed natural to do so. They smiled happily at each other, hidden away here whilst people danced downstairs. For a time, they merely held each other, kissing and cuddling. There was no urgency. Eleanor thought of the times she had studied Simon's body, and now began to explore it with her hands, feeling the hardness of his pectoral muscles, the firm strength of his arms and legs. At length, Simon's fingers went gently into her, and he watched her face as he manipulated her slowly to orgasm. Eleanor cupped his face and looked into his blue eyes. Then she sat back and looked at him.

'You're not going to start drawing me?' Simon asked in mock dismay. 'You're like Louis . . .'

Eleanor looked down at Simon's extended penis.

'Go on, touch me,' he whispered.

Eleanor looked at his penis. It was clean and long, and smooth, the hood clearly defined. She extended her hand slowly, and began to stroke his erect manhood with her fingers.

'That's nice . . .' said Simon, smiling at her. He lay, watching her as she explored him, seeming to enjoy her gentle touch.

'Touch the vein,' Simon suggested, indicating the thick vein which ran from his testicles to the head of his member. He squirmed in pleasure as Eleanor's slender hand examined his penis, fingering its hood, and then moved down to fondle his balls.

'Just grab it, and pull, from the base to the head,' Simon said. 'And then back.'

'Show me,' she said, then watching Simon as he pleasured himself for a few moments.

He released himself and Eleanor began to masturbate him. She was aware of Simon's pleasure increasing, as he moved in time to her pulling. She gradually quickened her rate, seeing Simon becoming increasingly tensed and sexual. He reached up to take her breasts, holding one in each hand and moving them round and round in time to her pulling on him. That he was holding her breasts raised his pitch of excitement. He smiled at Eleanor and closed his eyes. He moved his head from side to side, and, pleased with her ability, Eleanor continued to wank Simon, until he tensed dramatically and began to toss. Eleanor pulled faster, until Simon reached for her, to hold her close, kissing her as the creamy substance shot from his cock and over Eleanor's stomach and breasts. Eleanor smiled and held him, kissing his head as he relaxed.

'Listen . . .'

In the space from the rock music, Eleanor heard the plaintive sounds of piano and clarinet.

'It's Louis and Jake. They're excellent musicians . . .'

'Simon . . .'

He smiled sleepily, but opened his eyes as she began to stroke his chest.

'Yes . . .'

'You know Louis kissed you?'

'Yes?'

'Is he gay?'

She felt Simon hesitate. 'I suppose he's bisexual,' he answered. 'But I reckon he likes women, probably more than he does men.'

'Have you – had sex with him?'

Simon looked away from her.

'It doesn't bother me,' she assured him, smiling and caressing him. 'I suppose I'm just – interested – to know what it's like.'

'In some ways you know, there's no difference, but you – you're softer than Louis . . .' He pulled her to him, kissing her.

'Don't let's talk about Louis now . . .'

Simon held her close, his penis swelling against Eleanor's sex. Simon kissed her and began to caress her breasts. Eleanor nodded as Simon held the head of his penis against the opening of her vagina, he kissed her tenderly as he slipped it gently in. Eleanor's womb responded with exquisite pleasure as Simon began to make love to her, at first very, very slowly. Gradually, Eleanor responded until they were both contained in a steady, mutually satisfying rhythm. They smiled at each other as their young bodies reached orgasm simultaneously.

Amy heard the music from upstairs, now that Sam had turned down the CD player. Some of the guests left to go and listen, but she was too comfortable, lounging here against Sarah. The room was almost empty and the few remaining were locked in earnest, if inebriate, conversation, or love-making. She nestled closer to Sarah, relaxing even further as the woman began to stroke her hair. She was drowsy with wine and warmth, and the cordial ambience of the party. It took her a moment to remember and to assess, as Sarah's hand touched her bosom. She was surprised at the quickening of her blood and the rush of sensation to her vulva, though she told herself that she was drunk and really she knew it did not matter who touched you . . . after all she could always arouse herself with the help of her vivid imagination.

So, she did not prevent Sarah as her other hand went to her crotch, and fingered her most accurately. And it was an easy thing to allow her gentle kiss when it came. Part of her was bemused and canny, thinking how different it was from the hard demanding kiss of a man, how generous and knowing, and how knowledgeable the hand that slipped into her silk panties and explored her sensitised sex. Sarah's kiss became more seeking, her tongue wanting entry into her mouth as her fingers simultaneously entered her wet vagina.

Amy murmured her assent and enjoyment and began to return the other woman's attentions as she fondled Sarah's ample breasts, feeling the other woman's urgent response. Soon, the woman was on top of her as they spread out on the opulent sofa in the comforting darkness of the warm room. The people who were dancing, now to The Doors' *Riders on the Storm* took little notice of them. Amy took it for granted that the artists' friends would think nothing of two women affectionately entwined. She complied as Sarah positioned herself on top of her, her fanny against Amy's as the two women clung hungrily together, moving in accord. Amy gasped at the richness of the sensation as their pussies met, feeling the hard ridge of Sarah's clitoris against her own. She could not help thinking that Louis had been in both of their minds. She kissed Sarah fervently as gushes of pleasure throbbed through her. This was different. Amy felt excited at this unexpected expansion of her sexual enjoyment. She massaged wildly at the woman's generous bottom and breasts; thinking of the exquisite portrait, groaning loudly in ecstasy as they came together, unaware of more people returning to the room to dance as the live music ceased. And of Jacob in search of a drink, watching them and wondering whether he would get either of them tonight. He had allowed for the possibility that Amy and Louis would succumb to their obvious passion, but he had thought he stood a good chance with Sarah, whom he had fancied for a long time. How ironic if he was left alone with Louis. He laughed cynically into his drink. The women kissed, meeting each other's eyes smilingly.

Eleanor watched Simon for a while as he slept and then rose, looked round for something to wear and found Jacob's scarlet satin gown. It smelt of him and its silky feel was luscious on her skin as she wrapped it around her and went quietly from the room and along the corridor to the bathroom.

Piano music still came softly from the room at the other end of the long corridor. Intrigued, she was drawn to it. Louis was alone. She stood at the door, watching Louis play Debussy's 'Arabesque'. She was captivated by him as he played on, in his own world of concentrated magic. She leaned against the door frame, taken in by Debussy's undulating and graceful music. After a time, Louis looked up at her happily, and then indicated his empty glass and bottle regretfully. But Eleanor was too shy, and too young, to go down into a roomful of strangers in Jacob's gown to bring him another bottle.

Louis shrugged, and smiled; understanding. He stopped playing and rose, crossing the room to come to her. He was lovely, and he had given her a gift. He stopped in front of her, seeing Jacob's scarlet robe hiding her nakedness, he must know that she had just made love. His eyes took in her slim form, her black hair and her round dark eyes. He traced the tender lines of her small face with his eyes and then reached out slowly to cup her pointed chin with his hand. Hands that had played so exquisitely, and painted so wonderfully. He saw that her dark lashes fluttered as her eyelids drooped.

'You're beautiful . . .' was all he said, though Eleanor felt that she should be saying this herself to this dark man. Then, she waited as with exquisite slowness his head came down and his passionate mouth met hers, brushed hers for an exquisite moment as he kissed her lips. Eleanor felt an unfamiliar and deep thrill. She saw that his eyes were soft and gentle as he regarded her silently. Stillness contained them both, enveloped them. Louis placed an elegant thumb on her mouth for another moment and, as he lifted it, she turned to go, aware that Louis looked after her.

As she reached Jacob's door, she turned to see that Louis was still watching her. Inside the room, she leant against the door, her breathing rapid as her heart raced. She looked over to see Simon, naked on Jacob's bed, his body painted with light from the flickering fire. She crossed the room and gazed down on him, thinking what a marvellous painting this would make. Simon, with one hand on his thigh, close to his detumescent penis, the other tangled in his bright hair, his mouth slightly parted. His body seemed to glow a little in youthful health, and in the comforting light from candles and fire. She wondered about Louis, and the kind of new world she had entered. She smiled to herself as she unfastened Jacob's gown and let it fall in a crimson pool around her feet. She stepped out of it and lay next to Simon, imagining Louis, kissing him.

'He's good, isn't he?' Simon murmured.

Eleanor began to understand Simon's admiration for the attractive man.

'Yes,' she agreed softly.

'I'll show you his studio, if you like,' Simon offered as he embraced her.

'Yes, I'd really like that. In a little while . . .'

'Mmmm . . .'

Simon led Eleanor proudly around Louis' studio, showing her each portrait, and telling her a little about each, and that there were more, and that he would take her to Lavenham, tomorrow, after the class, to show her the one of him. It had earned its painter prizes. Eleanor was silent. An artist herself, she regarded each proffered picture critically and came to the same conclusion as more ignorant viewers: the man was a genius. She wondered at the time and patience each had taken, and considered what personal pain it had cost its executor. At the end of this magical tour, she was silent, though Simon waited for some comment. Eleanor was thinking: I will succeed, like this. I too can expend time and patience and suspend my life, to achieve this. And she touched her face where he had touched her, and marvelled.

Before she left, Eleanor came to say goodbye to Louis in his studio. She lingered, at last saying to him:

'I'm going to Art School, next year . . .'

Louis nodded. Eleanor was unable to do as she wished: to ask Louis if he would be willing to give her advice on painting. And Louis could not yet ask Eleanor to pose for him. A refusal would be too raw, just now.

'Bye, then – thanks – it was a good party.'

'See you, Elli . . . Bye, Simon.'

Eleanor was aware of the lingering look of warmth between the two men.

Jacob supposed he was lucky to get into his room as he saw Amy and Sarah, naked and entwined in each other's arms. They smiled to see him and pulled back the duvet to welcome him in. He quickly took off his clothes. They watched him undress, fondling each other, completely at ease. They smiled at his immediate erection.

It was lovely, between the warmth of their bodies. Jacob thrilled at being in the middle of two naked and sexually aroused women. They pampered him, kissing and caressing each other, easily inciting the concupiscent Jacob further, and then they caressed and fondled him, kissing him with affection. They moved their hands quickly all over his body. Jacob was an object of their sexual desire. He reached out to grab them, revelling in this double femininity. Sarah took him close to her, kissing him eagerly. Almost immediately, he entered her: he could not help himself, he was in a frenzy of desire. The women had excited him beyond endurance. Sarah responded to him lovingly: his greedy cock found its own way home. He slid with tremendous relief into the comforting warmth of her muscular passage, crying out as he felt the strong walls of her vagina gripping him. He kissed her, kneading her breasts and slamming impatiently into her. He felt Amy against his back, he felt her sex between his buttocks and knew that he must soon ejaculate.

'It's okay Jake, come on . . .' Sarah said generously, encouraging his rapid thrusting with her own movements.

Jacob kissed both her and Amy as he fucked Sarah. He could feel Amy's hands on his abdomen, reaching down to his balls. He gasped. Sarah encouraged him to be below her, thus leaving his hands free to fondle both her and Amy's breasts. Sarah took up a sitting position on his groin, easing herself up and down his cock, while Amy caressed his body and pushed her breast into his face, so that he could lick and suck at it. Jacob closed his eyes in bliss and suckled greedily at her teat. Sarah raised her voluptuous body along his penis, then grasped him back with her muscles and ground down on him. He felt the hard ridge of her clitoris tantalising his sensitive skin, her anus against his balls. Jacob was in sweet agony. He suckled on Amy's breast, and pulled on her other nipple. He fondled her dripping labia and squeezed her engorged clitoris, all the time heading inexorably to his climax. His excitement reached fever-pitch as Amy moved her sex to his face. He lapped at it noisily. The women exchanged a triumphant smile as Jacob ejaculated, dramatically and with gusto, swearing and cursing as though reluctant to let his seed go. Sarah's body echoed his joy.

He slept instantly and Sarah snuggled down with him. Amy dressed and went downstairs. Jacob woke refreshed to take Sarah into his arms and to caress with satisfaction the body he had seen so often, and craved. Sarah was opulent and comforting, with generous curves. For a time, she kissed and caressed him, gradually teasing him back to life, until he was rigid in her hands. Jacob recalled all the times he had gazed longingly at Louis' lascivious portrait and, gently turning her over, stroked her buttocks and explored the secret cleft between. Sarah laughed dirtily, with her legs spread-eagled and raised.

'Have you got cream?' Sarah asked, sensing his intent as he gazed lasciviously at her parted sex-lips.

Jacob nodded and, taking the tube from his bedside cabinet,

applied this generously to her tight hole and lavishly to his cock. Before entering her, he concentrated on ensuring she was aroused, attending to her clitoris, stimulating her breasts and gently preparing her anus for his entrance.

'I've thought of having you, so many times, Jake.'

'Me too, Sarah . . . is this alright?'

'Yeah, it's what I imagined – lying there for hours. . . You're very gentle . . . very sweet.'

Biting the tip of his tongue in concentration, Jacob inserted his prick by degrees, so that Sarah's sphincter muscle expanded gradually to accommodate him. And all the time, his other hand was fondling her sex, so that she writhed in absolute pleasure under him. At last, unable to control himself for much longer, Jacob thrust into her, ignoring a picture, which filled his head for a fraction, of doing this to a compliant Louis – or Louis to him. His own anus throbbed. He shook his head forcefully and grasped Sarah's ample breasts. He concentrated on Sarah as he lay along her, moving at first as slowly as he could, and then speeding up, enjoying the unusual tightness of Sarah's secret passage.

He felt Sarah's own pleasure as she moved sexily under him. He alternated between both hands kneading her breasts, to one rubbing at her clitoris and one pinching her nipples. They came together, Jacob jerking the last few thrusts extravagantly as Sarah stilled. He rolled off her, but pulled her to him, lapsing into deep sleep.

Louis removed the portrait of Sarah from his easel and placed it carefully against the wall. Now it was complete, he could move on.

Amy wandered around the lovely house. It was almost morning and the house was warm and peaceful. Everyone was asleep, but for Louis. Whenever she saw him, Amy was filled with a reflex appreciation of his perfection, quickly repressed. He was, she knew, as restless and hungry as she was. The trouble between them was that they read each other all too well. And they were both very proud. She saw the lust in his wonderful eyes as he eyed her as candidly as she did him. He did not look away, and once more they were engaged in some kind of complex game. But tonight, it could be simple. They had no audience. They had a simple animal need, which could be satisfied with any one here (should chance allow). But, they both knew, it would be best if they partnered each other. Amy wondered whether she could get Louis for tonight without any concession, without losing face. She wanted him. She had wanted him since she first saw him. The problem was, he knew that. He had recognised her adoration, and her need, and – well used to this – had scorned her. But she had to face, too, her dismissive attitude towards him.

As she stood watching him in silence, when all the world was asleep and they were alone in their hunger, Amy was aware of how her body was becoming attuned to Louis'. As her breasts firmed and her sex pulsed, this state transmitted to the receptive Louis. Amy had to admit that this was a last chance to do what she had come tonight to do, what she had denied to Jacob and adamantly, to Sarah, but had craved all along. To fuck Louis. The very thought gripped at her body, turning her into a completely sexual being. She had no doubt they would be very, very good together.

All evening, she had watched him, been aware of his every action, followed his seductive movements, gazed at his expressive face. She had seen how he gesticulated with his hands when he talked, how heartily he laughed when amused, how he watched others avidly, with an artist's hunger. She had seen how people loved him, how he got away with temperamental behaviour, was indulged and treasured. She had noted how he looked at Jacob, with great affection, and observed how Jacob could not do enough for him. She had heard them play music together, witnessed how they ran their house – to perfection.

She was aware of Louis' cruelty and how he used people, and determined that she would use him too. But she was also aware of his vulnerability, and knew that he had made some overture to his oldest friend, but had not been entirely accepted.

90

Most of all, she was more than ever aware of his masculine beauty, and her own very natural response to him. She herself had sought solace with a woman, as he had with a man, as though it would not do for them to be with a partner of the opposite sex – and not each other. Jacob's wild attentions had fed her need. Still, she was not prepared to make the first move – to admit that she wanted Louis. Why had she come down then? She wanted Louis to say: 'Can I fuck you?' or 'Let's call a truce.' But Louis was at least as proud as she. She had never had quite this response to a man she had not even touched. Overwhelmingly physical and needy. It was relatively new to her to look at a man's body and desire him. Hitherto, she had concentrated on her own body, and attracting men to her. Would he be chivalrous, even in a chauvinistic way and come over and show her that he understood?

But Louis Joseph understood only too well. He remained where he was, waiting. Anger surged in Amy. Then, she rationalised with herself – why, when they had both been born after 'Women's Lib' should she expect him to take the chance? She reasoned that he may not want her, after all. Would she let this stop her? She knew that he was vulnerable and desperate for sex – a perfect opportunity for her to show her domination. That settled, Amy went across the acres of studio that separated them, aware of Louis all around her. In his paintings and drawings. Louis continued to survey her calmly.

She glanced at his crotch, but his trousers were too loose to reveal him. Deliberately so, she assumed, as she caught the flicker of amusement in his eyes. She wondered if she would have to do some kind of erotic dance to please him. She would hate herself for her weakness were she not so overwhelmed with desire to be thus close to him. It was scary, to be so liberated and dominant. She longed for Louis to help her out.

'Okay – I want to fuck you,' she threw at him condescendingly. She could not fail to see that, despite her off-putting tone, her admission had raised a light of victory in Louis' beautiful eyes. Damn the man, damn, damn the man and his beautiful eyes!

Louis shrugged, as if to convey that he would not actually stop her. Amy sighed, exasperated, then sat beside him and began to tug at his buttons, not exactly seductively. However, with no help from Louis, she eventually had his shirt off. His skin was warm and of a deep mediterranean hue. Amy could smell his musky sweat. She wanted to kiss his shoulder. She had no idea of the enormity of her achievement, in getting his shirt off. Until she recalled Sarah's complaint that Louis would not take his clothes off. Amy longed to kiss his neck, beneath the intricate curls, to suck on his muscular shoulders; to lick down the middle of his breast-plate. She met his eyes. They were still and watchful. Amy felt breathless. She had no doubt that he would prevent her from unfastening his trousers.

So she was surprised when he stood up. Less so, when he made off, but, determined, she followed him up to his room. Louis had heard, before she had, the movement from the other room. Already, people were rising. Would he have been bothered if she had not followed? Anyway, here she was, in his room. Louis stood in front of the mirror, his back to it. In his reflection, Amy could see the complex curls of his thick black hair, and the clear olive-brown smoothness of his skin. She came to him, aware of the blinking of his clear eyes, and the unusual length of their dark lashes, because it was his only movement. Amy reached out and unfastened his buckle, and then his button, and then slid down his zip. She opened her eyes wide at him as she became aware of the tumescence beneath. Louis' breath came more quickly now. Amy wondered what extent of control it took for him to remain so passive.

She slithered his loose trousers down and Louis stepped out of them obligingly. She caught a pungent and arousing scent of spunk and sweat. Amy looked at him in admiration, clad only now in his red satin shorts, which bulged at his erection. She ran her hands over his shoulders and down his back to his waistband. It felt wonderful to touch him, at last . . . and Amy enjoyed being in control in this way. She slipped her fingers just under the elastic and smiled at Louis, who did not exactly return her smile, in fact, she thought that he was smouldering –

with anger? She did not let it bother her as she swept her hands deliberately all over the less erogenous parts of his perfect body.

Then, though she was going to take off her own clothes first – brief as they were – she decided to divest Louis of his last remaining garment. With some delay, because of the size of his swollen member, Amy pulled his pants off slowly, wondering what effort it took for him to remain still, and what he would do if she should laughingly leave him now. If only, Amy thought – that would show him! But it was impossible. She wanted him like crazy, her body gave evidence of that. She could not resist kissing his lovely prick, licking at it, breathing in his provocative perfume.

Amy stood, placed her hands on Louis' waist and moved close to him, parting her thighs and taking his erect member between them. She moved along him, raising herself on her tip-toes to do this. She slid her silken-sheathed crotch along his stiffened rod, moving her hands to his buttocks to support herself. It was possible that he would not move at all. The soft fine material of her pants trailed tantalisingly along his prick. Louis shivered.

Amy slipped off her damp knickers and felt his hard warmth against her wet vulva. She gripped him between her thighs. She pulled off her dress and pushed her breasts against his chest. Louis placed his hands under her abdomen as she rubbed her sex along him. Amy thrilled at this first, potent touch. She sank her teeth into the soft flesh of his neck and bit very hard. Louis lifted her, with one deft movement thrusting his prick deeply into her and crashing her against the cupboard, where he could support her. His own teeth responded to Amy's threat by teasing at her stiffened nipples. His sudden masterful possession excited Amy.

She leaned back, glorying in the feel of his big cock deeply inside her, nudging at her womb. She wanted to laugh with relief. She seemed filled with exhilarating gas. Louis pulled her back to him, holding her breasts against his chest as he worked her along his cock. They were maddened now with this admission and their mouths met, kissing and biting savagely, further frenzied as their bodies slammed powerfully together. Nothing existed for them except this desire and its fulfilment. Amy felt her temperature and blood-pressure soar. She was dizzy with Louis, never had she experienced such overwhelming longing for any man. It possessed her entirely. They crashed about the room, fucking wildly, not caring about the sharp corners and edges of furniture against their tender flesh. Amy was radiant, convinced of Louis' equal passion for her.

Louis got Amy onto the edge of his bed, and raised her legs around his shoulders so that he could penetrate as deeply as possible into her. Amy could not think – all she was aware of was the incredible impact this man was having on her body. And the feel of his huge cock within her. He appeared to be tireless, managing to raise her to a peak of arousal without making her come, almost as adept as she at delaying and protracting her enjoyment. At last, he reached for her aching breasts, though he touched them only lightly, encircling her aureolae with finger and thumb. He held her as she climaxed, stilling his own thrusting. But he did not release her. He drew her onto the bed and turned her over, caressing her bottom lovingly, slow now as though he was not still rampantly turned on. He stroked her back and nibbled at her ear-lobe and pressed on her abdomen, forcing her against the mattress repeatedly. Finally he slipped his fingers between her cheeks and teased at her anus, while inserting another finger deeply inside and feeling for her clitoris. He stimulated both these delightful places in an increasing rhythm until Amy was obviously ready for him again, as her copious juices wet Louis' fingers. He lay along her back, and inserted his penis from this angle, into her vagina, whilst at the same time, he slipped his finger into her anal passage. Amy's enjoyment was increased by this added manipulation.

She was filled with wonder, as still Louis did not rush to his own fulfilment. When she had reached her climax once more, her orgasm wracking her body, he withdrew and turned her over, beginning to lick from her breasts and down to her sex, lapping at her swollen labia, as if healing her, after his frenzied attentions. She tousled his thick curls. Whatever their relationship, she had rarely had such an attentive lover. She was filled with gratitude as her body flooded with contentment and warmth. She was considering how she should make him come: that was the challenge as she drifted off to sleep.

She awoke, alone, her body throbbing as she recalled Louis' love-making. Perhaps he had won this round, because he had not ejaculated. One up to him maybe, Amy grinned, but she had benefited. Her body thrilled at his potency. Caressing herself lovingly, thinking of Louis' wild passion, she went back to sleep until Jacob came to tell her that they were going to the Life Class. He did not seem to give her a choice. Still, he was the teacher. Amy smiled dreamily up at him. He shook his head at her, silently acknowledging that he understood that she had had her desire. Sarah was still asleep. Amy wondered whether he imagined, as she did, that Sarah and Louis would get together, once alone. Would Jacob mind? She did not want the voluptuous model to have what was rightly hers. Louis' orgasm. Jacob was smartly dressed, his hair neat and clean, though his eyes were shadowed with weariness. Amy got out of bed, deciding that it was best to leave Louis this way, rather than to hang around him hungrily. She smiled at Jacob's reflex appraisal of her naked body as he handed her Louis' black satin gown. Amy hugged it around her. She requested a quick shower, and Jacob said that he would prepare some breakfast for her. Amy looked in on Sarah.

'Do you want to show me some of your jewellery – to see if I could sell it in my shop?' she asked the sleepy woman.

'Yeah . . .' Sarah smiled sleazily up at her.

Amy gave her a card.

When they left, Louis was in his studio, playing his guitar. He had scarcely acknowledged their presence. Amy tried to convince herself that he would likewise not be bothered with Sarah.

95

Four

'*Are* you coming on this gallery trip?' Jacob asked Louis.

Louis shrugged moodily. Louis without a project in hand, without a painting on which to concentrate his energies, could be pretty unbearable, though he did have his exhibition to plan. At times like this, it seemed that all his creative imaginative energy became negative and destructive. Jacob sighed: perhaps it wasn't such a good idea to invite him, anyway. At his best, he would be an asset, adding to Jacob's own comments valuable ones of his own, but like this, he would be more of a liability, temperamental and sullen. It would be best if he had a new model lined up as soon as he finished a portrait, but that was not really viable, as he had to rest and refocus. However, he could paint Amy or even Eleanor, now. As if translating Jacob's thoughts, Louis suddenly brightened.

'Are we meeting them all at the National Gallery?'

'It's best that way, Louis,' Jacob assured him, recalling past occasions when he had agreed to give lifts, but things had gone wrong. 'Anyway – we're going to the Dominion to see "Artists".' He wondered whether Louis had plans to offer Eleanor a lift. Louis had scarcely spoken of the young woman, but from his initial reaction to her, and because of her obvious appeal, Jacob was convinced that Eleanor, rather than Amy, was Louis' next victim, or – rather – subject. He wondered, with sympathy, how Eleanor would deal with such a possibility. She was very shy, and still young. Though a gifted artist herself; she probably had much in common with Louis. She could refuse him, of course, but it was difficult to refuse Louis once he had his mind set on something. But – more than the painting – Jacob wondered whether she was ready for the sex which would doubtless derive from this. He told himself that she would probably enjoy it and wondered how Amy would react.

They were early, waiting in the foyer, looking out for their group, when Jacob noticed Louis' face light up: Eleanor was the first to arrive – with Simon. Jacob felt that his callous friend would disregard Simon, especially considering Simon's 'idolisation' of the artist. However, surprisingly, Louis did not try to take Eleanor over. He was going to play it cool, Jacob scoffed silently to himself, all through the morning keeping a wary eye on his calculating companion, as they examined the paintings he had chosen, including 'The Rokeby Venus'; 'Saint Sebastian'; 'An Allegory with Venus and Cupid' and Botticelli's 'Venus and Mars', in which Venus, goddess of love and beauty, watches whilst her lover, Mars, god of war, sleeps. He caught Amy's eye as he laughingly relayed the interpretation: 'Making love exhausts a man, but invigorates a woman.'

Louis shone. He radiated enthusiasm as he took his turn in talking about each painting they studied, and his remit was to convince the eager students how good it was to be remembered as such a wonderful model; how gifted to be capable of posing – not all were. Oh, no, it was not in the eye of the artist – or beholder – alone: the model had to have an indefinable something. Jacob smiled wryly to himself. When he caught Louis' eye, Louis looked quickly away and Jacob wanted to laugh. He saw that Eleanor looked at Louis with reverence. Louis was winning. Louis told them something of the models whose images they gazed on. Some of what he said was authentic (with additions), some was completely fabricated. He became very imaginative, in recreating the lives of the artists, and their relationships to their models. And Louis stood before the paintings, looking as stunning as any, a successful modern artist whom they all admired, these would-be painters, someone who possessed in abundance the gift they all cherished.

Devil! thought Jacob, rescuing them as Louis threatened to break into hyperbole. He had convinced Eleanor. Perhaps some of the others would take it into their heads to ask Louis to paint them. He could be inundated with offers. Certainly Amy was aware of his intent. Jacob caught her eyeing the innocent Eleanor murderously. She had consummated her tempestuous relationship with Louis, and was obviously unwilling to share him but she would have to get used to the idea, thought Jacob. He had never known any female pin Louis down.

As Jacob continued his lecture, he noticed that Eleanor and Simon were now cloistered with Louis, and scarcely listening to him, or looking at the pictures. Louis was really in danger of getting carried away with himself. He was certainly safer behind a canvas. Amy's green eyes were full of jealousy. She and Louis had scarcely spoken, despite their intimacy at the party.

'I expect you reckon you could paint any of these yourself!' she sneered at him, as they made their way to the restaurant.

Louis shrugged and splayed his arms as though, naturally, this would be within his power. Jacob imagined that he saw himself as some kind of Raphael, with a band of ardent admirers, hanging on his every word. God knows what he would be like let loose in Florence with these gullible students. Still, Jacob thought soberly, insufferable though he may seem at present, it was little to compensate for the darkness he experienced at times. Louis may be gifted and imbued with creative energy, but his imagination also led him into despair from the depths of which nothing seemed to comfort him. And occupied thus was better than hanging around the house sullenly. Or careering dangerously round the Suffolk lanes on his motor-bike.

Fortuitously for Louis, he managed to get on a table alone with Eleanor and Simon. Jacob realised that Simon would be no barrier for Louis; he would simply disregard him if necessary. It was quite likely, however, that Simon would back up anything the artist suggested. Amy fumed invisibly behind Jacob; she was also watching Louis and Eleanor. Jacob turned to smile at her. She had not looked really happy even when she had arrived, and Jacob surmised that something else had also upset her. Surely she would not take Louis so very seriously?

He paid for her coffee and sandwich, and in tacit consent,

they went to sit, apart from the others, at a table for two. They were still in a good vantage point to see Louis though. He seemed engaged in earnest conversation with the young couple. No doubt the innocent Eleanor was flattered to have his attention. She could not yet know that nothing was freely given, for such as Louis.

'He's taken over a bit . . .' Jacob said vaguely, his comment as pertinent to the morning as to Eleanor.

Amy shrugged. So, it was obviously something else which was bothering her.

'Reuben phoned last night,' she blurted out, obviously keen to share her grievances with a sympathetic listener.

'Reuben?' Jacob frowned. 'Oh – your boyfriend – in Italy?' he recalled.

'Ha!'

'He's in Florence at present?'

Amy nodded.

'So – how's he doing?'

'Absolutely fine,' Amy said, her green eyes flashing as she shot an accusing glance at Jacob.

Realising what was coming, Jacob wanted to laugh at her unreasonable rage. He now had no doubt that Louis' indifference had added to her gall.

Amy went on to describe how Reuben, keen to share his Italian experiences, had regaled Amy with tales of his sexual exploits with a young Florentine girl on the course. Francesca! Jacob desisted from asking whether Amy had returned this candour by telling Reuben of her liaisons with him, with Sarah and with Louis. He knew that she had not. The unfortunate Reuben had called at a time when Amy had been feeling lonely, or confused by Louis.

'Have you been to Florence?' he asked.

'Yes.'

She did not seem open to reliving the splendours of the Renaissance city, so intent was she on Reuben's audacity. Personally, he had to suppress a small surge of excitement at the mere thought of actually being in the magical city soon.

'Will Reuben still be there when we go?'

'I'm not sure if he'll actually be studying there, he may be in Rome or Venice – but he says he'll come back there – at least for some of that week.'

Jacob nodded, imagining that there would be fireworks then. They had an Italian friend, Claudio, who ran a small hotel. He had booked their party in. Louis usually accompanied him, but spent most of the time on his own, either in galleries or sketching. He had the feeling that Louis would spend more time with the group than he generally did, this time. An ex-student friend of theirs, Nicky, had a studio by the Arno, and Louis often worked there, staying with her. More often than not, he could not bear to leave Florence when the week was up, and stayed on. Jacob knew that this visit would be different.

Jacob glanced across to Louis. He would love to be able to witness Louis' approach to Eleanor, being aware of its probable outcome. He was obviously treating the girl with great charm and gentleness, rogue that he was. Jacob shook his head.

'He wants to paint Elli?' Amy said miserably, following his look.

'You really shouldn't take him too seriously, Amy . . .' Jacob said kindly, putting his hand on hers.

'He's a calculating swine,' Amy observed.

Jacob could not disagree. Anyway, he understood, all men were anathema to Amy today.

'He couldn't not want to paint you, Amy,' he said before she snatched her hand away and glared at him. It was true. Amy, with her magnificent colouring and inner fire was a must for every painter; he only wished he could do her justice himself. He had been aware, even if she had not, of the admiration that she drew as men passed her, invariably giving her a second or third look. She was no doubt accustomed to such blatant affirmation of her desirability.

'But Elli is more of a challenge,' she said, accurately.

Jacob smiled. Amy softened a little at the admiration in his gentle eyes.

'Elli is little more than a girl. What is between you and Louis is – more adult – more—'

'Sexual?'

Jacob smiled again.

'It's inevitable that he will ask you to pose.'

'I may refuse!' Amy said with dignity.

Jacob nodded doubtfully and they both laughed.

'And what about you?' she challenged almost viciously.

'Oh I've posed for him, as you know.'

'You know I don't mean that, how do you – cope with him?'

'Oh . . .' Jacob sighed, 'With difficulty sometimes . . .' A rare admission.

It was now Amy's turn to squeeze Jacob's hand in sympathy.

Eleanor had not really touched her expensive soup. Something strange was happening to her. Something which had begun, calmly, at Louis' party, when he had welcomed her, and continued when she had watched him play piano, had then been confirmed somehow when he had come quietly to her and looked – into her soul, it seemed. And this morning she had been bewitched by him, by his knowledge, and his enthusiasm for the wonderful paintings. She had watched as his eyes filled with vitality as he talked of the portraits, it was as if he knew just how the painters felt. Eleanor had not visited the London galleries as often as she would have liked, and being here was still magical to her. So she was in a sensitised and receptive state, especially enchanted by the colours and richness of the Sainsbury wing. To her, it was indeed like a chapel, as someone had once described it. It was as though all her nerve ends were invisibly extended, reaching out to the life emanating from the old Italian paintings. And Louis was somehow entangled with this, weaving in and out of its spell, himself as beautiful as any oils.

He was beautiful. More so than she had ever imagined a man. Such beauty was rare. Eleanor was able to watch him closely now as he talked softly to Simon, who he obviously knew very well. And Simon too was under his potent spell. He had confessed to sleeping with Louis and told her that he enjoyed it. She tried to imagine the men in bed together, but this thought made her feel shy. As Louis talked to Simon about the paintings, and she was hypnotised by his rich, musical voice, she looked at him (so she thought) secretly, able to trace with her keen eyes the classical perfection of his face, his lovely rich curls and the fullness of his lips. His colouring was vivid. His eyes met hers lazily, and he smiled slowly, keeping her gaze. Eyes so filled with mysterious depth. Louis gave (Jacob would have known) a wonderful performance of selling himself for his own ends.

Eleanor was not sure even what Louis said to her, and she said little, not trusting herself. She was tremulous, and filled with new and exciting sensations. She could not believe that the great man was taking such an interest in her – it must be because she was Simon's friend, she convinced herself. Louis' dark eyes rested on her for a long time, full of warmth and friendliness. Eleanor thought of the paintings from Greek mythology, and, with a secret blush, imagined what it would be like to paint this glorious male. One day – she was not ready for that now. She shuddered with the audacity of such an idea. She would be honoured to talk to Louis Joseph of his art sometime. His advice would be very useful. Would he do this? Some artists were very unwilling to discuss the elusive process of creativity. She herself became anxious if people tried to dissect a painting with words, trying to ascertain exactly what made it work. Still, he could help her with technique. She was very glad that Louis Joseph had not touched on the subject of her own ambitions.

It was time to return to the galleries. They were going to see 'The Wallace Collection' later. Simon took her hand as they rose to follow Jacob.

'I'm going outside for a fag,' Louis told Jacob, grasping his arm, speaking quietly.

Jacob raised his eyebrows. Perhaps Louis thought that absence would best serve his purposes with Eleanor now.

'Philistine,' he said.

Louis grinned at him and went off down the stairs and

through the swing doors to Trafalgar Square. Jacob tutted to himself as Amy followed. At least his afternoon would be easier.

Louis actually smiled ironically at Amy as she pulled on his sleeve, asking for a light. They went across the busy road to the square and walked in silence to a bench.

'I've got you a ticket for *Artists* at the Coliseum tonight,' Louis said, without looking at Amy.

Amy was amazed; she did not show her delight as she replied:

'Arrogant bastard.'

Louis smiled.

'I'm going for a drink.' He rose and turned to her. He took her hand, assured that she would wish to accompany him, as they began to walk towards Soho. Although she should have been annoyed at his forceful self-confidence, Amy felt her body flood with increased desire for him at this physical touch. She suppressed her need to talk to him, so as to fully experience this. By the time they reached his chosen pub she was mad with the desire to possess him. And soon. Anywhere. She thought of how, especially at the beginning of their very sexual relationship, she and Reuben had often found it necessary to screw in semi-public places. Even now, sometimes. It added further zest.

Louis indicated the corner they should sit in and she went towards it. He asked her what she wanted to drink and she requested a pint of cider. Louis made his way through the crowded lounge to the bar and Amy watched him. She was so obsessed with Louis that it took her a few minutes to realise that the clientele of the pub were mainly men dressed up as women and several of them regarded her with disdain. One attractive transvestite, sitting close to where Louis was waiting to be served, eyed him hungrily. Amy seethed.

'You're going to paint Eleanor?' Amy accused, as Louis lit another cigarette. She refused one, and then grabbed one from his packet. He lit it for her, inhaled deeply and then exhaled, looking with interest around the pub. He was regarded with more favourable speculation than Amy. In fact, his favour rather increased their hostility for the interloper. Amy wondered whether Louis had come as voyeur, to obtain inspiration, or as client. She realised that several of the men were thinking of approaching him.

'So what . . .' Louis said, in delayed response to her observation. 'Eleanor is beautiful – she'd be perfect.'

'She's too young!' Amy protested with assumed indignation and protectiveness.

Louis turned his head to look archly at her.

'She's eighteen, for God's sake. I'm going to paint her, not rape her!'

He turned away as Amy raised her eyebrows questioningly.

'I'd be grateful, Amy, if you did not discuss it with her,' he said in a dignified yet imploring tone.

'She doesn't know?' Amy realised. 'She must be the only one who doesn't.' She laughed falsely.

Louis got up to go the toilet. Amy smouldered as she saw the flamboyant transvestite from the bar follow him. She fumed as too much time passed. She lit another cigarette from Louis' packet, and gulped down cider. She tried not to meet the amused gazes, though one man even regarded her with pity.

Louis stood by the wall, watching the newcomer. He leaned against it. The man did not even bother to pretend to have a pee. He met Louis' eyes and Louis opened them, dark and wide, and they went into the cubicle. Louis stood passively, as the older man unfastened his trousers and released his penis. He closed his eyes as the man went down on him, taking his cock into his mouth, and administering to it lovingly, whilst forcing his fingers with their false nails into his crack. Louis felt the sharpness invade his anus as the man pulled on his cock. He moaned, feeling his body flush with pleasure. He allowed himself to come, quickly. The man stood, wanting to kiss him, pushing him harder against the dirty tiles. Louis shook his head, killing the man with his sultry eyes.

'Lou . . . ?' he pleaded.

Louis caressed him, moving his hands to his breasts and squeezing the silicone implants as if they were real. The man wanted to kiss him. He put his fingers to Louis' mouth and

Louis sucked on them, regarding the man through lascivious eyes as he pressed on the hard flesh of his penis, pushed back to his anus, to form a mound.

Louis pushed the man away and dragged up his pants. Resigned (such beauty was not given cheaply), the man left him.

Amy saw the transvestite reappear and go to his mates by the window. They glowered at her, and she became increasingly uncomfortable. Louis appeared moments later. Amy was enraged by his obvious lasciviousness. Louis did not even sit down. He drained his pint, drank his whisky and said to Amy, in a drawl that further maddened her, whilst ripping through her raging body:

'We can go to a place near here where I can tie you to a bed and fuck the arse off you.' His tone was matter of fact: take it or leave it.

Amy's body jolted with the suddenness of his invitation. She could make him come. In some dark corner of her mind, Amy hoped that the watching men heard.

Amy thought she must be dreaming, or drunk. She saw that Louis was amused as her eyes flashed fire at him. But her wild body responded dramatically, her sex already throbbing, cursing her if she refused. So, she shrugged nonchalantly and stood, albeit unsteadily. Perhaps her blood-pressure was raised, she felt so strange: everything seemed in a different hue. She knew, though, that what she felt was pure lust at the exciting prospect of Louis' abrupt suggestion. Together with a little fear.

Eventually they entered a narrow door, hidden between shops, like many others, and Amy hung back as Louis completed the transaction with a young man behind a counter. She had fully expected some seedy establishment, and was surprised at the opulence of her surroundings. Deep crimson carpets, plum velvet curtains, elegant gilded furniture, classical music.

They went up narrow stairs, and entered a small room with no window. It was decorated in scarlet embossed wallpaper, with a bed covered with red velvet and with black satin sheets.

There was a mirror above the bed. Amy noticed the metal cuffs at the iron head and base of the bed.

'Do you want to do this?' Louis asked, meeting her eyes.

Amy nodded.

'Can you get undressed?'

Louis watched as Amy stripped until she was naked, then she lay on the bed and Louis, still clothed, secured her wrists and ankles. She was spread-eagled on the bed, her sex opened to him. Amy squirmed, feeling her breasts fill and her vagina burn, as he let his eye rove over her nakedness. She looked at herself in the mirror above: ready for penetration. It occurred to her that Louis may well be assessing her pose as to its suitability for a portrait. Perhaps he would calmly sit down, take his sketch-pad from his shoulder-bag, and begin to draw her. A devoted artist. But Louis needed sex. He reached out and touched one breast, trailed his hand down to her parted legs and inserted his fingers very deeply into her moist hole. Amy tensed around him, and he pressed his thumb on her clitoris, sending excited spasms to her womb. He looked at her through hooded eyes. Amy saw the fullness of his lips. She had to admit that he looked wonderful, sultry and passionate. She tossed her restrained body, exciting Louis deliberately. She knew that he was aroused. Louis removed his hand and, still meeting Amy's eyes, he put it to his mouth and sucked on it, narrowing his eyes and tasting Amy's honeyed juices. Amy wondered whether he would keep his clothes on.

But Louis slowly removed his long black coat, his white silk scarf and his shoes and socks. Regarding her with a seductive smile, he loosened his black satin shirt, and then the buckle of his black trousers. Teasingly, he unfastened the buttons slowly, and then removed his shirt. Amy feasted her eyes on his muscular body. She threw her body about, desperate for his touch. She secreted sexual fluid as Louis' black eyes rested deliberately on her swollen vulva whilst he removed his trousers.

Amy moaned as she saw his cock, sticking out hugely and sheathed in fine black silk. She bounced her body against the bed, feeling her breasts shaking. Louis looked at them as he pulled down his boxer shorts. Amy could not prevent a gasp of delight at the magnificence of his protuberance. She licked her lips in anticipation as he stood still for a moment. It was a lovely cock, Amy thought, thick and long and smooth, with a big head. She saw the dew at its eye.

Louis advanced and she writhed enticingly, knowing that she looked wonderful. Her rampant sexuality was pre-eminent, confirmed by her reflected image. Louis straddled her and as he held his cock to her mouth to be kissed, Amy lapped at it eagerly. Louis then trailed it lovingly down to her breasts, encircling them and rubbing at each nipple with its head. Amy's pussy pulsed in anticipation; she relished the moment of entry, the delicious time before she was filled absolutely with his manhood. As Louis took his rigid prick over her belly and down to her pubis, Amy glanced repeatedly at the glass above them, excited by the enhanced view.

Louis brushed his cock fleetingly over engorged clitoris and swollen labia to nuzzle at her tight anus and then back to thrust himself into her. Amy grunted as he entered and then yelled out in unadulterated pleasure as her tight muscular passage was filled with Louis. He placed his hands under her buttocks and raised her. Then, slowly at first, but with a steadily increasing pace, he began to slide his rigid penis up and down her welcoming muscle. Amy saw his actions repeated in the mirror: it was extremely exciting to be able to watch his muscular body on hers. Amy moved in complete accord with him, building as he did. He was in no hurry, and he wriggled in enjoyment as he glided with her, continually deliberately pressing on her clit; arousing her to a fevered pitch so easily.

Very gradually, he increased his rate and depth of penetration, he seemed aware of Amy's growing capacity, and reacted to help her increase this to its ultimate. Once more, she was amazed at his consideration. It was probably better for him, in the long run, she tried to convince herself. That he did not touch her excited breasts, or kiss her, merely seemed to add to the simplicity of this act. Long after the furthest time when Amy had thought he would reach his orgasm, Louis continued, so that her intense enjoyment was increased by her wonder at his capacity. Being fucked for so long made her enter another dimension – as if she had been fed some life-enhancing drug. She forgave Louis anything – everything – for this.

Louis' pace fascinated Amy as she gave herself up to him, confident that he read her body accurately. Sometimes he raised his body so as to rut more deeply into her, shaking her with his force, sometimes he seemed to glide easily, writhing on her clitoris for added stimulus. She did not know whether he read her state, or dictated it, neither did she care: she was lost in this heady liaison. She could raise her eyes to see his pumping buttocks moving sexily up and down. She could gaze into his eyes, fascinated by their stillness and by the depth of passion contained in them, and in his full, pouting mouth.

'Louis, Louis! . . .' she screamed at last as her body was taken over by the most magnificent orgasm she had ever had, her body reverberating with the depth of feeling that exploded and grew.

Louis smiled and became rigid, pressing on her bud, allowing his cock to vibrate within her as he ejaculated. Amy tossed her head in abandon, as, at his release, her body was wracked with further ecstasy as he exploded within her. Louis was still and calm; a flicker of his long dark lashes as lassitude overcame him. He sank on Amy who was relaxed now. Her entire body was flooded with warmth and relief as she entered into a sensual swoon and she could scarcely focus on Louis as he unfastened her. She curled up as he pulled the soft cover over her and held her close, kissing her head as she drifted off. But soon, he was gone, to shower in the adjoining bathroom.

Through her languid haze, Amy could hear the running of water as he prepared a bath for her. She became aware of the aching of her limbs, though considered this a small price to pay for the immense pleasure the man had given her. Louis . . . Amy gave in to her dreaming.

She was lifted, lifted into light. She opened her eyes to look into Louis' face, and to realise that he was about to drop her into a full bath of foaming water. She shrieked.

'It will be good for you,' he assured her as he lowered her into the warm water.

He was dressed in his shirt and trousers. His hair was wet, falling over his brow. Amy looked dreamily at him.

'Don't be too long, though,' he warned, 'We'll have to meet Jake at the Coliseum at seven, and I'm starving.'

With that, he left her to sink deeply into the fragrant foam. But not for long; too soon, he returned with a thick towel to urge her out. He dried her long hair tenderly, seeming to glory in its length and weight, watching its colour return as it dried. His eyes were still filled with tenderness towards her.

Amy had thought that her love-making with Louis would satisfy her for – well – days, but she had not reckoned on the potent effect he had on her. Even whilst they were in the restaurant, she found that his proximity was driving her crazy. It did not come, as often, from her own natural desire, but directly from Louis. The man's power was daemonic in its intensity. She was sure that he was aware of this as he looked laughingly into her eyes and ate all the food she was too distracted to manage. As they went out into the busy evening, Amy realised that she was not released, but in further thrall to this diabolic angel.

Jacob waited wearily outside the Coliseum. The group had long since dispersed and he had eaten drearily alone in a pub. He saw Louis and Amy coming, arms around each other, stopping to kiss and embrace en route. Jacob was filled with anger at Louis.

Louis smiled enchantingly and kissed him on the cheek. Jacob met Amy's eyes. She was radiant. She shrugged at him, obviously, she had had sweet revenge on Reuben. They went into the foyer, and now that he no longer had to wait for them, Jacob went to get a drink. He felt out of sorts, and did not want to display his irritability. He told himself that he had had an arduous day. He ached all over. He wondered whether he would fidget uncomfortably in the theatre seats. Still, the play was unusually short. He wished that Louis had not had so much to drink; he did not relish the drive back to Suffolk.

Amy sat between the men, not really concentrating on the play which had some kind of experimental existential plot. Louis dubbed it 'pretentious', though many critics had raved about its originality, and the more generous Jacob was able to see its merits. She took Jacob's hand in the darkened theatre, and though he did not refuse this, she felt that he was cooler towards her. He told her that he was tired and it did not occur to Amy that he was jealous, and jaded with Louis.

Amy had been the first student to arrive at the centre and now she watched Jacob as he prepared for the lesson. As she surveyed him, dressed in his smart clothes, and with his hair curling crisply, she thought of how much had happened since she had first seen him. And how much time was left for pleasurable encounters. She was very glad she had come along to these classes. As well as the personal opportunities which had been opened to her, Jacob was an excellent tutor, and she felt she had already learnt much about technique and art history. From her conversations with Reuben, he seemed to be being at least as liberal as she, in Italy and if his encounters were fewer then his partners were more. It was enjoyable, to think of Jacob, naked and sensual, so different from now – in his professional guise. Eleanor arrived next and Amy experienced a sharp stab of envy as she saw the look of appraisal Jacob gave the young girl as Eleanor went to her desk, smiling at Amy, who gave her a nod. Soon, the room was filled with the noise and chatter of the others as they arrived for their life class. Amy wondered at Jacob's present detached and professional approach. Who would believe his uninhibited love-making? But then, she noticed how Marie-Anne was looking at him, and Eleanor, and Amy shrugged.

'Today, and for the next couple of weeks, we're going to have a female model – Sarah,' Jacob said, as they were all settled. 'Both Sarah and Simon are going to accompany the group to Florence. It's my idea that in the evenings they can pose – perhaps in the position of the paintings you have seen and you can draw them. During the day, you will probably want to sketch some of the paintings we'll study in the galleries, and then you'll have to come to some agreement on the poses you want them to take up.

'By the way, the week before we go, we'll have both Sarah and Simon pose as Titian's "Bacchus and Ariadne", which we saw at the National, so you can have a go at a composite rendering. Now, Sarah . . .' Sarah smiled at them as she advanced, dressed only in her pink robe. 'If you'll take up your position—' Amy smiled at Sarah as the woman disrobed and sat on the same chair as Simon had occupied on the first week. 'Sarah will take up a similar position to Simon's first one, and I'll come round, as usual, to look at how you're all doing.' He smiled around at them as they began to draw.

Amy began her drawing, concentrating on the woman's generous curves, and the graceful arch of her neck. She executed her work with confidence, thinking of how she had made love with Sarah at Louis' party, and wondering whether Sarah would come home with her this afternoon. She had agreed to bring some of her jewellery for Amy to look at. Amy thought that it would be restful to indulge in some sweet feminine love-making. As she had completed her sketch of the woman's body efficiently, she now paid special attention to her facial features, and her sex. Later, she listened dreamily as Jacob talked of the history of Venus in art, and Plato's concept of the Celestial and Vulgar, the latter most evident in nineteenth century paintings, when Venus resembled a knowing prostitute in the pose of her more innocent forerunners. The lights were dimmed and once more they were taken into Jacob's world of wonderful slides as Sarah imitated the portraits, much as Simon had played Apollo for them. The class had got to know each other well, and its individual members were at ease with one another and their teacher and models now.

In the break, Sarah said she had brought lots of her creations for Amy to examine, and would be delighted to go home with Amy after the lesson. As she now drew the standing model, and in the silent atmosphere of intense concentration and effort as the class grappled with this new challenge, Amy thought of how they would no doubt take their physical relationship further. She began to be gently turned on, with a slow-growing awareness of incipient pleasure in her belly and sex. It was very enjoyable to sit here, amongst these serious students, in such a pleasant atmosphere. However, she could not help but wonder what Louis was doing, and whether Eleanor was ready to respond to Jacob's obvious interest in her. Jacob continued to be warm towards Amy, but she had begun to feel that he was secretly jealous, though this was controlled, at the obvious power of her attraction for Louis. That was natural. She smiled tenderly as she left with Sarah, relieved at this simplicity. She did not stop to consider that Jacob would have taken Sarah home . . . In many ways, Amy was as self-centred as Louis.

Eleanor lingered after the others had left, plucking up courage to speak to Jacob as he packed away his things. Sarah had left with Amy: they were obviously great friends now.

'Mr Laurence . . .' she began.

'Jacob – or Jake . . .' Jacob smiled at her encouragingly.

'You live with Louis Joseph?' She had made the assumption at the party, but could not be quite sure. Anyway, it was a beginning.

'Yes.' He nodded.

'I thought – as you know him so well . . . Well, I wondered whether you would know if he would be prepared to talk to me about his work, just his technique. As you know, I'm going to Art School in September, and – well – if he would talk to me – it would really help me. I know not all artists like to discuss their methods, etcetera – I could understand if— '

Lucky Louis, thought Jacob, thinking of his friend, still at a loose end. Despite his encounters with Amy, he was obviously not prepared to succumb completely – however attracted. That would not be Louis. And never had he had such a challenge . . . He would not paint Amy yet: he was too embroiled in his sexual games with her. Jacob considered, with amused cruelty, just turning up with the young woman, and catching Louis unprepared. That would pay him back for taking Amy. However, though Amy would respond well to Louis, caught in his pit, he knew that Eleanor would not. It would not be fair to expose Eleanor to Louis' decadence. He wondered if Louis would be drunk, now, wallowing in self-pity and no doubt at present alone, trying to satisfy himself with hand and imagination, perhaps even as he thought of this striking young woman.

Anyway, Jacob sighed to himself, it would be very good for Louis to have a model now. He had not pursued courting Eleanor himself for this end, but Jacob had no doubt that Louis' mind was obsessed by it. Perhaps, if he had not been waylaid by Amy, he would have concentrated entirely on Eleanor.

'I think he would be prepared to talk to you, Elli,' he told the girl kindly. 'If you like I'll phone him and make sure he's in, and then, if you're free, you could come back to Dedham with me. Would that be alright? Are you free this afternoon?'

Eleanor flushed with pleasure and nodded keenly. Jacob felt a pang at her eagerness.

Jacob went to the public phone in the corridor. The phone rang on for a long time in their house and he imagined Louis' reluctance to be recalled to the world of reality. At last, he answered perfunctorily.

'You've taken your hand off it for long enough?' Jacob joked.

'Jake! Aren't you coming home?' Louis sounded drunk – or perhaps he was just exhausted with masturbation.

'Getting hungry, are you? I've got someone here who perceives you as an oracle on modern painting and would be honoured if you would just pass on a few gems to her, as she begins her own career. Your technique has obviously impressed her! Or maybe she just swallowed your act, hook, line and sinker.'

Louis was silent for a few minutes before saying, in some disbelief:

'Elli?'

'Why do I have the idea that I'm bringing a virgin to the lion's den? Do you reckon you could shower all that spunk off before I arrive home?'

114

'She asked?' Louis actually sounded quite touched.

'I'll take that as a yes, then?'

'Jake—?'

'What?'

'Can you bring some food back?'

Jacob slammed down the receiver.

He took the drive back to Dedham quite slowly, so as to give Louis time to prepare. This also gave Eleanor the opportunity to ask about Louis. Great. Jacob told her that they had gone to the same boarding school, but that, as their mothers had been friends from Art School, they had actually known each other all their lives. Louis' parents had been tragically killed in a car accident when he was a toddler, so Louis had spent a lot of his childhood with Jacob. They had gone to college together, and had travelled quite extensively, especially around Italy and Greece, and to Spain, before Jacob had taken various jobs teaching, and Louis had devoted himself to his painting. He realised that he was incidentally giving Eleanor his own history too.

'I've seen his work at exhibitions,' Eleanor said.

'He's arranging another one for the spring,' Jacob told her.

'So, you don't think he'll mind – talking about his work?' Jake shook his head, smiling. She was obviously tremulous at the prospect. Jacob felt quite protective towards her. He imagined Louis unnecessarily bundling off his sheets and stuffing them in the machine, finding new ones. He smiled: he was being unfair to his friend, and he realised that his imaginings hid envy. Eleanor was not really an innocent, not *really* – and he himself was very taken with her. He loved her air of gentleness and quietness; he admired her talent, and her ability to concentrate, and he found her delicate beauty and exquisite features extremely attractive. He allowed himself to float in an idyll of slow, deliberate exploration with her, shutting Louis out. He found that he was filled with sexual languor, and wondered what Eleanor would think if she became aware that his prick was stiff at the thought of her, and that Louis' sexual fantasies were probably focused on her.

115

He smiled ironically to himself as he parked by the church, and opposite the delicatessen. He nodded vaguely as Eleanor talked enthusiastically about the church and Flatford and Constable. He wondered how difficult it would be for him to get through the afternoon, and why he hadn't had the foresight to go and pick up Amy and Sarah on some pretext – invite them to tea, for instance. Eleanor continued chatting, a little nervously, as they shopped.

Jacob told himself that he should not really have been amazed at Louis' approach to Eleanor. He was charming and gentle, and if she was beguiled by his appearance (Louis was at his best, his sable hair gleaming, set off by his poet's shirt, his demeanour steady and calm, his black eyes steady and intelligent), he did not trade on this. He remained detached, but friendly. Eleanor could not be aware of how rare this aspect was. Jacob doubted Amy would recognise Louis. As he prepared a meal of soup and various pâtés and assorted rolls and salads, he amused himself by wondering, idly, how it would be if Amy was here too. He rather thought that Louis would ignore her. But Amy was so volatile that she would probably seek to disenchant the younger woman. He doubted he would get a look in, except as a shoulder to cry on. For either, or both of them. He had been there before, in Louis' complex life.

Eleanor was certainly enchanted as Louis took her round his studio, showing her his portraits. She lingered critically over each one, asking questions on how he had achieved certain results, admiring the richness of the colours. She was thankful to have been given a preliminary viewing by Simon. Louis seemed impressed by the incisiveness of her observations. They agreed in their dismissive opinion of how much modern art was concentrated on computer. Neither of them knew the first thing about how they worked, though Jacob was adept at graphics, and had sold some of his work.

Eleanor regarded Louis' wonderful studio as a haven she would die to possess, and wondered whether anything like this would ever be possible for her. Louis admitted that he had been very lucky, having had financial backing from his parents' will, and from Clarissa Laurence's patronage. It occurred to him that perhaps he may eventually be able to help the younger artist.

Eleanor accepted the wine Jacob brought, and lingered before the portrait of Jacob looking extremely sensual, captured in his naked longing by his intimate friend. She did not flinch as she examined it closely, and then she told Louis how much she liked Jacob, and how she admired him, and admitted that she was jealous of Amy, but that Jacob would not think of her in such a way. She turned to smile at Louis too late to catch the sudden fire of jealousy in his own lovely eyes. She wanted Jake! Louis was filled with pain. He thought of her, spending hours looking at his attractive friend as she drew, confiding in him, and submitting her attempts for his scrutiny. She probably did not think of him, Louis, sexually at all, just as some kind of god, worshipping his talent. Simon had told him that Eleanor had thought he was gay! That was amusing, considering his attraction towards her. Louis' fretful sexuality distracted him. Then he told himself that that was good. He did not want to make love to her. Not yet. That she could be involved with Jake was good. Yes, it would give him chance to talk her into posing for him. It would keep her safely within his sphere, and Jacob would persuade her to pose. There was no way he could seduce her, and then paint her. He needed her innocence – to him, at least. All the same, it was difficult to control his ardent need. But then, there was Amy – though she would be possessive and distracting if he did begin to paint Eleanor.

He watched Eleanor as she walked around his private place, glass of wine in hand, from which she sipped occasionally and little. Louis drained his glass. There was no doubt that she was impressed with his work. Perhaps she would be willing to be his model. However, Louis could not be sure of this. He felt insecure and wished that he was immersed in a portrait, getting all his life from that, and with no need for all the complexities of 'real' life. He went for another drink.

'Tea is almost ready,' Jacob informed him as Louis sloshed

Minervois into his glass. He frowned at Louis' sullenness, asking, 'Won't she pose for you?'

'I haven't asked her yet . . .' Louis threw at him, irritably, 'She fancies you!' he added with incredulity, as though that would be the least likely thing he would have expected from anyone.

'No . . .' Jacob said with disbelief, recalling how enthusiastically Eleanor had talked of Louis. Louis glared at him as he perceived that his friend was pleased and returned Eleanor's interest. 'Anyway,' Jacob added reasonably as he dished the vegetable soup he had made into bowls, 'You want to paint her, Louis.'

Louis nodded moodily. He had to pull himself together. As his studio was not free to him, he wondered whether he had time to play his piano. Would Elli think that odd? It was important to him not to put her off him, to give her the impression that he was in some way strange. For the thousandth time, the extremes of his nature fretted him.

'I'm just going for a pee,' he told Jacob.

His friend looked at him in sympathy, and went to tell Eleanor that tea was ready. She followed him back, helping him carry the dishes through. Once Louis had gone, Jacob was pleased that Eleanor was interested in him. They began the meal without Louis, hearing the strains of Schubert floating down to them.

'Sometimes, he finds it hard to resist his piano as he passes,' Jacob explained.

Eleanor nodded in complete understanding of an artist's different needs. She did not seem to be at all disturbed by Louis' moodiness. She had quickly finished her soup and was tucking hungrily into hunks of wholemeal bread and pâté and cheese, helping herself to lashings of salad and guzzling down wine. Watching her, Jacob recalled how hungry he always was at her age. He wondered if Louis would unwittingly starve her, and decided that he would look after her. He poured her some more wine, and wondered whether he should go and get Louis. However, Louis appeared quite soon, seemingly in command of his wilder self. Jacob realised how important it was for Louis to

118

paint Eleanor. He smiled and joined them, eventually participating in their light chatter.

Louis could not help but stare at Eleanor, rejoicing in the clarity of her smooth, unblemished skin, and the perfection of her delicate face. It would feel like satin to the touch. He drank her in, as if, in some way, consuming her with his eyes, so that he could possess her, in order to give her back to his canvas. By concentrating thus, his obsession for her was purified, made spiritual, the sexual energy redirected. He seemed as if in a trance, withdrawn from them, but full of radiant power. He was ready to draw her: his fingers tingled with this need, and he wondered whether he could just do a few sketches.

Jacob was aware of his state, and the intense pitch of creativity and ability he had reached. He had the energy of weeks of rest. A portrait of Eleanor would be good. Time was short before they went to Florence, and all sorts of things could muddle his pure state. For once, he jumped in . . .

'You know, Elli, Louis would be very honoured to paint you . . .'

Jacob felt Louis stiffen beside him as Elli paused in her drinking to turn her coal black eyes on them in turn. He could almost feel Louis' heart race.

Eleanor was in a delicious, languorous mood, unexpectedly at ease with these friends. She was drawn into their warmth, and relaxed by the delicious wine and food. She had been overjoyed at Louis' friendliness and the help and advice he had given her: she had not expected him to be so forthcoming.

'Do you, really?' she addressed him softly.

Louis narrowed his eyes, and nodded, filled with silent anguish. It was all he wanted, now . . .

Jacob saw how she looked away, how her white teeth chewed on her lip as she struggled with herself. At last she sighed:

'It's not that I'm against it, Louis – I'm flattered, honoured that you should want to, but . . .' she shrugged, dejected, unable now to meet his eyes, feeling that she was about to let him down, and she herself, after all, lived for art.

Louis reached for her hand and squeezed it.

'Don't worry, Elli,' he said gently.

She looked up at him. He smiled tenderly. Her stomach seemed to somersault.

'Don't say no, not yet. Promise me you'll think about it? There's no hurry . . .'

Eleanor nodded.

'Let's go for a walk!' Louis said with sudden brightness, standing up and stretching, infecting them with his sudden energy.

They went down to the river, and the old mill, laughing and joking, running around like children, shaking off the seriousness of the impending ordeal for Eleanor. Jacob then drove her home.

Amy and Sarah had gone shopping for new clothes for Florence, then, delighted with their purchases, and after a meal and a few drinks, had decided to go and see a film. Then, agreeing that they would go to London the following day, they went back to Amy's, where they drank wine and listened to music. It felt gentle to be without men, and they basked in the warmth of their friendship. It was therefore natural for them eventually to begin to make love; this had been the exciting secret at the base of their day together.

They took it slowly, standing and kissing before they started to undress each other. Once naked, Sarah knelt to lick at Amy's sex, holding onto her bottom as she tongued her lovingly, giving her her whole attention as she explored Amy's salty flesh with her mouth. Amy held onto her head, parting her legs over Sarah's face as the woman aroused her, moving her body in pleasure. She was relaxed – this seemed right.

Then they lay on the bed, and lying face to bottom, continued to perform cunnilingus on each other before resuming a sex to sex position, Amy on top, as they pressed their sensitised fannies intimately together, caressing each other's breasts, and sucking nipples as they each experienced identical responses. They prolonged their enjoyment, gaining orgasm after orgasm as their ecstasy spiralled, at last lost in heady explosion, their bodies writhing and entwining passionately.

In the early hours they woke, once more greedy and energised by each other's willingness.

'Look at this.' Sarah delved into her bag to show Amy a double-headed dildo. Amy laughed, realising that it was not she alone who had anticipated this encounter. First making each other's fanny wet and ready, they eased the instrument of pleasure into place, until they were both filled with its soft manipulative rubber, yet also able to pound magnificently on one another's artificially stimulated and enlarged clitoris. They kissed and squeezed at each other's swollen breasts, writhing with increased abandon, their wet vaginas squeezing on the extended hard rubber within and then pressing firmly on each other as they reached orgasm.

The next day, they went off to London, still drunk on sex and novelty and laughter, indulging in private fondling and sex in all the places two people of the same sex could do so. They were empowered by this temporary exclusion of the powerful and potent men necessary in their normal lives.

Five

Jacob had organised an extra class on Sunday evening, for them to have a go at sketching Simon and Sarah in the poses of Titian's 'Bacchus and Ariadne', a painting they had studied in detail during their visit to the National Gallery. Though, in their preliminary drawings they would capture the models naked and not semi-clothed in red and blue as in the picture. Jacob told them that artists had traditionally drawn their figures naked first. Some of them, including Eleanor, had already practised drawing these two figures from the complex scene, from postcards they had purchased at the Gallery. There were other figures they could draw later. Simon had to maintain a flamboyant pose with his body bent forward, his left arm swung back and his right over his lower torso, legs likewise outstretched, one behind and one in front of his twisted body – though, unlike the wild god, he was firmly on the ground.

As Ariadne, Sarah also had to take up a turning pose, though more gently, with her eyes meeting those of Bacchus, whose head was inclined towards her, her right arm crossing her body and raised to the height of her head, her right leg back, and her body turned so that her left arm was back, her hand curled at her buttocks. Their eyes met in a dramatic moment where Bacchus swept down to carry off the abandoned Ariadne.

Jacob got the models into these complex poses, his clothed body close to their naked ones as he lifted arms, moved back legs and instructed them as they laughingly complied. He turned to the class and smiled at their trepidation.

'Right, have a go – a quick sketch first. Observe the twisting and straining of the muscles and sinews as the bodies yearn in these unusual positions. Do a few sketches, concentrate on different parts if you like. Try to capture the invisible force between them, the dynamics holding the pair. Then we'll have a short break, for the models to flex their muscles before we have another shot. Okay? Ariadne is terror stricken as the lascivious god leaps down to take her as his bride . . .'

'Lucky Ariadne,' quipped Sam, and the class laughed.

They worked keenly, attempting to do as Jacob suggested. As he came round to take a look at their efforts, Amy found her lustful mind taken up with the promised ardent sexuality between the abandoned mortal and the wild god. She smiled sleazily at Jacob, whose eyes held hers in shared humour for an instant before he passed on to Eleanor. Jacob knew that Louis had gone to Amy the night before.

While Amy was well aware of Jacob's budding relationship with Eleanor, sexually involved with him herself, she was attuned to any nuance between them. As she was passionately obsessed with Louis, and would soon see Reuben in Florence, she could scarcely be possessive of Jacob too, however, she would like to maintain an easy (sometimes physical) relationship with him. Somehow, she did not mind sharing him with Sarah.

'Do you fancy a drink, later, Jake?' she asked in an undertone as he paused once more to trace her pencil-lines, to point to the twisting of muscles on Simon's young body and offer a few salient words of advice. He nodded and smiled.

'Louis is coming along, to "The Raven",' he told her.

'Right.' Amy sighed to herself: no chance for a quiet time with Jacob then. Still, her body responded excitedly to think of seeing Louis soon.

As she drew, Amy found herself conjecturing on the relationship between the models, who had so much in common and the romance of their subject added glamour to this. So when it transpired that not only Louis, but they, and some other members of the class, including the lively trio of Marie-Anne, Sam and Robbie also planned to join them at the 'The Raven', to discuss the trip to Florence, she was not too dispirited.

* * *

Eleanor was trying hard to concentrate, but she was repeatedly filled with flutters of nervousness as she thought of posing for Louis. She had almost decided . . . At break, she chanced to be standing by Amy as they collected their coffee.

'Difficult?' Amy commented, regarding the young woman with interest.

Eleanor nodded. 'I wonder what it's like . . . ?'

'Posing?' asked Amy, narrowing her eyes speculatively at Eleanor. The girl seemed preoccupied. 'It's okay, I'm sure. I expect you soon forget to be self-conscious, float off in your own world.'

'Yes . . . That's what Simon says.'

'Has Louis asked you to pose for him?' Amy could not prevent herself from narrowing her eyes at Eleanor.

Eleanor lowered her own eyes, embarrassed as Amy tried to submerge the rising jealousy. *She* wanted to be his next subject.

'You'd be much better,' Eleanor said candidly.

'Oh,' Amy turned away to put her mug down. 'I'm much too busy with my shop at present.'

Eleanor nodded uncertainly. Amy felt that she was very anxious about what she perceived as an ordeal.

'Think of the money,' she advised, adding to herself – don't think of Louis Joseph. It suddenly seemed to Amy that Eleanor could usurp her place with both Jacob and Louis. She toyed with the idea of putting Eleanor off sitting for Louis.

For a moment, Eleanor imagined that the older woman saw her as some kind of prostitute.

At the end of the class, everyone went on to the pub, while Jake was detained for a few moments by the caretaker, but as he left the building, he found Eleanor waiting for him.

'Jake?'

'Yes, Elli? Are you coming for a drink with us? Louis will be there and we can have a chat about Florence. Not too long now, hey?' He smiled, transmitting his enthusiasm.

'I don't know . . .' she hesitated now.

'What is it?'

'I was going to ask you to tell Louis, that I will pose for him.

125

But, if – you know – I feel too uncomfortable, I won't be able to continue . . .' she let it all out in a rush.

'That seems fair enough . . .' Jacob smiled at her, squeezing her forearm in empathy. 'Louis will understand that, Elli,' he assured her. 'Don't worry. Do you want to come and tell him yourself? Lay down the ground rules?'

Eleanor was torn between joining the lively group in the pub, with whom she had come to feel quite at home, and leaving Louis to discover her acquiescence whilst not in her company. She thought of Simon and Sarah, and the intimacy between them and then she thought of Amy's shifting moods towards her and decided against it. Besides, although she had, after much thought, decided to pose for Louis, she did not want to discuss it with him, now, in public. She did not relish Amy's envy.

'Fair enough. Louis will be pleased. He's free now. When could you begin?'

She shrugged, 'I do have quite a bit of free time during the week now.'

'Tomorrow?' he persisted, his tone patient, 'I could collect you if you like. I'm going to do some landscape sketches.'

Eleanor's eyes lit up. Jacob smiled.

'Would you like to join me, in the morning, and then we could go back and you could begin with a short session?'

'Yes, I'd like that. Jake—?'

'Yes?'

'Will you be around, when Louis is drawing me?'

Jacob wondered if Eleanor was afraid of Louis, but he did not ask her. He simply nodded in assurance, adding,

'You can bring your mum, if you like, Louis is so keen to do your portrait . . .'

Elli laughed and then said, 'I don't know why . . .'

'Don't you, Elli?' Jacob asked seriously, meeting her eyes.

Eleanor blushed.

They walked along the lane which led to the main road, and to the pub, where Eleanor saw Louis waiting at the end. Jacob was surprised to see him (thinking he would be waiting in the pub), until Louis approached Eleanor, lingering behind with her.

126

'We'll be in "The Raven", Louis,' Jacob told him, seeing that his preoccupied friend merely nodded. Jacob went ahead.

Louis was dressed all in black leather, his dark curls hung into his eyes and Eleanor thought that he looked wonderful. She smiled shyly.

'Are you coming to the pub?'

Eleanor shook her head, not looking at Louis, who was so close to her.

'I told Jacob – that I would do the portrait, pose for you, but . . .'

Louis nodded, his dark eyes shining, looking down into hers. He smiled at her.

'Don't worry, Elli. Completely on your terms. Thank you . . . I'm delighted. Let's have one drink – to celebrate?'

'Alright, then . . .' Eleanor agreed, flattered that Louis was so pleased. 'Louis?'

'Yes?'

'Wouldn't you rather paint Amy?'

Louis laughed and shook his head.

Amy watched Eleanor and Louis with intense jealousy as Louis chatted to the young woman. He had eyes for no-one but her: Jacob knew that he was overjoyed and no doubt intent on discussing the painting, but all Amy could think of was that Louis may prefer Eleanor to her. Jacob could see that she was in danger of storming in and breaking the fragile understanding between Louis and Eleanor, so he asked her how Reuben was.

'Alright, I suppose,' she shrugged, darting another quick glance at Louis and Eleanor.

'It won't be long before you see him, again.'

'I know what you're doing, Jake, but I'm not going to let Louis mess me around . . .'

'He really only wants to paint Elli—'

'Hah!'

'You know, Amy—'

'What?'

'I've never known Louis to paint a current lover.'

To Amy's relief, Eleanor *was* leaving, without so much as a kiss from Louis, and Louis was coming to join them, smiling at Jacob, glancing at Amy.

'Do you want a drink?' he asked her, ignoring her loaded look. He always treated her as if she was an old friend to whom he owed recognition, but not necessarily courtesy. Almost like a man would treat another man – with feigned casualness. Watching him carefully, she could not miss his reflex glance towards Simon, and over his agile body – at Sarah, speculatively, and she wondered whether he saw everyone as a possible sexual partner. If she was honest, she had to admit that she herself was as predatory. And that Louis was avoiding meeting her eyes because he was all too aware of her interest. Perhaps if she flirted with Jacob . . .

Louis went to the bar, and Amy used the time to look at his firm buttocks, under the sheath of his expensive leather trousers. The trousers caressed his bottom intimately. The choice of this supple animal skin with the soft cotton shirt and its touches of lace and embroidery was a beguiling juxtaposition of hard masculinity and tender femininity. An indication of the make-up of Louis' character? Amy's body heated up as she imagined the leather against her naked skin.

'Louis' in biker mode . . .' laughed Jacob.

'So he has got a bike?' Amy demanded to know, as if she supposed Louis sufficiently ludicrous simply to get himself dressed up like that for effect. Not that she really cared. He looked stunning.

'Oh, yes, but I wouldn't ask for a ride unless you've got a death-wish. He's pretty wild on it.' But even as he warned her, Jacob could see that Amy couldn't wait to get Louis' bike – and soon Louis himself – between her thighs. He looked across to Sarah, who met his smile immediately. Jacob anticipated a passionate night with the generous and sexy woman. Giving his attention back to Amy, he perceived that she saw Louis' death-machine as yet another aspect of her challenging relationship with him.

'Amy wants a ride,' he said helpfully as his friend returned, still seemingly interested in Simon, probably for Amy's benefit.

Louis shot a disgusted look at Jacob's unworthy double-entendre. He looked Amy up and down sleazily, and then into her bewitching eyes.

Amy's body responded powerfully to him as he suddenly looked directly at her. She was struck by the contrast in the white of his eyes and the darkness of the irises. Every time he looked at her, it was as though she had been given a blow in her guts, and she was weak with sickness. Overwhelming lust. No man had the right to be that beautiful. Louis was smiling at her and she realised that he had been teasing her with his interest in Simon and Sarah. She knew that he wanted her. She felt very excited and a surge of sexual readiness caused sudden wetness in her pants. She was aware that Louis moved closer to Jacob, perhaps merely to take his cigarette from him. Amy excused herself and went to the Ladies, nearby, partly to allow Louis a tantalising look at her bottom as she wiggled it provocatively.

'So – come on then,' Louis said as she returned. He was already standing, which, even for Louis, was a little abrupt. Jacob had gone over to join the others.

'It's a lovely bike, a Yamaha,' Louis said, his dark eyes twinkling.

Amy finished her drink, raised her hand to Jacob as they left. Louis flamboyantly blew Simon a kiss.

They roared through the country lanes on Louis' black and silver motor bike. Amy felt the machine trembling between her thighs and under her sex as she clung to Louis, enjoying the leather and feeling that this was another display of power as he drove at speed through Essex and into the Suffolk night. A silent challenge to her. She was confident of Louis' riding, but the excitement of hanging onto him as he speeded dramatically round corners, was exhilarating and a little frightening. Louis seemed genuinely intent on terrifying her at times, but she would not give him the pleasure of knowing that he succeeded. Her knickers were sodden against the leather of the seat. With sex and sweat. Louis zoomed to a sudden halt down a narrow lane, dismounted and took off his helmet, shaking his hair loose.

Amy followed suit. They were by the old stone wall of a churchyard.

'Great, isn't it?' He grinned at her.

Amy agreed breathlessly; she certainly felt elated. Louis indicated the wild grass beyond the low wall, and Amy realised that he wanted them to make love there, out in the open. Well, she was game. She nodded.

'Keep your leathers on,' she commanded.

Louis shrugged in agreement.

'You'll get cold,' he joked, watching her strip.

'I'm sure you can manage to heat me up. Just take me – forcefully and quickly, Louis. I'll just be lying asleep here, and you stop off, getting off your bike for a pee, say, and you see me . . .'

'I think I can work out the rest,' Louis laughed.

Amy lay on the damp earth, already burning in the cold wet grass. Louis even obligingly started up his bike and drove it up the road and back. As she lay, fingering herself and waiting eagerly, it flickered across her mind that Louis could, if he chose, sadistically leave her here. But, of course, he never would have. He made her jump by leaping over the wall beside her. He stood above her, eyeing her. Amy pushed her thighs tightly together and covered her breasts. Louis sprang upon her, pulling away her arms from her naked breasts. He writhed dramatically upon her, giving her the pleasure of wrapping her naked body around his leathers, before parting her legs forcefully with his thigh, and deftly unzipping his leather trousers to release his throbbing cock against her. Though she had intended to pretend to fight Louis off, Amy succumbed immediately as Louis' huge prick forced open her vagina and rapidly penetrated her. His hands began to knead her breasts mercilessly, tearing at her flesh with primal need. His hot tongue was in her mouth as he possessed her entirely and greedily, taking her roughly. Amy clutched at the leather, delighting in the feel against her nakedness, but more aware of Louis' dominant sexuality as he fucked her savagely. They came together dramatically and noisily in the dark night. Louis kissed Amy passionately as he shuddered to his overwhelming orgasm.

'So – you *are* going to paint poor Eleanor?' Amy asked as Louis dropped her off.

Louis merely nodded, refusing to be trapped by her, not wanting her jealousy to hinder him.

'I'll warn her about you.'

'You do that,' Louis called as he roared off into the night.

Eleanor's fantasies were now sometimes pervaded by the enchanting Louis, though he came from her unconscious, so determined was she to suppress these dark imaginings. Thinking of him like this stirred her in a way she did not yet recognise. The ordeal of posing for him was almost too much for her to think of, without being reminded of his sexuality. She decided that she must be business-like and only think of him as an artist.

Jacob collected her early on Monday morning. It was an unusually mild, bright day. She felt at ease now with this gentle, sensitive man. She was looking forward to spending the morning sketching with him. Once engrossed in this enjoyable activity, she would be able to control the anxiety she felt at the impending sitting. She looked out at the Suffolk countryside as they drove in companionable silence.

They settled themselves at the edge of a churchyard, and Jacob, no longer the teacher, became engrossed in his sketches. Jacob was well aware of the young woman's superior talent as he glanced at her work, though, as her teacher he drew attention to one or two points of craftsmanship, and she nodded seriously. The morning continued in quiet solitude each engrossed in studying the church.

They went to the nearby pub for lunch, and Jacob became aware of Eleanor's increasing anxiety, now that she was devoid of the solace of drawing.

'Louis is like you,' he assured her, 'Once he is painting, that's all he thinks of, he'll only be aware of you as a model.' Jacob wondered whether he was being entirely truthful in his attempts to reassure Eleanor, but he knew that Louis would treat her with infinite respect, and it need not matter to the young woman what was in the lascivious artist's mind . . .

But thinking of the beautiful Amy, and her interest in Louis, Eleanor was not sure she really wanted to be seen just as a model, not really . . .

Louis was already in his studio when they arrived. Jacob wondered what he had been doing all morning. Had he prowled around the empty house restlessly? Played sporadically on his piano? Driven people wild on his motorbike? Anyhow, he had not done the washing or cleared away his breakfast things. Jacob noticed that Louis and Eleanor regarded each other with almost the same silent trepidation. Though the young woman was probably not conscious of Louis' anxiety – usual before a new venture, before his dominant confidence was justified once more to him in his proven ability. Eleanor's eyes were as black as Louis', Jacob realised with a sudden knot in his stomach. He left them to it, telling them he would be in the kitchen. Whilst engaged in mundane tasks, he felt that he was full of concern for both of them: fragile creatures, they seemed just now . . .

'What I thought— ' Louis said to Eleanor, after clearing his throat: his voice was still husky. He'd also smoked himself to death all morning. He advanced, showing her a picture, in a huge book of Titian's *Venus of Urbino*, '—was something like this for the portrait.'

Eleanor saw with relief that the model's thighs were closed, though of course she was naked. The woman was very sensual, obviously aware of her own beauty. She lay on a white sheet on a bed, covered in red, with her right arm resting on pillows. Her long red curls fell over her right shoulder. In her hand she held crushed red flowers. Her knowing eyes looked out of the picture, at the artist or observer. Her breasts were softly rounded. Her right leg was bent, her knee raised slightly, and her lower leg crossed under the calf of her left leg. Her left arm was resting casually down over her body, following the gentle swell of her stomach, her hand resting over her pubis, her fingers between her legs. Her body was much more voluptuous than her own,

132

thought Eleanor. Would Louis be disappointed?

She was aware that Louis regarded her patiently as she nodded slowly. For some reason – probably because of Venus's lovely long curls, but perhaps because of her sensual expression, Eleanor was reminded of Amy. She would surely be more suitable for Louis? Eleanor did not have the model's generous curls.

'Good, okay,' Louis was saying; he sounded relieved. 'You can undress in there – there's a gown.' Louis indicated the conservatory with its blinds down. He watched her as she went slowly towards it.

He was desperate for a drink or a cigarette. This was ridiculous. He already felt ill, having had so many cigarettes this morning. She took ages to prepare . . . He went restlessly to his easel. He felt better, thus ensconced, though he only planned pencil sketches. He flipped through his battered sketch book, looking at old drawings of Simon, Jacob and Sarah as well as preliminary ones for other paintings of his various friends and many models.

Eleanor was sitting on a chair and looking at Jacob's aunt's strange plants. What was she doing here? She felt that her body trembled, though it was not cold in here. She had noticed that Louis had put an extra electric fire by the couch. She thought of the sultry look on the model's face. Venus. She recalled Jacob's lecture about prostitutes posing as the goddess of love, and her mouth went dry, her heart pounded. Already she needed the lavatory. She told herself not to be stupid, and thought of how blasé Simon and Sarah were. She had asked Simon how he felt and he told her that he became quite relaxed, in his imposed position, and his mind floated off. It was a kind of freedom. He had been quite impressed that she was posing for Louis, and told her that the portrait would be delicious. He told her that she could save the money Louis paid her for Florence.

She stood and undressed quickly, put on the gown and then fiddled about, tidying her clothes and delaying the return to the studio. Her belly was a mass of nerves. It would almost be easier

133

to go to bed with Louis, she thought, at least it would not seem so calculated and clinical . . . So cold.

Louis saw the fear in her eyes as she came through the door, like an abandoned waif, her black eyes huge. He was filled with warmth for her, but it would not do now to take her in his arms and comfort her. He smiled at her, Eleanor returned this, confirming to him the wisdom of his detachment. Now, he must do his best to remain aloof and business-like. He must subdue his natural arousal. In time, it would be easier.

'Take off your robe and lie on the bed,' he said, sounding like a doctor as he busied himself unnecessarily with materials.

Taking a deep breath, Elli took off the gown, turning her back to Louis as she put it down and got onto the bed. Louis smiled in admiration at her slim yet womanly form, taking in her small neat buttocks and suppressing his animal desire to grasp them. His impetuous cock quickened inconveniently. Despite his continued and frenzied masturbation all morning, he still felt hungry for it. His sexy interlude with Amy in the churchyard made him want more. He should have stayed with her last night. Though she would have gone on about Eleanor. He regretted complicating his life. Still, this stage would pass, and he would soon be able to transmute his sexual energy into creativity.

Elli felt exposed and lonely as she lay on the old sofa, where so many of Louis' lovers had lain. She knew that he was not yet looking at her, but studying the book which contained the painting he was going to base his on. She tried to get into that pose, with one leg under the other. It wasn't easy. She did not want to move, to expose herself to Louis. She was all too aware of her hidden sex. And of her breasts, raised tantalisingly. It was not at all like going to the doctor's – and she was little enough experienced in that. Louis seemed more attractive than ever, and she was very conscious of his age and experience.

'Right . . .' said Louis, feeling that he had given her sufficient time, and turning round. *Oh God*, he thought, as his narrowed eyes took in her young, pure body. A body seemingly only just into young womanhood, and infinitely desirable. Elli must be aware of the sensual flush of his face, of the desire in his too-eloquent eyes. He took refuge in the book, as if it contained a complex puzzle they both had to solve – were committed to solving together. His cock nudged at the tight constraint of his jeans, urging him to get it between those young thighs. He should have worn looser trousers, he told himself.

'Okay. . . usually, I do several sketches of my models – in different positions, so that I can get used to their bodies. But if you're comfortable like that I'll make a start. Think of Simon or Sarah . . . tell me if you want a break, or don't feel happy. Just tell me, Elli . . .'

Eleanor nodded in miserable silence, thinking of the possible double meanings of his words, aware of her slender nakedness under this man's minutest perusal. Thinking of him, getting used to her body. She thought of his older and beautiful lovers – Amy; Sarah . . . She closed her eyes. She sensed a withdrawal as Louis began to draw. She concentrated on the sound of his rapid pencil sketching. Such a familiar soothing sound. She thought of herself subjugating her dread of people by this method, and wondered whether she feared Louis' ability to do this to her. But she was eventually assured by succeeding in thinking of him primarily as an artist.

Louis relaxed, his keen eyes glancing repeatedly at the delicious young body as he took in its form, remoulding it in his mind and recreating it on paper. It seemed to him as if she *was* a virgin, though he knew she was not. She seemed so innocent. He must not get carried away, and draw for too long. He was thankful that Jacob was about; he tended to forget time. They had agreed on a short session. If Eleanor felt okay with this, then she may agree to another sitting after a break. Louis drank in the warm tones and clear lines of her body, his mind racing ahead to how he would mix his colours; he loved the sensuous qualities of rich, thick oils. The challenge of getting the colours right. The vivid colours of her face – the heightened flush of her cheeks, the brightness of her eyes and the silky-black of her short hair made him itch to portray these. Her skin was dark, easily tanned.

'Would you like some tea?' Jacob asked Elli. 'Is that alright, Louis?'

'Sure – I was about to say it was time for a break . . .'

Eleanor sat up, reached for her robe and quickly put it on. She had not been aware of Jacob's appreciative glance. She was merely pleased to see him. She was surprised at how quickly the time had passed, though she could not honestly say that she had felt relaxed. Jacob was smiling at Louis' first sketch. He nodded reassuringly to her as she handed her the mug of tea. Elli held it to her, savouring its comfort, sipping often, like a thirsty child. Louis looked at her, silently inviting her to see. Eleanor gasped inwardly. The sketch was one of great accomplishment and workmanship. Achieved so rapidly. She smiled at Louis, forgetting that it was her, thus exposed, her body rendered in confident strokes, and impressed only by his innate ability. How very many hours he must have spent practising to have acquired such ability. Could *she* be this good, one day? She burned to be. Louis excused himself and went to the garden for a cigarette.

Eleanor drank her tea and stared at the sketch. Jacob could see that she was tremendously pleased that Louis had achieved so much and wondered whether she was imagining the glory of the finished product. He wondered whether Louis would be able to complete the portrait before they went to Florence. He hoped so, as it could cause problems all round if not.

'He'll do a good likeness of you . . .' Jacob said.

'I know he's good . . . He's brilliant.' Eleanor sounded more confident now. Relieved.

'You said you had quite a lot of free time?' Jacob fished on Louis' behalf.

Eleanor nodded. She finished her tea and went off to the bathroom. Jacob went to the garden, thinking, well done, Louis. Louis turned to smile at him. He too looked as if a weight had been lifted. Their smile lingered. After all, under all the trappings of art was the very ordinary masculine understanding that this was a very pretty, very desirable girl.

As Eleanor was alone in the luxurious bathroom, she lingered to experience the overwhelming sense of relief, now that she had successfully completed this first sitting. She was full of admiration for the lovely house, and the organised way in which it was run: she thought that this was down to Jacob, rather than Louis. Though the men seemed to live together very amicably. When she went back down, Louis asked her:

'Do you mind if I do a few more sketches?'

Eleanor shot a quick look at Jacob, who smiled at her.

'Okay . . .' she agreed, though her voice was a little uncertain.

The rest of the afternoon was spent in her taking up various poses – some similar to those Simon and Sarah had modelled for them during their Life Classes. Louis sketched rapidly, seemingly in a concentrated and businesslike way. He did not make her keep any one position for more than a few minutes. After all, he was an accomplished artist, and looked now only for detail. And though this was true, she could not know of the effect she had on him, and how he ached to touch that young, smooth flesh, to experience its warmth and softness. To kiss her full, generous mouth, and to take her in his arms and hold her close. It was as if all his avid gazing at her body fed his sensual mind and its culmination would be in touching the figure he drew, tracing its undulating shape with his sensitive fingertips. Distracted, at last, he nodded and put down his pencil and Eleanor went to get dressed.

Jacob, who had been popping in and out throughout the session, sometimes to smile reassurance at the young woman, came to look at Louis' work. He grasped his arm, expressing his admiration and pleasure at the keenly executed line drawings. Louis shook his head in weariness. He felt empty and exhausted. Jacob saw the near-wildness in his drooping eyes. He nodded as Louis explained that he was going to rest.

Eleanor was surprised that Louis had gone, sensing, Jacob surmised, some dissatisfaction with her.

'He'll be lying on his bed – shattered,' Jacob explained, going to the kitchen to make her coffee and offering her food.

Eleanor nodded, herself familiar with this sudden withdrawal of adrenaline. She was ravenous, and eyed the food Jacob was preparing, with the hunger of a starving adolescent. He smiled and gave her an apple.

'Can I go and see him?' she asked.

'Sure,' Jacob replied, a little surprised, wondering whether Louis would be able to resist her, now.

Eleanor looked at the drawings. They were excellent. She felt very special.

Louis was lying on the bed, very still, one arm under his head. He looked lovely, though his down-turned mouth expressed his fatigue. He felt strange – a familiar state, rectified partly by eating and perhaps walking. He was too tired to prepare anything, though he knew it was imperative for him to begin to replenish his energy. He hoped Jacob would bring him food. He looked across at Eleanor, standing uncertainly at his bedroom door, looking at him. She held a half-eaten apple in her hand.

'I could begin the painting tomorrow, if you're free,' he told her. Even his voice expressed his weary state.

Eleanor understood. She herself would sometimes become so engrossed that she would forget the time; forget to eat. Though she was lucky – her mother still provided for her, and nagged her to take a break. Sometimes, though, she painted all night. She surveyed Louis, lying in so relaxed a state in this room, surrounded by his art. His body was strong and supple. She did not think he would have an inch of flab under those jeans, that scarlet shirt. One hand was deep in his pocket.

Though she had been filled with gladness to hear how confident he was, she realised that she had not answered him. Now, she nodded, going further into the room, beguiled by the drawings. She turned from Louis' dark gaze now to look at them. Very many were of Jacob, less of Simon and Sarah. Some she recognised as being preliminary sketches for the portraits in his studio, or in local art galleries. She became engrossed in her study of them, oblivious to Louis' hungry watchfulness. She recognised the drawings copied from Raphael and Michelangelo: the latter's Adam from the Sistine Chapel; *The Dying Captive* from the Louvre; Raphael's ravishingly beautiful mistress . . . Absently, she continued to eat her apple. She glanced at the reproductions – some of them familiar from art books – of Apollo, Bacchus, and of various naked men and women, painted by renowned artists. Eleanor did not consider Louis Joseph's talent to be less than these.

Louis bit his lip as he watched her from his bed. He ached to rise and go to Eleanor. How close seemed the simplicity of the act that would bring her to him, to lie beside him. He imagined slowly turning to her, and bringing her so close that her flesh would meld into his. He closed his eyes in anguish, feeling the familiar wave of sensuality surge through him. He needed physical contact now, after all that cerebral concentration. He looked again at her long, slim legs, which parted, he knew, invitingly at the top. He saw her naked body under her loose clothes as she moved gracefully round his room, no longer conscious of him, but only of his art.

He felt his penis become painfully even more rigid under the coarse denim, so close to his hand. He was burning and it made him feel dizzy not to grasp it. If she should come and lay along his body, her hard mound, with its fine down of black hair pressing on his cock, and he could run his palms down her back to cup those tight muscular hemispheres. He felt pre-orgasmic just to imagine this. Louis knew that he had more to suffer than this before he dared even approach her. He sighed. Why did he put himself through it? Next year, he would draw old buildings.

'Food's ready,' Jacob said from the door, looking in with interest.

'Great!' Eleanor said, turning to him and smiling.

'Are you coming down, Louis? Or shall I being you something?'

Louis turned to him, and Jacob nodded, the laughter rising in his throat. He understood all too well his friend's state, though most men experienced it more simply. It was as though he put himself through the masochism of his art deliberately to torture himself.

Jacob followed Eleanor out of Louis room, 'Come down when you're ready.' He looked back at Louis and indicated his aroused state with an oblique glance.

Eleanor chatted gaily throughout tea, thoroughly relieved, perhaps even proud of herself now, looking forward to the portrait proper. Jacob smiled at her child-like excitement. She was probably more relaxed than she would have been if Louis had joined them.

'How long do you think it'll take?'

'It varies. He has to let the oils dry . . .'

'Do you think that he'll finish it before we go to Florence?'

'That's his intention. And – you seem to be free?'

Eleanor nodded enthusiastically, then frowned.

'What is it?' Jacob asked.

'Well, I'd forgotten, but although I'm free – I mean, I have some work to do, but can do it in the evenings – occasionally I have to look after Katy, my little sister. She's three. That's when my mum has to go on a few courses – she's a teacher. I had arranged to do this, though I suppose Mum could make other arrangements . . .' she wondered doubtfully. 'My brother, Robin's got a job . . .'

'Don't worry. Bring her with you.' Jacob said, wondering how Louis would cope with this.

'I don't really want her – you know – watching . . . Anyway, she wouldn't leave me in peace.'

'Fair enough. I'll see what I can arrange in the way of entertainment. By the way, did Louis discuss your rates with you? No? He's quite generous, so you'll have some money – for Italy?'

Eleanor nodded.

'Don't worry, he will. He'll put it in writing for you if you like. A contract.'

Louis began the painting the next day. Eleanor lay in the ordained pose for a long time whilst he laid down the preliminary lines. She could sense Louis' intense concentration, and thought she picked up on his underlying anxiety at this crucial time. It was as if he hovered on the brink, once he had entered this new world – and it would not be without some pain, as he gave himself up to this – he would be increasingly taken into it, and calmer, but obsessed.

He actually made some lunch for them, though Eleanor had to suppress her mirth at his abstractedness. It was the first time she had really been alone with Louis. He was quiet and pre-occupied. Eleanor began to feel a little more at ease with him, though she could not imagine ever feeling as easy as she did with Jacob. Half-way through the afternoon session, she began to relax into a kind of enjoyable stupor.

Both Eleanor and (especially) Jacob were surprised at the enjoyment with which Louis played with the little Katy. He also sketched an enchanting picture of her, and expressed his desire to paint her. She was a delightful child, with massed dark curls and deep black eyes. Seeing Louis with her, Jacob thought with a pang of Louis as a father. He could be her father, they looked so alike. Perhaps Eleanor looked more like Louis than he had realised. Perhaps he did not want to realise . . .

It was as though she daily existed in another world as Eleanor became accustomed to the intense stillness and silence of her lengthy sessions of posing for Louis over the next days. They existed in an enforced meditation, in which Louis slowly took her material being to express on his canvas. Eleanor was able to observe him directly as she lay, naked on his couch. But she became increasingly aware of the spirit of the man, and, when they rested, she observed him closely, gradually more convinced of his very special quality and in awe of his physical beauty. She did not look at the portrait yet, as Louis had not invited her to, though she was curious at his progress. She was keen to discuss the various uses of colours, and brush-strokes but Louis was never very talkative, seemingly drained by his work.

Predictably, Amy turned up one evening. Jacob could not be sure whether Louis was relieved at the prospect of sexual release, or angry that she should come to disturb him now. But he was off to see Sarah and left them to it. Louis did not manage to prevent Amy from going into his studio, and her eyes sparked cold steel as he followed her. Amy had looked at the painting, still in its early stages, but she was astute enough to recognise its eroticism. Who better to, than Louis' lover?

'You've got no right to come in here,' Louis told her, anger smouldering in his eyes.

'No? And what have I got a right to, Louis?'

He shrugged carelessly, turning away and Amy grabbed at him angrily. Louis caught her and brought his mouth down hard on hers, stopping her from shouting at him. When she could, Amy flung him off.

'Elli hasn't even looked at the painting yet,' Louis explained.

'I bet. You're trying to convince her it's not sexual . . .' To Amy, Louis was smouldering with repressed sexuality. 'You equate sex with art. That's wrong!'

'Why?' asked Louis calmly.

Amy met his eyes. She could not help but look over his body. Lingeringly. She wanted him. Louis went from the studio to the lounge. He lit a cigarette and went over to the CD player.

'Where's Jacob gone?' Amy demanded.

Louis slotted in a John Williams CD, and turned to her, sadistic laughter in his eyes.

'To fuck Sarah.' Louis lingered eloquently on the verb.

'You're all the same!' Amy yelled in exasperation.

'Oh, and *you're* different?' Louis asked, pouring brandy, handing her a glass.

'Yes!' said Amy, amazed, accepting the drink.

'How did you get here, Amy?'

'Tttt . . . by car.'

'I mean . . .' Louis explained with exaggerated patience, 'into this house – the first time?'

'With Jacob.'

'To see his aunt's paintings?'

'Tttt . . .' Amy guiltily recalled her ulterior intent, but then Jacob was silently privy to it, surely?

'It's not quite the same as a sensual response to art, or an interpretation of life in art, but you came to screw Jake. Using art.'

Amy recalled how she had also gone to the first class intent on finding a man.

'You can't really tell me that you aren't moved by beautiful paintings. You feel a response to them . . . You chose to do the course. You can draw . . . Art is the ultimate sensual experience . . .' Louis drew her to him and kissed her more gently this time. 'Or is it sex?'

'So – you are involved sensually in your art?'

Louis thought he could get trapped into admitting his desire for Eleanor. He clasped his hands under Amy's bottom so that she could not escape. He was not always articulate, especially when he had been immersed in painting.

'Come on. Let's go to bed,' he suggested.

'Why?'

'That's what you came for.'

'You are the most arrogant swine I've ever met in my entire life.'

Louis smiled. 'I'm not complaining at being used to indulge your overwhelming libido.'

'Louis!'

They were much better at communicating with their bodies than in conversation. As soon as they got to his room, Louis ripped off Amy's clothes and began to squeeze and fondle her roughly, sending spasms of sexual electricity through their bodies. However, he did graciously allow Amy dominance as she lay outstretched along his strong, naked body. She held his hands above his head and undulated her eager pubis against his glorious erection. She felt fantastic, very aware of her own body on Louis'. Louis was passive, responding to her mouth as she traced his, thrusting his prick against her clitoris in response to her sensual movements. Amy knew that he could choose to be dominant at any second. This latent power fired her as she urged him deeply into her, and took control, riding him as she stimulated her clitoris against him. Louis patiently matched her pace until she began to move faster, and allowed himself to ejaculate as she reached her orgasm. He moved his hands to hold her. Amy felt him throbbing inside her, his sex-beats echoing hers. She kissed him madly.

* * *

143

Even when she was not present, it seemed to Eleanor that Louis worked on her portrait, devoting all his energy to this. Eleanor was very moved by his absorption and dedication. The gift, he was born with, but he had nourished this and expended great energy and patience, as no doubt he did on all of his paintings. If hers was as good as those, it would be, she was certain, marvellous. Whilst lying there, she imagined herself, in the future, in his place. She did discuss technical details with him as they ate – increasingly it was Eleanor who prepared their food – or walked. Occasionally, Louis admitted to the need for exercise, especially when Jacob cajoled him. Sometimes the three of them would walk in the countryside around Dedham: it was lovely and mild. Even then, Louis would smoke constantly, seemingly continuing to be immersed in thinking of the portrait.

For his part, the silent Louis was becoming increasingly aware of the delicate beauty of the young woman, now that he knew her tender body with such precarious intimacy. His compelling need for sexual release became increasingly dominant as Eleanor's likeness reached maturity on his easel. It was a very good resemblance: he captured the personality and dawning sexual maturity of his model.

Now, as he added final details, his eyes flickered to the secret hidden bud of her femininity, hidden under her dark triangle of hair, and within the warm folds of her sweet-smelling skin. He imagined putting the tip of his aching forefinger gently upon it, whilst looking into those round black eyes, and then slipping it into the moist crimson depths as she parted her legs for him. He became restless at the reflex stiffening of his hungry prick, and it was difficult to concentrate. He saw that Eleanor was becoming aware of the lust in his eyes, and he tutted to himself.

'Are you alright, Louis?' she asked in innocent concern. Surely she could not think that he was made of stone?

'Yes . . .' he said, passing his hand wearily across his eyes, closing them to shut out her images, the false one close to him, and the potent reality just yards away. Would it be beneficial to leave her, to go and lock himself away and try to appease his destructive sexual urge? But Louis had spent hours at night

144

pleasuring himself in his fabricated images of her. Her form alone, so familiar to him, was enough to feed his fantasies. He did not need to conjure it to arouse himself. He was constantly turned on by now and it was making him feel crazy. He was, as a consequence of this, irritable and angry towards her. His fantasies were sometimes of him taking her with violent and savage enjoyment.

'Shall we take a break?' Eleanor had got up and put on her gown, tying it around her as if in protection against his secret urge. She went to the kitchen, perhaps to revive him with coffee. He sensed that she was a little afraid of him. Unwisely, he followed her, cursing the masculinity which made him want to behave like a savage beast. All civilised veneer was stripped from him now and all he wanted to do as he leaned against the sink and watched her was to rip her wretched robe from her and hold her young naked body to his. His hands yearned to touch the warm flesh, to satisfy his physical need. He could not now feel cerebral.

Eleanor was shocked by the intensity in his eyes. She was going to hand him his mug of coffee, but changed her mind about going closer to him, and placed it on the cupboard.

What if he should kiss her now? thought Louis. If he could calm himself and build up to seducing her? He could do that . . .

'Can I see the portrait?' Elli asked, going back into the studio. Louis followed her.

Eleanor stood in silence before her image. It was like being filled with sudden and extreme sexuality, a sensation like before making love to herself. She had not expected this. Suddenly, she was extremely shy, naked before this man.

'It's very good . . .' she said with difficulty, feeling that something was due, some reaction – though the artist did not need to be told of his excellence. With a pang, she realised that it was also almost complete, and she realised how empty her life would seem now. What had begun in trepidation and reluctance had become a kind of communion. She was very close to Louis, and could feel the heat from his body. Deliberately and with an ensuing sense of loss, she moved away. Louis was bereft.

Surely he could have kissed her, then?

As she dressed, Eleanor was confused by her state of sexual arousal. It seemed wrong. She could not understand its genesis. She was intensely relieved when she heard the sound of Jacob returning. She had brought Katy with her today and they had gone to the park and now her little sister ran to her, to show her the leaves they had collected before they took her home.

Jacob immediately recognised his friend's state of helpless longing; the war within that made Louis wild with desire, whilst shackled by the needs of his art. He smiled at him, but Louis merely glowered, and Jacob shrugged this off with a laugh and turned to lift Katy onto the work surface as he made her a drink.

Louis went off to his room. Eleanor was still worried by Louis' mood, as they sat in the car, but Jacob explained that he was tired – drained of energy, and she seemed convinced by this. They took Katy home, but Eleanor felt too restless to remain indoors and jumped at the chance to accompany Jacob across to the other side of the river to get a view of the village. She collected her things.

It was reassuring and relaxing to sit on the river bank beside him in companionable silence, each immersed in their rendering of the old mill and the ancient cottages with their whimsical roofs and pretty gardens. As Jacob came close to her, to scrutinise her sketch, she felt a sudden rush of warmth for him, and was brave enough to move closer, asking to be kissed, as he looked up, to comment on the work. Louis had disturbed her in some subtle way. She needed reassurance and Jacob could not resist, as the black eyes yearned into his. He kissed her soft mouth gently, and as she pressed herself to him, he enfolded her in his arms and luxuriated in the feel of her young, slim body against his. He could feel the soaring sexuality in her, and though he knew that it was a result of Louis' prolonged attentions, he could not suppress the answering action of his own body, neither did he want to. He felt her pubis pushing against his growing erection and he ran his palms down her back, feeling her excitement as he caressed her bottom tenderly. As her kisses became more eager, his own sexual response was increasingly

146

urgent as his penis nudged against her crotch.

'Elli . . .' he said huskily, thinking that really, he ought to pull away, take her home. But he was possessed with need for her. He wondered if she knew the effect she had on him as she concentrated on her own enjoyment, pressing herself against him, clinging to him, kissing him deeply. With a groan, he reached for her small, perfect breasts, and Elli said yes – yes . . . as he caressed her, pressing at the small erect nipples. He ached to enter her. He slipped his hand between her thighs, which parted willingly. Desire swept through Jacob. He pulled her closer to him as she writhed hungrily against him. Then Jacob pulled away. Eleanor smiled at him. It must be her youth which made her so easy-going.

He had planned to invite her to eat with him at the pub nearby, but now it seemed best to drive her home. She lay back in the seat in a dreamlike state, humming softly to herself. Jacob glanced at her often – he could not help it. She looked adorable, her lips red and sensual, her dark eyes gleaming; her small breasts jutting under her soft purple jumper, and her long legs, encased in black velvet leggings. He could see the outline of her hips and pubis. It was difficult to drive. She still looked extremely sexually aroused, and Jacob's erection was so painful that he could think of nothing but how sweet it would be to ravish her.

'Come in for a coffee, a sandwich? There's no one in, they've gone to my auntie's . . .'

Jacob began to shake his head, but she laughed at him, and took his hand.

'I'm starving – aren't you?'

And she was. She eyed him flirtatiously as she prepared masses of sandwiches, eating cheese and tomatoes ravenously as she worked, laughing at him as he watched her. Jacob was filled with fascination for her – at this bewitching mixture of womanhood and teenager.

He drove home, wondering just how crazy Louis could feel; empathising, in his own frustration.

* * *

147

The next morning, he went to collect Eleanor as usual. Louis was not up, and had responded dreamily when Jacob had taken him tea. Eleanor gave Jacob a kiss as she got into his car, and his crazy body, already aroused in anticipation, responded dramatically. Eleanor chatted happily on the way; she seemed full of bright laughter. However, as they neared Dedham, she fell silent, apprehensive, no doubt, of the sullen artist. Jacob tried to reassure her, and she brushed off her nervousness.

Louis was not in. Eleanor seemed relieved. They waited for him, drinking coffee and listening to music in the lounge. They sat closer on the settee, becoming increasingly aware of each other's proximity.

'I really like you, Jake . . .' she said to him.

Jacob turned to smile at her. He reached out and placed the palm of his hand on the base of her skull, feeling the silkiness of her black hair. He touched the knuckles of his other hand gently against her cheek bone, smiling deeply into her dark eyes. She moved her face to kiss his hand, her mouth looked very soft and inviting. Jacob moved to kiss her gently, taking her close to him. Eleanor lay back on the settee, smiling up at him. He touched her breast gently, kissing her once more. His penis unfurled as he fondled her sweetly, hearing her moan softly in response.

Jacob moved his hand down to her pubis, and pressed tenderly through the warm material. Eleanor began to writhe against his caresses. Then, thinking of Simon's advice she put her hand out slowly to Jacob's crotch, her heart rate increasing as she reached his hardness. Jacob gasped, smiling at her. Eleanor ran her hands along his sex as Jacob lifted Eleanor's jumper and thrilled at the touch of her naked breast. Eleanor smiled, feeling his other hand stimulate her clitoris excitedly.

'I'm not a virgin, Jake – you can, you know, make love to me . . .'

Jacob stopped and regarded her steadily. Eleanor nodded. Together, they got her leggings off, and Eleanor pulled off her jumper and T-shirt. Jacob kissed and caressed the body he had so often looked at, slipping his hand to her sex and fingering her labia. He took off his clothes, and lay in Eleanor's arms as she explored his firm body, kissing and nibbling at him. His prick lay maddeningly against her sex. He took it and began to rub it against her moist hole. He kissed Eleanor and he penetrated her as carefully as if she *was* a virgin, then he lay still for a moment, holding her gently before he began to move along her tight passage, gradually increasing his rate of thrust. All the time, he kissed her, and caressed her swollen breasts. Eleanor was now moving in response to him. Jacob pressed his sharp bone against her clitoris as he began to move more quickly.

They were lost in their sensual world when the door burst open. They jumped and then froze as Louis came in, full of fire and anger:

'How could you, Jake – how could you!'

Elli looked up from under Jake, seeing Louis' eyes flaming, his body filled with daemonic rage. Louis tried not to let the image of the couple making love, of Elli's face, and Jacob's lascivious eyes burn his soul.

Jacob rolled away from Elli, out of her, filled with anger at Louis. He bit his tongue, not wanting Eleanor to be caught in the masculine sexual rage between them. But Louis felt no such compunction as he ranted and raved about his painting, and Eleanor. Eleanor seemed mystified, pulling her clothes around her and snuggling closer to Jacob, who looked up at the ceiling. She stared at Louis, mesmerised by his dynamic movements, his consuming rage. Jacob wanted to get up and hit Louis. He felt that Louis wanted the same. More. To kill him.

'Can you go, Louis?' he said very calmly, silencing Louis with his controlled rage, and the unusual command.

Coming to a sense of himself, Louis looked at Eleanor, as if thinking of her for the first time.

'I'm sorry, Elli . . .' he said.

Jacob was aware of the intense effort it cost Louis, to see beyond himself and to address Eleanor.

Louis went.

'He's jealous,' Jacob said simply to Eleanor, turning to her, and kissing her on the forehead.

With a sigh, he sat up and got dressed. Despite his annoyance with Louis, his sexual frustration, and the fact that Louis had ruined such a tender moment, he was concerned for him, and did not want him to go off to drink himself into a stupor or – worse still – attack his painting in a rage.

'I don't want him to spoil his painting, by working on it now . . .' he said in explanation to Eleanor as he reached his door.

She nodded, a little shaken by the scene. However, once left alone, she dressed quickly, excited by the thought of these two older and very handsome men fighting over her.

'Don't go out, Louis—' Jacob called down the hall as his friend reached the door.

Louis turned and looked at him with infinite disdain.

'Why not?' he drawled as Jacob reached him, 'I though it would suit your purposes, you hadn't finished—' he glanced superciliously at Jacob's crotch.

Nevertheless, he remained, regarding Jacob with extreme hostility, his mouth expressing his hurt. He leaned back against the wall, and for a bewildering moment, Jacob did not know whether Louis wanted to hit him or kiss him, the sexual force from him was so strong. He was so aroused himself. Silently he cursed him. At the back of his mind, he realised Louis had been a long time leaving, and was apprehensive he had damaged Eleanor's portrait. An irrational fear, it seemed, though once, when very young, Louis had destroyed his own work. The shock of this had remained with Jacob.

'I haven't touched the painting,' Louis said, and then as if he had caught Jacob's fleeting confusion, or as if he was so turned on that anyone would do, and feeling justified in taking advantage under the circumstances, he moved deliberately towards Jacob and kissed him roughly on his mouth. Jacob realised that it was a toss-up between this, and hitting him.

Eleanor was filled with astonishment to witness their kiss from the lounge door. Jacob moved away, and Louis met her eyes, realising that she would be unsure now whether he was possessive of her, or Jacob. He opened the door, filled with the image of the lovers, his penis rigid, his mind hurting.

'I'm just going to get some cigarettes,' he said patiently to Jacob and Eleanor as he closed the door behind him.

Jacob saw him go in his mind's eye, a dark figure in a long black coat. He smiled at Eleanor. 'Artists . . .' He shrugged, leading her back to the lounge.

'Are you, are you and he – are you lovers?' she asked.

Jacob shook his head.

'No, we're not, Elli.' Though Louis would have it so, he added to himself. He did not think it pertinent to tell Eleanor of Louis' expansive nature, but wondered who he should be fairer to – Louis, or Eleanor. 'Louis is – pretty flexible, in his partners . . .' he told her, not looking at her, pouring himself a Scotch. Eleanor shook her head as he offered her one, and he wondered if she would rather have Coke. He went restlessly to the kitchen and put the kettle on. Eleanor followed him.

'He's slept with all those models?' Eleanor said, in slow realisation.

Jacob thought that Louis had been lucky she had not thought of this before, but, perhaps because she was an artist, and not an ordinary young woman, she would understand. He made tea and poured some for them both.

'That isn't his intent,' Jacob felt he should explain. 'And – perhaps not *all* of them.' He smiled with difficulty.

'I knew about Simon,' said Eleanor, wonderingly.

Jacob nodded. They sat in the breakfast room, drinking tea. Jacob had thought to provide Eleanor with cake, and she ate almost absently.

'How do you feel about that?'

Eleanor looked thoughtful. 'It doesn't bother me,' she replied, at last.

Jacob wanted to resume making love to her.

'Can I have a bath, Jake?' Eleanor asked.

'Sure – there are towels in the cupboard.'

'Thanks.' She rose to go, finishing her cake as she stood, taking the remains of her tea with her.

She was probably beguiled by the thought of the lascivious

artist making love to her. So, that was that, thought Jacob, left alone to finish his tea. He took their cups through to the kitchen to wash. The ringing of the phone jarred his mind. It was Amy, just returned from visiting her sister in London. A God-send! Jacob had thought that she had planned the trip to avoid the complications of Louis painting Eleanor.

'Hi, Jake – I've just got back, and am at a bit of a loose end. Are you busy?'

'I'm going to the opening of an exhibition at the Minories tonight – Jacinta King.'

'Never heard of her,' Amy confessed.

'She's good – very colourful. There's a piano recital, and free wine – you're welcome to come along if you like?'

'Yeah, that would be great. Why don't you come round here, first?'

'Okay, Amy . . .' Jacob grinned to himself, relieved.

As he replaced the receiver, he heard Louis returning.

'Has Elli gone?' he asked Jacob.

'No – she's having a bath.'

'Who was that?'

'Amy – I'm going to see her, and we're going to the Jacinta King exhibition tonight. Will you go?'

'Maybe . . . I should, I told Jacinta I'd go. I'll see you there if I do.'

'Right. I suppose I ought to see whether Elli wants a lift home?'

'Yes . . .' Louis regarded him sadly.

'Did you intend to do any work on the painting with her?' Jacob asked, unable to meet his friend's black eyes.

'I don't know. Do you think she'll want to stay?'

Jacob grinned ruefully at the sudden insecurity of his sensitive friend. He squeezed his arm.

'I don't see why not – do you? Ask her.'

Louis smiled.

'I'm sorry, Jake.'

'So am I, Louis . . .'

'At least you'll be alright with Amy.'

Jacob nodded.

Eleanor came down dressed, her short dark hair still damp from her bath. She was glowing with vitality. Jacob's look lingered over her.

'Shall we get on with the portrait?' Louis asked.

'Okay,' she replied simply, perhaps assured at continuing a known practice.

She smiled at Jacob, who thought: Ah! the simplicity of youth . . .

'Can we eat first?' asked Eleanor. 'I'm starving.'

Jacob grinned as Louis looked a little vaguely around the kitchen.

'Why don't you take Elli to the "Rose" for lunch, Louis?' he suggested.

Louis looked relieved not to be immersed in domesticity.

Louis wasn't very talkative as they drank wine and waited for their meal to be prepared. Eleanor began to talk about art, about his methods, gleaning more for her future work. Louis was impressed by her single-mindedness, and her intention to gain knowledge wherever she could. It was easy to respond on this level.

'I'd like to see some of your work,' he said.

'I've done studies of Katy and my brother, Robin. With clothes on.' She laughed. 'Louis?'

'Yes?'

'Perhaps you'd sit for me?'

He looked down into his wine glass, and then smiled and nodded slowly, meeting her eyes, thinking how alike they were, in some ways.

'With my clothes on?' he joked.

Eleanor nodded.

Louis scarcely ate anything, despite Eleanor's encouragement.

'You remind me of Jake,' he told her.

'You don't look after yourself. Don't you paint too much, and get weak?'

'I suppose. Then I get beyond preparing anything,' Louis admitted.

153

'I know what you mean. When I live on my own, I'm going to prepare lots of stuff to leave in the fridge – if I can afford one. You should eat fruit . . .' Eleanor suggested.

'Too much effort.'

Louis indicated his acquiescence as Eleanor began to tuck into his vegetable lasagne.

Amy's hunger seemed as extreme as Jacob's own as she dragged him into her cottage. Jacob surmised that she had not seen too much of Louis lately: that would run true to course for Louis, painting. And she obviously hadn't met any convenient partners in London.

Amy laughed, dragging off his clothes as she did hers, going down on his standing cock, digging her sharp finger nails into his buttocks. Jacob shuddered, energised with the possibility of appeasement as his starving member went deeply into her throat. This fulfilment was what he needed, after Louis' interruption. Amy sucked on his prick strongly, sometimes drawing her teeth along its length. He wondered whether, despite his bath, Amy could unconsciously sense Eleanor. He moved his penis rapidly along her sucking, ready to come. Amy released him and stood up.

'Let's go to bed . . .'

Jacob nodded, dizzied by this sudden abandonment. He wondered at the significance of his course of action as he turned her smooth white body over and lavished her anus with gel, penetrating it with dark enjoyment, which Amy obviously shared as she writhed beneath his hard, directed body. Jacob closed his eyes, and did not touch her elsewhere as he began to thrust into her, his mind on his stiffened cock moving carefully along her tight muscle, crying out as his penis was gripped by its strength. Shutting out dark images, he supported himself on his hands as he began to concentrate on this selfish act; his face and throat – his entire body – flushed with deep pleasure. He began to pump rapidly into her, caught between decadence and delight. Amy did not complain, but simply moved her buttocks against him as his abdomen descended to bang repeatedly against her.

His brain filled with forbidden and exciting images, Jacob sodomised her mercilessly, nurturing the ripening pleasure of his cock until the final thrust, when he ejaculated with loud anguished cries, shuddered and then fell from her, warm and soft.

Amy turned over and kissed him.

'Thinking of Louis, were you?' she teased, lifting his relaxed hand to her swollen breasts.

'*No!*' Jacob denied vehemently.

There was an anger she had never seen before in Jacob's eyes. 'Okay...' she smiled, kissing his hot mouth and moving onto his hand to press her clitoris against him, finishing what he had started.

After a while, she teased him into renewed life, encouraging him between her wet, inviting thighs and Jacob fucked her skilfully, and with energy, as if to assure her of his imperative heterosexuality. Amy smiled dirtily, imagining him making love to the decadent artist as she caressed him.

Eleanor lay in the familiar pose aware, in a way she had not been before, of the warm languor of her body as she lay exposed to Louis. She was lulled by Louis' concentration, and warmed by the time she had spent with him before this session. After lunch, they had walked along the river, and she had wanted to take his hand, but was not sure that he would want that. (They had not mentioned her and Jacob at all.) She could not quite understand him, but was very aware of his eyes now as they flickered between her and her painted image. This was certainly something more than an artist's scrutiny of his model. Eleanor felt pleased.

When he came to her, she felt her heart race. He had never before approached her as she lay naked. She had an urge to cover her body, to hide it from his smouldering eyes, and dragged the drape over her. But Louis pulled it away, and she was bewitched by the animal magnetisim of his eyes, in the strength of his body as he sat beside her, his clothed thigh against her naked hip. He reached his hand out slowly towards

155

her and cupped her small, pointed chin. She gazed up adoringly into his wonderful eyes, longing for him to lean over and kiss her. She looked yearningly at his full mouth, a thrill of desire making her feel weak.

She wanted to cry, though she was not sure why. The bewitching power that came from Louis was all-consuming. She shivered and let out a deep sob. She closed her eyes, feeling tears well from them. When she opened them, she saw that Louis' mouth was parted, and he was looking at her breasts. The warmth of his touch was lifted from her chin as his hand went towards her small, flattened breast. Eleanor was torn between welcoming Louis' touch, and running away from him. She gasped, when at last he allowed his hand to take one breast and hold it still. A sudden spurt of vaginal fluid tricked from her. Louis slowly tightened his gentle hold, though still he merely caressed her tenderly, and it was hard for Eleanor to remain still under his touch.

He moved his hand to her other breast and fondled it, teasing it to firmness as his eyes returned to hers. Eleanor's soul seemed to stand still at the lasciviousness of his expression. Louis merely touched her pink nipple before moving the warmth of his elegant hand to her concave belly, and then to the gentle roundness of her hip.

It was as though they were slowly breaking through something, he as the driving force and she the obligingly willing partner. She had lain here, separate from him, mutually engaged with him in his supreme creative act. If he had desired her, it was in the purity of his mind. Eleanor began to cry silently as his fingers trailed down to her secret pink bud. But she did not want him to stop. It was merely the emotion released by this change.

Louis lingered around her clitoris, working his finger gently over it, looking directly into her eyes as he pleasured her, taking up her fluid with his finger before easing it more deeply into the sensitised folds of her labia. Eleanor felt spasms of sexual excitement chase each other up into her womb and along the delicate mass of nerves in her thighs. Her breasts throbbed. She could feel them expand. She did not part her legs as Louis encircled her vaginal opening, looking back now at her eyes. His face was beautiful. She wanted him to kiss her.

He did not yet penetrate her, though Eleanor waited, wanting this. Instead, he kept one finger just a little inside her, manipulating her gently, whilst another found her tighter, more private hole. Eleanor met his eyes quickly at the shock of this unusual familiarity. Then, it was pleasant to feel both fingers stimulating her simultaneously. As if trained to stay still, Eleanor remained very passive, as if it was necessary for this exploration. She let out a shuddering breath.

Louis smiled beautifully at her as he explored only a little way into her vagina, and less into her anal passage, with the very tips of his long fingers. Eleanor felt herself throbbing spontaneously around him. She watched his dilated eyes, the fullness of his mouth as he experienced this. When she had finished, though her pleasure would increase easily, she thought, he slowly withdrew his fingers and then, using both hands for the first time, placed them on the insides of her thighs and urged them apart gently, to look with delight at the opening flower within. He seemed to drink in the magic of her scarlet depths. (Eleanor had the feeling that he really *was* worshipping her womanhood.) She saw the tip of Louis' tongue come out between his lips as if he imagined tasting the nectar there.

But he smiled at her, and as tenderly as he had parted her legs, he moved them back to their original position and looked deeply into her eyes. Then, holding only on to her shoulders, gently, he covered her mouth with his and kissed her. His kiss stirred her breasts and womb dramatically. Eleanor sat and hugged him, and he embraced her, holding her to him as she sobbed. Eleanor felt the comforting warmth of his body. In time, he released her, looking into her face and smiling gloriously at her. He wiped the tears from her face, and then taking up his cigarettes, he held them up to her and went through the conservatory and into the garden.

A little shakily, Eleanor got off the couch and got dressed. She was not sure of her tremulous emotions, and she was surprised at Louis now, unsure of his attitude towards her.

'Would you like to go to Jacinta King's exhibition?' he asked her as she went out to find him in the garden. 'She's very good. Have you seen any of her work?'

He was sprawled on the wrought-iron bench and had watched her approach keenly.

'Emmm . . . Yes – I've heard of her . . . Yes. That would be nice . . .' Eleanor was not sure why she felt as shaky as though she had only just met him, and that he was like a stranger. As she had walked across the garden, she felt just like he had never seen her naked, and was trying to imagine what she would look like without her dress on, which was ridiculous. Louis probably now knew her body better than she did herself.

Louis dressed in a dark, generously-cut suit, with a long jacket, and a soft white shirt. He looked debonair and charming; extremely handsome . . .

'Do I look alright like this?' Eleanor asked anxiously, watching him ruffle his dark curls, regarding himself, and her, in the mirror.

'You look beautiful, Elli,' he told her sincerely. She flushed. Perhaps clothes did not matter to Louis. Though he looked dashing enough himself.

Jacob was aware of the change of light in Amy's eyes, and turned to see Louis and Eleanor arriving. Louis had been greeted by the artist herself, Jacinta King, and had stopped to exchange a friendly hug and a few words with her. Eleanor smiled at Jacob. Jacob was aware of Amy's speculation, and then, as Louis turned to them, of the cold arrogance which flashed between them. He wondered what Eleanor would make of the games between Louis and Amy, but she seemed preoccupied. Later, when Louis and Amy were arguing over the paintings, Amy deliberately goading Louis, Eleanor moved closer to Jacob and he took her hand, wondering what was worrying her. Louis and Amy, he thought, were as solipsistic as each other, and had no regard for anyone else. No doubt now Louis had painted Eleanor, he was ready for his next – very difficult – victim. But he had not *quite* finished . . .

'What is it, between those two?' asked Eleanor, for the first time bothered by Amy's possessiveness of Louis. She was losing her special, exclusive time with Louis. She had hoped to advance their friendship before he had finished.

'Oh, they're as crazy as each other – don't let them get to you, Elli . . .' For he was well aware of the older woman's savage envy of Eleanor, and hoped that she could suppress her sexual jealousy.

'You slept with her, didn't you?' Eleanor asked, a little sadly.

Though Jacob was not sure on which occasion she referred to, he nodded.

'Is she – is she very good?'

Jacob sighed, frowning.

'What's the matter, Elli?'

'Louis doesn't want *me* . . .'

Jacob understood Eleanor's mood now. He wanted to laugh out loud at this, but he was sensitive to her insecurity, and leaned close to her ear, to whisper:

'I can assure you that he does, Elli . . . Of that I'm absolutely certain . . .'

Eleanor looked into his eyes a little disbelievingly, and Jacob thought how lucky Louis was, and hoped he would not hurt her. He was surprised at Louis' unaccustomed reticence. As if to verify his interest in Eleanor, Louis had turned to them, regarding their obvious intimacy with keen interest. Jacob sighed again, wondering whether he should warn Eleanor off these complexities of the art group. She was sufficiently proud not to let Amy see her frequent glances at Louis. He was glad for her when Simon came along, and Eleanor went to him naturally, one of her own age, whom she could relate to more easily. As for himself, he had decided that it would be better not to pursue his sexual interest in Eleanor.

'How's the portrait going?' Simon asked Eleanor.

'Oh, it's more or less finished.'

'Great – I'd like to see it.'

'Do you go and see Louis – and Jake,' she added the last hastily, 'often?'

Simon glanced at her, puzzled, then shrugged.

'Simon—?' she said quietly, glancing over towards the men and Amy.

'What is it, Elli?'

'You've – you know – slept with Louis?'

Simon laughed. 'Yes.'

'Well – I mean – is he really gay?'

'Louis . . .' Simon looked over at him with warmth in his blue eyes. 'No . . . He's very liberal I suppose. I told you – he's bisexual. As I am, I suppose . . . He loves women – look at him with Amy . . .'

Eleanor looked. Though it cost her to do so.

'What's it like? I mean—'

'You know, Elli, in some ways – I told you – there's no difference. It's someone else with you. I expect a partner of the same sex should know what to do. That's not necessarily the case – some people don't know what to do to themselves. You're sweeter than Louis, Elli . . . Kinder . . .' Simon put his arms around her waist and pulled her close to him, to kiss her. 'Come home with me, tonight?'

Eleanor nodded, relieved to feel close to Simon.

Amy was taken up with observing the natural intimacy between Jacob and Louis, as well as seeing the way in which Louis' eyes would constantly flicker towards the young woman, now released from her constraints and laughing gaily with Simon, who often touched her affectionately.

Perhaps from watching the young people together, Louis had the idea that he would pose Simon and Eleanor as 'Cupid and Psyche', and lost no time in putting this to them: a few quick sketches before Florence? Simon and Eleanor laughed at him. Eleanor felt stronger now.

'You're incorrigible, Louis!' Jacob said.

'So, he's finished the portrait of Eleanor?' Amy asked him bitterly as the others went off to chat to Jacinta King about her new exhibition.

'Don't ask, Amy . . .' Jacob warned her, knowing that she

needed to know if he had seduced her. 'I'm sure he's saving you for his piece de resistance,' he drawled, taking up a lock of her glorious hair. It would be wonderful to be able to paint this glamorous creature.

Amy snatched it away and shot him a hostile look.

'I'll be relieved to see Reuben in Florence next week,' she told him.

'Aren't we enough for you?' Jacob laughed, recalling, as he knew she did, her abandonment of the afternoon.

'Can I give you a lift?' Louis asked Amy in an off-hand manner as they watched Jacob leaving with Eleanor and Simon. They had agreed to pose for Louis as Cupid and Psyche. Eleanor seemed glad of Simon's easy company, and Simon was a practised model. They were coming the next day. He could easily fit in the finishing touches to Eleanor's portrait.

'Can't get your little lover-girl tonight, then, Lou – or maybe – boy?'

'Whatever.' Louis shrugged in a nonchalant manner and Amy wanted to kick him.

'Jacob wasn't too keen to stay with you?' he enquired cattily.

'He was with me all afternoon, when I expect you'd rather he'd have been with you?' she countered triumphantly.

'I live with him,' he reminded her, 'so he's there any time.'

'Hmmm . . .'

Louis was turning to leave.

'I take it you don't want a lift?'

'May as well save the taxi fare, since I was brought here.'

They completed the short drive to Amy's cottage in angry silence.

'Aren't you even going to offer me coffee?' Louis asked in a tone of mock complaint as Amy made to leave his Jag.

'It isn't coffee you want.'

'You should be so lucky!'

'Ha!'

Amy slammed the car door, a little concerned lest Louis should not follow her, but drive off in a huff. However, she had read him well enough to know how much he needed sex.

'Huh . . .' she sneered at him, green eyes flashing, red hair flying, as she unlocked the door.

'Shall I do it for you?' he offered, as she struggled in her preoccupation.

'Anything I want – I can do for myself!' she assured him as she stormed inside.

'Oh, yeah? Just doing Jake a favour were you?'

It was quite something, having this beautiful man here, more needy than she, and though she knew that she could lose him on the twist of a word. At heart he was vulnerable, she thought, cold towards him, angry at him for wanting Eleanor – anyone could see that he did. Except that stupid girl herself. Still, she was getting Reuben back – for a week at least – and she had no doubt that Louis was at least a little jealous of her and Jake. She felt mighty powerful.

And Louis, enraged by all, countered with savagery towards her. As he turned to her, closing the door behind him, and leaning on it, she suddenly felt like his trapped prey. But why? She had invited him here. She wanted him. There was no doubt of that. And Louis was aware of it. She backed away from the rage in his eyes and flew upstairs, full of excitement and just a hint of that heady aphrodisiac – fear. He was a strong, fit man and she had goaded him – touching on sensitive and secret places. He knew that she was equal to him.

Amy ran along the corridor. Louis was soon close behind her. She was incredibly aroused at the thought of him taking her by force, her panties gave evidence of this. She ran into her room. He was close behind her now. She pushed the door to and tried to shut him out as he reached it. Louis flung the door open and grasped her arm, but Amy pulled free and ran to the bed. Louis took off his coat and his jacket and dropped them on the floor, then he advanced, his eyes glowering, and grabbed her. At the terrific force of his hands on her, Amy was a mass of expectation. She prayed that he would not laugh and leave her. She wanted to lie on the bed, spread her legs, and invite him in, but she would not show such need.

She struggled against the intense force of his passion, feeling him getting more and more aroused as their bodies struggled and writhed against each other.

'Do you want to tie me to the bed?'

'I don't think that will be necessary,' said Louis, making her cry out at his sudden deft caress between her legs.

Louis pushed her back onto her bed, parting her legs with his knee and tearing off her soaking pants. Then, with a practised speed, he released his cock and entered her. Amy felt a rush of excited joy at the size of him, filling her up, penetrating so deeply into her depths as she grunted gutturally and stretched up her legs, feeling his hands tearing off her blouse, kneading her breasts hungrily as he rammed his cock repeatedly into her. She held onto him as he fucked her savagely, sending powerful echoes of sexual feeling through her body with the increased force of each thrust. Louis held on to her clenched abdomen, digging his nails into her taut flesh, scratching her legs and buttocks.

'Louis, Louis . . .' she cried, urging him on with her willing body, feeling successive orgasms wrack her body as he continued relentlessly. She held his head, making him kiss her as she felt his orgasm begin. He took her higher as he writhed against her fanny, his cock throbbing hugely within her. Her body was possessed by pure sexual ecstasy as she joined his massive climax.

'Jacob came and buggered me, Louis, after he had left you . . . Don't you wish it was your arse he stuck his cock up?' Amy fingered Louis' anus as she woke him there teasingly.

'Stop it, Amy . . .'

His anger resembled Jacob's. Amy stuck her fingers further into him.

'What, Louis? Stop talking about randy, sleazy Jake . . .' Here she pulled on his quickening cock. 'Or stop doing this . . .' she penetrated his tight hole very deeply with her fingers, feeling the muscle quicken around them. At the same time, she fondled his growing prick. Then, with dark excitement at Louis' likely reaction, she inserted Sarah's dildo (still covered in recent oil) sharply into Louis' anus. Louis did not prevent her as she thrust inside his tight ring. He moaned expressively as she pushed more deeply. She thrilled to see his lovely face fill with sensual pleasure, and she wanked on his stiffened cock as she slid the rubber device up and down in his hole, clutching onto the slippery phallus. Louis reached for her breasts, but she moved away, her green eyes glittering at him.

'Think of Jake, Louis . . .'

With her double stimulation, Louis could not help but give in to her manipulation of him, writhing on the bed as his body filled with sex. It was something else, Amy thought, to have this man so completely in her power. Louis undulated his muscular body against her hands, his cock slithering easily along her tightening grip. She watched his increasingly lascivious expression in fascination. She rammed the phallus more deeply into him, making him move faster against its invasion, and speeding up her masturbation of his generous cock. Louis grunted, low growls coming from deep within him as he closed his eyes. He bit on his bent finger wildly as Amy kept changing her pace to tease him, to prolong his agony and to make him think she was about to hasten his orgasm. God, he was beautiful, she thought, her stomach wrenched at the sight of him as his lovely body demonstrated his narcissistic sexuality. She would make sure he was starving for little Eleanor.

Louis came loudly and extravagantly, shooting along her tightened grasp as she shoved the phallus faster into him.

Then she straddled his face and he sucked greedily at her honeyed sex. She bore down on him until she came, and then went to have a shower. After this, she went down to the kitchen, made tea and toast for herself, and ate it in front of the gas-fire. Then she returned to the exhausted Louis and began to work on his cock, licking and sucking him back to life, and then lying on his belly and taking immense pleasure in riding him, caressing her own tits and grinding her clitoris on his pubic bone. It took a long time to make him come again, but she could not, after all, afford to let him go home hungry. Louis held onto her, watching her face dispassionately. Then, with a sudden movement, he had her under him, her legs raised, bent at her knees and pushed down as he moved his penis as he pleased inside her, savouring his freedom. Cruelty filled his eyes as he subjected her to his prolonged indulgence. But Amy was indomitable, and she was aware that she had reached a raw place. Louis was still as he ejaculated and then he went to have a shower.

Louis was weary the following morning as he posed Simon and Eleanor as Cupid and Psyche, though he soon forgot his weariness as he became lost in his work. He was also fired by anger towards the powerful Amy, and determined to get even with her.

Eleanor was glad she was with Simon, and in an altogether different, though extremely erotic, pose with him. She wondered whether Louis was trying to tell her something by choosing to do this now. Simon did not seem in the least troubled by Louis' moody silence. Eleanor found that this sexy pose with a young man she knew found her attractive, and with whom she had nice easy sex, redressed the balance in her relationship with the artist. It made her feel independent of him, and able to demonstrate her adult relationship with a handsome youth. Someone, after all, Louis found attractive too. She felt that Louis' sullenness was divorced from his dealings with them. He did several sketches, concentrating intensely on their pose, and asked them if they could pose again for him after their trip to Italy. He seemed very businesslike, and did not show any particular interest in either of them – at least outwardly. Eleanor guessed that he had been with Amy.

Louis did not seem to mind at all that she and Simon hung around the house after he had finished, playing music in the lounge and eating copious amounts in between laughter in the kitchen. When Jacob came home, they helped him make dinner. It was interesting for Eleanor to observe the quiet Louis, and to spend some more time in his company, under the shelter of Simon's friendship. She had feared that Louis would specifically want Simon's company, but he seemed more interested in playing his guitar. He played very well, concentrating on classical pieces. Eleanor wondered at the kind of homosexual relationship which was only sometimes physical, and not constantly demanding, and wondered whether this would last longer than a heterosexual relationship.

It was a very enjoyable evening, and Eleanor looked forward to spending time with these friends in Florence the next week.

Six

Only a small proportion of the group had elected to participate in the trip to Florence. This included Marie-Anne and Sam and Robbie, who were good fun, and Sarah and Simon, who were to pose for them. Amy was very much looking forward to seeing Reuben again, and he had promised to meet them at the airport. She had spent much time over the past few days fastasising about how they would find somewhere to make love – perhaps even straight off the plane. She was assured, from past experience, that Reuben would be as eager as she. The flight had been coloured by this expectation and she was physically more than ready when she saw him. She suspected that her anticipation was exaggerated because she had alienated Louis, and could not expect sex with him at present. Perhaps she had done this with the sanctuary of her lover in mind. To simplify her life – so she had thought. She could not wait to get into bed with Reuben. She was relieved at the simplicity of their relationship as a contrast to her intensity with Louis. The others smiled to witness the enthusiasm with which they greeted each other, caressing and kissing as though they had both been denied any physical release since they had parted. Jacob shook his head indulgently at Amy.

Amy delighted in Reuben's bodily closeness as they embraced. But, as she was released and looked hazily around at the group, she became aware, with a mixture of irritation and foreboding, of the speculative looks that Louis was giving the young man. She should not have been surprised. With his lush golden curls, unusually dark eyes, and perfectly proportioned body, Reuben was an artist's dream. And, a lover of art himself, she had no doubt he would be willing to pose for the artist. How crazy she had been not to foresee this! Reuben knew of Louis Joseph's prowess and returned the artist's friendly greeting as Amy was forced to introduce them immediately when Louis came forward. She noticed how the men's eyes met in intelligent interest as they shook hands. Anger surged inside her. Louis steadfastly ignored her darts of warning. Amy clung to Reuben's hand as they made their way to the shuttle which would take them the few kilometres to Santa Maria Novella. Claudio's hotel was not very far from there. On the bus, Amy realised that Louis would take delight in getting equal with her for her jibes about him and Jacob.

As Reuben became engrossed in talking to Louis about art, Amy turned away from Louis' arch smile at her. Apart from anything else, he probably felt he had to punish her for her cavalier and sadistic treatment of him last week. She had been in the ascendant in their stormy relationship and he was obviously determined to regain a superior position. No doubt he resented her personal comments about him and Jacob. Indeed, even she felt she had trespassed. Amy looked out of the window distractedly, she had visited Florence before – with Reuben – and had hoped to rekindle the romance of it with him. But both Reuben and Louis were even more familiar with the city than she, and were free to chat about other things. They got on very well, she thought ironically. They had a lot in common. Perhaps they also discussed her. A fear crept into her mind, that Louis would seduce Reuben in retaliation for her biting comments about him and Jacob. She knew that Reuben had had no homo-sexual proclivities, but he was liberal-minded . . . Would even he be seduced by Louis' lascivious nature? Although she was attracted to the idea of two men making love, she was not at all sure she was in a mood to be excluded. Amy simmered. They were talking about San Marco and the work of Fra Angelica. She glanced at Reuben. Did he know – did he care – that he was being courted for his looks? She felt sure he did not mind. He was vain, really. She was annoyed and filled with self-pity. Her vulnerability was exaggerated by her readiness for sex –

anywhere, soon – being thwarted. If they had been alone, they would have found somewhere to make love by now.

Jacob regarded her with sympathetic understanding, but she could not yet even respond to this. She felt a little guilty at trading on her perception of his attitude to Louis. Disloyal to Jacob. Grrrr . . . she could strangle the artistic demon! Claudio's sons met them at Santa Maria Novella, and drove them, past the Duomo to the hotel. Amy saw that Eleanor was captivated by the beautiful Renaissance cathedral, with its intricate marble exterior.

Claudio greeted Jacob and Louis with affection when they arrived at the hotel. Amy watched as the men chatted effusively in Italian. Then Claudio extended his friendly welcome to embrace all of his new guests, smiling and bustling around, organising his staff to show them to their various rooms. He was obviously enchanted by the pretty women in the party. He invited them all to join him for welcoming drinks as soon as they had settled in.

Reuben did have the grace to respond physically to Amy in their room. It was a relief to close the door and go to him, run her hungry fingers over his firm, willing body and to receive his passionate kiss. But Louis came in, ostensibly to show Reuben some book or other concerned with their earlier conversation. Now ragingly turned on, Amy glared at him in hatred. He eyed her near-nakedness superciliously, and had the audacity to stay in the room even though she caressed Reuben possessively. Although Reuben continued to fondle her, absent-mindedly, it was as though she was more or less forgotten between their other mutual interests. Amy was reminded of being with a group of young male football fans in a pub, when she was younger, and how, though she had been turned on by her boyfriend, he seemed to have forgotten her in his enthusiasm with his male buddies. She had no doubt that Louis remained to thwart her. Though there was the chance that he was jealous . . . Perhaps she should cut her losses and concentrate on Jacob. But this was more of a challenge, and she was not going to let Louis win that easily.

Anyway, she did not want to hurt Sarah, who seemed close to Jacob at present.

'Okay—' Jacob smiled around at the group, assembled in the lounge after unpacking, and settled in with drinks. 'You've all got a copy of the proposed schedule for museum and gallery visits,' he said. 'As you can see, there is personal time for you to explore. There are seventy museums and twenty-four historic churches in Florence – all of them worth visiting – but no one could take in so much in one visit.' He grinned, particularly at Eleanor. 'As you will see, I've indicated the particular works we'll concentrate on in the museums and galleries we'll see together. We'll meet at the times specified to look at some of the sculptures and paintings we've seen on slides, and you can draw these. In the evenings, I'll get Simon, and Sarah to take up the same poses, and you can draw from life. Today, I thought you would like the chance to look around Florence generally, perhaps taking the opportunity to visit the Duomo, which is very close to this hotel, and the Baptistery; the Ponte Vecchio? San Lorenzo is not far. Anywhere you choose to visit is within easy walking distance. Those of you who haven't visited the city before will find that it is a delight, just to wander round. There's a wonderful view over Florence, if you are up to the four hundred and sixty-three steps up to the Cupula of the Duomo.' They all grinned. 'It's a good introduction . . .' he added, smiling. 'You could cross the Arno and go up to the Forte di Belvedere, and then on up to the beautiful church of San Miniato al Monte. It's worth the climb, and there's a good view of the city. You will also enjoy the view from Fiesole, merely a five mile bus ride into the hills.'

'The most beautiful bus journey in the world,' agreed Louis, standing close to him.

Jacob glanced at his friend affectionately.

'We'll do that in a couple of days,' Jacob told them.

'Tomorrow morning we'll visit the Bargello. I've suggested walks, sites, etcetera, on the notes, but do come and ask me – or Louis – if you need any help or information.'

They split into small groups or pairs to look around the city. Eleanor was delighted to be with Jacob and Louis. Their joy at being re-acquainted with Florence was infectious as they wandered around the wonderful city, drawing Eleanor's attention to the important buildings. Despite her determination to be detached, Eleanor could not help but be very conscious of the dark artist, and very aware of his charisma, and the sense that he was in a place where he felt spiritually at home. To all, he was charming and beguiling. Eleanor had decided not to allow anxiety about him, and what he thought of her, prevent her from enjoying her holiday and gaining all she could from this wonderful visit. It had been with difficulty that she had scraped together the money, even with the payments for her modelling, and could not tell when she would be able to return. She doubted she would ever be as successful as Louis in selling her work. Still, one never knew, and she was of an optimistic frame of mind. She had great confidence in her ability, regarding it as a fortunate gift, but one which had to be nurtured. Art was the one thing she had always been good at. She also worked very hard at it. Louis, as well as Jacob, could tell her much about the works on display here, and it was on this aspect of their knowledge that she would concentrate. It would be a waste, she thought sensibly, not to do so. She intended to make up her own portfolio of the trip. This would be something to build on for next year, and who knows – she may, one day, be able to gain a scholarship on the strength of it. And so she planned to spend the whole of the week making sketches of Florence. Louis had told her that the Uffizi had masses of paintings not on show and that, with a special pass from an academic institution, a student could gain access. This was Eleanor's dream. She imagined returning one day, in a few years, perhaps with Louis, to extend her knowledge. That thought excited her. Though she knew that she was physically attracted to Louis, she wanted much more than to be a discarded model, or lover. She wanted to remain his friend and felt that they had much in common. Such an opportunity to visit these stores would be wasted now, though; she knew that she had much to learn first. She felt that Louis understood this: she was sure that he could gain access. Even on her first day, Eleanor knew that this had to be just the beginning of her love affair with Florence.

The next day they went to the Bargello, where Louis enchanted them all with his obsession with his beloved Bacchus, by Michelangelo. Amy could not help but stare at him in fascination, too sexually responsive to concentrate on Jacob's talk as Louis prowled around the tipsy god, with his satyr and goblet of wine. She envied the god his lascivious drunkenness and suppressed an annoying image of Louis, naked and posing as an embodiment of ecstasy. As beautiful as the god and as cold as the marble. Bacchus was sensual, his body seeming soft and sinuous. She saw the artist touch the forbidden statue as though he could not resist this sensual gratification: as though he alone, as an artist himself, had the right to do so. He was clever enough to keep a wary eye on the guard. Amy thought of his conception of Simon: perhaps men and statues were interchangeable to the tactile artist? Jacob told them that Michelangelo believed, as he sculpted, that he was merely releasing the figure already within the marble. They began to draw. Jacob became engaged in deep conversation with Eleanor who was taking her work extremely seriously. Amy was surprised that the young woman seemed oblivious to the sexual opportunities available to her. Both Jacob and Louis obviously fancied her like crazy, and even Reuben declared that she was very pretty. She was annoyingly friendly to everyone, and captured their interest in her questions about Florence. Reuben had gone off on a tour of his own around the museum. Well, at least he was not within Louis' dangerous sphere. The others were attempting, with varied success, to capture the three-dimensional figure onto paper.

Louis seemed at least as captivated by Donatello's David, as he had been with Bacchus, this time running his palm over the naked boy-king's pert bottom and smiling lasciviously, standing behind the bronze sculpture, and eyeing them with knowledge in his dark eyes. Amy imagined the decadent sculptor with his young boy models. Artists! Louis seemed to have taken over Jacob's role as he issued forth on the qualities of the statues, and how the sculptors had achieved various results. Jacob was still engrossed in giving Eleanor individual tuition. It would be nice to talk to Sarah, but she had gone to explore the craft and jewellery shops of the city. She and Simon were there primarily as models after all, and knew the pieces they were to pose. A quick look, and a chat with Louis or Jacob would suffice to prepare them. Amy became increasingly fretful, partly because of Louis' provocative response to the erotic statues. Reuben could not help but be aware of her state: perhaps she could persuade him to return with her to the hotel?

She caught up with him in the Palazzo Vecchio. The others were off to the Accademia to examine Michelangelo's 'David'. She whispered seductively to him, and he caressed her intimately and agreed to go back to their room to make love. As they left, Amy caught Louis narrowing his eyes at them, and cast him a triumphant backward glance.

'You are keen . . .' said Reuben, in between kissing her, as she tore off his clothes frantically, kissing him all over . . .

When they caught up with the others, for dinner in a trattoria on the Via dei Calzaiuoli, which seemed filled with elegant people constantly walking, Amy felt relaxed and contented. Louis could not help but be aware of her changed state as he looked darkly across at her and Reuben. With a delicious pang and feeling of confidence, Amy realised that he *was* jealous. She noticed that Jacob and Sarah seemed to be getting on very well together this evening. They were whispering and laughing together. Sarah, as did everyone else, evidently felt at ease with the man. And Simon, supposedly sitting by Eleanor, was making them all laugh, striking lascivious poses of 'Bacchus' and 'David'. Amy saw Louis' lecherous look as he regarded the young man. He drank chianti copiously. Amy made a show of her intimacy with Reuben on purpose to dig at him.

Louis was watching Reuben avidly, hungrily taking in his crisp golden curls and deep, expressive, brown eyes, keeping these knowing eyes in his gaze when Reuben became aware and

173

turned to smile at him. He took in the man's graceful movements as he talked and laughed with the others. The more he drank and watched, the more Louis was detached from them: on the edge, a voyeur. His brain was vividly alive, attuned to every nuance, silver-quick to perceive and understand. He was aware that this extreme and unusual sensitivity rendered his body sensual and receptive. He could take in all the dynamics between the group, and his mercury-rapid mind could translate and foretell. He narrowed his eyes at Reuben: he needed Reuben with a hunger that was all-consuming. His imagination swept over the man's loose clothing, making him naked. He was Louis the vampire, and he could suck out the man's red blood and make him still, so that he could paint him. He could use alchemy to render him into marble, then carve him out of the block as did Michelangelo. Freeing him from the solid state of his usual life. Louis' dominant need, though it could take sexual form, was to possess the man in order to paint him. If, perchance, he had him carnally, then though he would bask in this lust, he would afterwards feel disappointment. Art was more to him. His body was charged with this need, his brain burned and he knew he would feel strange and ill, especially with the tiny amount of time available to him, if he did not have his desire. For a moment, Reuben met his eyes and was stilled, amongst the laughter and noise, by the expression in them, then, as if bewildered, he looked away – though with difficulty – and was taken into the comfortingly familiar embrace of the treacherous Amy.

Louis regarded his adversary with hatred. Amy's eloquent eyes flashed molten at him. The thought of painting her in rich, coloured oils came to him, he suppressed it with an effort, though it would not be long before he would have to give in to this. Eleanor and Jacob were drawing on the table and Sarah was laughing and flirting outrageously with Sam and Robbie. Marie-Anne sat back with a happy smirk on her face. She met Louis' eyes and smiled. Louis thought of the happy simplicity of making love to this older, comfortable woman as he had, once last year. And his cock, motivated by unadulterated lust, stiffened. But it was too complex to get her. He whispered to Simon, now sitting close to him, and they left.

In Simon's room, Louis stripped the willing model and ran his sentient hands all over his firm muscular body and his silky blond hair. He knelt and sucked his erect cock and gained some comfort in this material touching of warm human, rather than marble, flesh. He drew on Simon's cock to pleasure him. For himself he gained something from the opportunity to feel warm flesh, to think of the wonderful sculptures as he caressed Simon's firm buttocks and explored, with his sensitive hands, every inch of his body, feeling the shape of muscles, bones and sinews, and nurturing the force that gave Simon vital life. He recalled his vivid painting of Simon, and back from this to the sensually indulgent art of painting him. He thought of the young man's perfect body rendered in marble. This thought excited him.

Simon pumped energetically into his mouth and Louis held his buttocks as he came. Simon smiled sleepily at him as he rose.

'Are you alright, Lou?' he asked, beginning to dress. He had been expecting Louis to fuck him, but he had not even released his own prick.

Louis continued to caress him, as if he was a piece of clay to be moulded and Simon laughed at him. He reached out to grasp the older man's concealed cock, but Louis moved away, picked up his coat.

'You want Amy . . .' Simon said, sympathetically, as though he held no grudge at Louis' preference.

Louis snorted, turning away and lit a cigarette.

'Louis . . .' Simon said reproachfully. Sometimes, he could not bear to think of this beautiful man's urge for self-destruction.

Louis turned away. Simon finished dressing, intending to rejoin the party. He did not need to go out, for they were now all noisily in the reception room opposite his door, planning the next day's visits. At some stage, Simon expected to pose for them. Although Louis accompanied him to the door, he did not follow Simon in. Amy looked up at him with interest, and caught his hungry look at Reuben. He had decided that there was no time to be wasted and he had to pluck up courage and approach Reuben – very soon, before Amy dissuaded him.

Marie Anne saw him lingering, aroused and lost, at the door, and came over. He allowed himself to be drawn outside, into the foyer. She knew that he had not been satisfied by his brief encounter with Simon, perhaps this was a unique opportunity to get the sexy young man. She had no illusion that it would be other than just once. This week, anyway. Louis was in a trance, created by his intellectual and sensual hunger, teetering on famine, for Reuben, with the still potent feel of Simon's young flesh under his seeking hands. Marie Anne thought that he was drunk.

''Come and have a coffee . . .' she said, pulling him away from the lounge and towards her room. Louis went. But he was not even offered coffee once within her small room. Marie-Anne kissed him and then began to undress him. He was not sure what he said, but her comforting voice lulled him, and it was a relief for once, to be passive, to allow himself to be undressed and given succour to.

She led him to her bed, lay him down and then began to caress him, glorying in his perfect form. She enjoyed stroking at his penis and fondling his balls before she took him into her generous body. She was overjoyed, if a little taken by surprise, at Louis' sudden potency and considerable energy as he quickly brought her to a shuddering climax.

Louis was lingering fretfully around the hotel, summoning up the energy to waylay Reuben. Would he understand? Would he be willing to give up so much time? Louis felt like some kind of criminal, some outsider who cannot be easily understood. At last he went to the suite he always shared with Jacob, as Claudio's honoured guests, at the top of the Renaissance building. He went out onto the balcony and took in the magnificent view of the cathedral. Then he poured a large Scotch and sat, in the dark on the wicker chair in the corner.

'Louis! I wondered where you'd gone!' exclaimed Jacob as he came in.

Louis blinked in the sudden blinding light.

'Are you alright?'

'I've got to paint Reuben.'

'Ah . . .' So that was the cause of his friend's extreme restlessness.

'Go and ask him. He's still in the bar,' Jacob said simply, foreseeing one of Louis' lapses into despair.

'With Amy,' Louis said with regret.

'Well, she's going to notice, if he agrees,' Jacob said reasonably.

'Jake – come with me . . .'

'Oh, no, Louis . . .' Jacob shook his head.

'Distract Amy whilst I ask him at least . . .'

'Tttt . . .'

'Jake?' Louis was on his feet, eager to go down now this solution had presented itself, before they went to bed. It would be more difficult to knock on their door, though he may have to do this: at least he could demand to speak to Reuben alone.

'I can't distract her all week, Louis . . .'

'I'm not bothered about that – it's only while I ask him.'

'Ttt . . .'

But Louis knew that Jacob revered his art, and that Jacob would do as he wished.

Louis lit a cigarette and waited until Jacob had taken Amy off and then approached Reuben. What would he do if the man refused him?

In the event, he merely took the bull by the horns, leapt in and said:

'I'd very much like to paint you, Reuben. We're only here for a week, and it would mean giving up much of that time. What do you think?'

'Yes, Louis, I'd be honoured,' answered Reuben simply, recalling the time he had attended an exhibition given by this talented local man.

Louis simply stared at him, as if he had encountered all kinds of difficulties.

'Let's drink to that, then . . .' Reuben suggested, pouring Louis some brandy.

'Drink to what?' enquired Amy suspiciously as she returned with Jacob.

Louis merely gave her the merest flicker of his lashes at Amy's anger as Reuben turned innocently to her and announced proudly:

'Louis is going to paint my portrait.'

'Really,' said Amy acidly, meeting Louis' steady look with intense animosity.

Jacob looked on with interest, seeing the gleam of victory in Louis' dark eyes and then making a quick getaway before he was trapped in their contemplexities.

Louis had the courtesy to leave Reuben with Amy. Though, Jacob imagined, Reuben probably had to face Amy's wrath. Louis could not sleep, and spent some time drawing and drinking, and then went out to haunt the sleeping city, fed by its quiet beauty as he crossed to the Oltrarno, and found some kind of temporary companionship.

'Why did you agree to it?' Amy shouted at Reuben as soon as they returned to their room.

Reuben was a little taken aback and bewildered by her tone and the venom in her eyes.

'We'll still have time together,' he tried to placate her, as he went to take her into his arms. 'You are supposed to be studying. We'll have every night.'

Amy shot away from him, fuming, her green eyes burning into him, her hands on her hips and her chin thrust out defiantly. Reuben was mystified, but his main reaction to her passion was to feel incredibly aroused and desperate to touch her, but Amy sneered at the lust in his eyes as they caressed her lightly-clad body. Reuben could not take his eyes from the lovely shape of her firm breasts under her silky top. His fingers itched to cup them, and he spoke to her dreamily.

'He's a good artist. I don't mind posing.' He couldn't help but sound pleased, and this seemed to rile Amy extravagantly.

'He's an arrogant, self-centred, selfish, narcissistic supercilious swine!' she shouted.

'You don't like him?' he said with amazement as Amy turned

178

away and folded her arms. Her back was shaking and he frowned to think that she was crying. Louis Joseph seemed to him to be a charming man. 'He's very good-looking,' he reasoned, thinking that Louis' sultry dark looks would appeal to Amy. Louis must have upset her in some way.

'Oh – you think so, do you?' she challenged, her wonderful curls flying as she turned back to him.

She certainly seemed full of passion and sex. Reuben advanced on her, pulled her forcefully to him, though she struggled to free herself, and drew her sharply into his arms. He enfolded her closely, though she tried to pull away, and brought his mouth down hard upon hers. As he held her tightly to him, he was aware that she trembled with anger, rather than passion. Knowing Amy, and recognising Louis Joseph's attraction, he surmised that she had been involved with him in some way. Had he rejected her? Reuben did not think it likely that any hot-blooded man could withstand Amy once she had set her mind on him. He had thought that Louis looked at her with desire. Reuben was intrigued. Perhaps Louis was gay? Many artists were . . .

To his surprise, Amy yielded to him, her hungry mouth feeding on his as he kissed her, her hands manipulating his body further into life. Flames of passion engulfed him. It was always the same between them. He moved towards the bed with Amy and went gratefully between her parted legs.

He pulled off Amy's silky top, and crushed her urging breasts in his greedy grasp. He was, as ever, filled with great relief – their shared lust made them wild and it was a tremendous joy to be allowed to indulge it. Sometimes, when they turned each other on – in public – they had to find somewhere to screw urgently. Though he had had lovers in Italy, the chemistry between Amy and him was unique. Despite their various partners, Reuben was sure that he and Amy were bound to each other for life, because of it. He clamped his mouth on her nipple and suckled, feeling her body toss under him. He was impatient for her manipulation as her hand was pulling at his buttons, releasing his cock and holding it tightly, wanking it energetically.

'Amy . . .' he murmured.

'Yes, Reuben?' Amy sounded as if he was lucky, really, to get her, under the circumstances.

Reuben moved down to kiss and nuzzle at Amy's mound, tantalisingly hidden under her gossamer-soft pants. He taunted her by manipulating her through the silky-wet material, catching her concealed clitoris between his finger and thumb. Amy writhed and tossed like a wild thing. He reached up his other hand to squeeze very tightly at her breast, holding her nipple firmly and increasing his stimulation on clit and teat. Amy's abdomen lifted invitingly. Reuben tore off her panties and moved his face to the musky warmth between her thighs. He licked at the fleshy pink lips and encircled her large bud with the sensitive end of his tongue. Then he ran his tongue along to her vagina and thrust it inside. Amy jerked rhythmically against him as he attended to her lovingly. She tore at his hair as he penetrated further, now adding to her delight by pressing on her clitoris with his fore-finger. He held her bottom as she began to moan softly. He worked her up to her orgasm, and he knew that Amy would be greedy for more immediately; that this was just a preliminary.

When she reached for him he lay on her, smiling into her eyes, his cock rigid against her vulva. Amy commanded with her devil-green eyes for him to insert his prick, but Reuben, though eager, delighted in delaying, feeding his hunger and ultimate enjoyment by teasing her. He ran his fingers over her full lips and inserted one into her mouth. She sucked and bit on him desperately, now banging her sex against him, giving him her urgent message. Reuben held both of her twin orbs in his hands. He watched her petulant eyes unflinchingly as he slowly moved to her nipples and squeezed them as tightly as she could endure. She had told him that it was as if there was an invisible chord from breast to sex, and he knew by her lascivious expression, and the rhythm of her body, the arching of her back and her sudden stiffness that she was having another orgasm.

'Tell me about your Italian lovers, Marie and—?'

'Giovanna and Francesca and—'

'Alright . . .'

Reuben laughed at her possessive unfairness as she smouldered under him. 'And what about you, my amiable Amy?' he challenged, his finger going once more into her sopping, tight hole. 'Have you been a naughty girl with Louis Joseph?'

'Jacob . . .' she confessed, her eyes closing as he impaled herself deeply on him, relieved as he went more deeply, and at his expert touch on her swollen bud.

'Jacob, hey?' asked Reuben, his eyes narrowing keenly. 'And—?'

'Sarah . . .' Amy admitted.

'Really?' he asked with interest. The image of his lover with the voluptuous Sarah further increased his appetite. By now, and fed by Amy's climaxes, his penis was painfully full and his balls burning to explode, but still, he delayed.

'And Louis . . .' she said grudgingly, as if making love with the handsome artist had been a chore.

Reuben was amused. 'I thought so! Well,' he teased, playing one of their familiar games, 'Amy Harrington, you've obviously been very very naughty.' He released her sex from his hold, and sat back on his haunches. Amy whimpered obligingly. 'Turn over onto your front, Amy . . . Let me see your bottom.' Amy obeyed. Reuben saw her buttocks tighten and raise in readiness. He gripped his penis and gave it a few swift pulls whilst watching Amy pressing her fanny into the mattress. He released his cock, raised his hand high and then brought it down with a resounding crack onto her small neat bottom. Amy winced but continued to murmur about her depravities, confessing to her lover what these men had done to her and what she had done to them. After several hard spanks on different parts of her body, he realised that she was about to have yet another orgasm. He turned her over and slapped hard at her tits, whilst holding onto his prick, beginning to wank in earnest, exaggerating his panting, as though he would take delight in coming all over her belly, and denying her his prick. And this, any moment now . . .

'Fuck me, Reuben, fuck me . . .' Amy pleaded, opening her legs wide for him, pulling up her knees.

Reuben continued to pleasure himself, looking now at her crimson flower, with the silvered sex-dew trailing all over. He gripped himself expertly, and masturbated rapidly. But then, he pretended to relent, kissed Amy, and plunged his long rod deeply into her, thinking with jealousy of those other men as he rammed furiously into her. Then, forgetting everything but the delightful home where his cock was, the feel of her warmth surrounding him, and the intense pleasure which originated in his genitals and spread throughout his body as he rapidly reached his release. They clung together as their bodies writhed and beat in unison.

Jacob could see that Amy was sulking as they waited outside the Uffizi early the next morning in the already long queue for the gallery to open. He shook his head, aware that Louis had taken the desirable Reuben off to Nicky's studio, along from the Ponte Vecchio. There he would lie, naked and under the inscrutable eye of the artist. No wonder Amy was fuming. She hung about the edge of the group, simmering and smoking, and looking wonderful in her blue velvet suit, and with her copious curls untamed, and her green eyes smouldering. She drew the eyes of every passing Italian male – and every tourist. Jacob had no doubt that she had spent the night in enjoyable love-making with Reuben, and wondered that she managed to behave as though she was sex-starved. He smiled affectionately at her. He was thankful that his own relationship with her was simpler. Though he could not help but be aroused when he looked at her.

Eleanor seemed filled with excitement to be on the brink of entering the hallowed grounds of the world-famous gallery. Jacob smiled to see that she hugged her battered sketch-pad to her. She returned his smile as he caught her eye. She was a delight to teach. And to look at, Jacob sighed. It seemed that too much of the female interest was going Louis' way. It was a relief to have him safely out of the way for a while. At least Sarah seemed to be free of his friend's enticing charm – for now.

They were to have more than one visit to the Uffizi. Jacob

began lecturing to them when they were allowed into the first room:

'As you probably know,' he said in his quiet, lilting voice, 'Uffizi means "offices". The gallery forms part of a building erected by Vasari to house the offices of the state of Tuscany in the sixteenth century. I thought it best if we concentrated on a few paintings this morning, and another selection tomorrow. Naturally, you will have time to wander around on your own as well.'

They followed Jacob from room to room. Eleanor delighted at the familiar pictures. They stood in front of Titian's lovely 'Flora', admiring this ideal of womanly beauty, with her placid, ethereal expression. Only her shoulder was bare. His 'St Mary Magdalen' was more sensual, with her long, luscious red-gold curls pulled around her body, whilst leaving her full, tempting breasts exposed. Jacob found it hard to resist surveying Amy, exuding sexuality, her hair as bright as these models'. Titian's 'Venus of Urbino' lay naked, facing the viewer frankly. It was as though they had watched a woman preparing for sex, first with the diaphanously clothed 'Flora', and then 'Mary', with her passionate glance heaven-ward, and now, at last, as Venus, she lay, completely naked, ready for sex. In her right hand she held roses, one of which had fallen. Symbolically, Jacob told them. Venus was sensual, with firmly-modelled limbs, and warm-seeming flesh. Eleanor looked with great interest at the original of the painting which had inspired Louis to paint her in this pose. She recalled her portrait, comparing it with this. She found her body filled with thoughts of Louis. Louis concentrating on her naked body, intent on rendering her in oils. Louis. Touching her . . .

Later they split up in the Uffizi and some of them concentrated on sketching a few of the paintings. Eleanor sat in front of Botticelli's 'Primavera', prints and cards of which she had seen many times. It was wonderful to see the real thing. This room was devoted to the works of Sandro Botticelli. Jacob was standing, with a group of students, before his 'Birth of Venus', in which the naked goddess stood on a giant shell, with one hand over her breast and the other holding her long golden hair to cover her sex. They gazed with admiration at her voluptuous, creamy-white body. Eleanor smiled at Jacob as he extolled the virtues of the painting: the ultimate Venus. She turned back to 'La Primavera', looking, with wonder at the various lightly-clad bodies within the complex group of allegorical figures, especially admiring the three graces, and the adjacent form of Mercury, his red cloak draped over his muscular body as he dispersed the mists with his wand. She would concentrate on drawing him.

Amy lingered restlessly by her, going from one marvellous painting to another. Eleanor sensed that she was agitated, and gleaned that this was because neither her handsome lover, Reuben, nor Louis were present. Though Amy was a competent artist, she seemed, to Eleanor, to be far more taken up with the men. Eleanor risked a sympathetic smile at her, and when she did not frown, or look archly away, she said:

'You would make a good model for Venus, with your hair . . .'

Amy smiled a little shyly.

'I expect he'll have us posing . . .' she complained.

Eleanor did not know whether she referred to Jacob or Louis. They walked over to scrutinise Botticelli's 'Calumny'.

'Men!' said Amy, apropos of nothing. 'They drive you crazy!'

Eleanor smiled sympathetically, and risked asking:

'Where's Reuben?'

'Lying naked for Louis by now, I don't doubt.'

Eleanor could not prevent her sudden, reflex flush.

'For his portrait . . .' Amy explained, her tone mocking and bored.

Eleanor nodded, understanding now why the older woman was so aggrieved, and wondering whether she would see much of Reuben now.

'Where are they?'

'Oh – they've got some friend here, who has a studio near the river . . .' Amy's tone was still filled with bitterness. 'If I knew exactly where, I'd be there.'

'I expect Reuben's colouring appeals to Louis. He's very attractive.'

'Quite,' agreed Amy cryptically, 'I'll see you later, I'm going up to the roof cafe to have a fag.'

Obviously, she could not concentrate. Eleanor nodded.

'We're going to the Pitti Palace tomorrow. There are some lovely Raphaels there.'

'Hmmm . . .' said Amy, her glance expressing puzzlement at the girl. She lingered. 'Louis painted you, Elli . . . Have you and he—?'

'No . . .' answered Eleanor, embarrassed, going to join Jacob's group and missing Amy's smirk of triumph. She immediately regretted giving so much away, in her tone, to this sophisticated older woman.

Amy sat on the roof terrace of the gallery, gazing unappreciatively at the crenallated tower of the Palazzo Vecchio. All she could see was her mind's-eye image of Reuben lying luxuriously on some couch for Louis as the latter drew him avidly. What a waste of two potent men, she thought scornfully, puffing furiously on the foul-tasting cigarette. Her sex-orientated body seethed with jealousy. It was no good, she would have to find out where they were. She drained her coffee and stormed off to demand of Jacob where the studio was.

The group lingered before Annibale Carracci's 'Bacchante', examining the heaviness of form of the back of the reclining nude, and the elegance of her face as she gazed at the darker semi-naked figure of Bacchus, offering her a silver dish of grapes. The painting was very sensuous. Eleanor could feel the sensuality, both of the figures and of the richness of the oils and depth of colours of the paintings, working on her spirit. As often in art galleries, she began to assume a trance-like state, her senses charged with the spirit of paintings. She could understand how Louis existed for days in his exclusive world of creativity. After all, he was as one of these acclaimed and treasured painters, gifted with the ability to pleasure others with the artifice of his craft. She was filled with great tenderness towards him, and what could only be described as considerable awe. Now, she could scarcely believe that she herself had lain for days, naked under his avid scrutiny. She picture for a moment her own portrait, hung like this, whilst gazers admired it. She smiled, filled with gratitude and warmth towards Louis, that he had chosen her. She still felt shy of him, although he had been very friendly and on occasion she had caught – something – in his dark eyes as sometimes she had looked up and caught him staring at her.

Amy's question had wounded her. Though she had been in trepidation of Louis expecting more of her, she had thought that his gentle exploration of her warm, nakedness would be a prelude to him making love to her. Still, she sighed, she could not blame him for turning to more experienced lovers. She had to admit that her dreams were once more filled with imagining painting Louis as he lay, naked, in her chosen position. The concept excited her, both intellectually and sexually. She sighed, disciplining her mind as they wandered from gallery to gallery. She had, at least, broached him with the idea of him sitting for her. And he had agreed!

Eleanor turned her thoughts back to the present and found herself transfixed by Caravaggio's 'Bacchus'. Caravaggio was a wild and decadent artist – he had even killed a man. He too, like many painters it seemed to Eleanor, preferred men – or even boys. He certainly painted his models with a sensuous brush, and captured the lasciviousness in their mouths and eyes. She gazed at the boy with his elaborate head-dress of dark, luscious grapes and vine-leaves of sumptuous varied colours, balancing the richness of greens, reds and oranges in the exquisitely painted bowl of fruit before him. The boy held a wine goblet between his delicate finger and thumb, and looked out at them a little blearily through hooded dark eyes, his full cheeks flushed, his mouth full and red. Eleanor invented a scenario whereby the artist later, smilingly, took off the model's crown and, taking the full glass from him, slipped his white robe from his muscular shoulder . . . She flushed to see that the artist was Louis Joseph.

'You have to tell me where they are.' Amy's voice, coming sharply and defiantly into the room, jarred Eleanor's erotic reverie, and made them all jump.

Jacob grasped her by the arm, and spoke calmly to her. Eleanor noted that she seemed to be soothed by his touch, and his closeness, rather than his words.

There was unaccustomed nervousness involved in sketching the man now standing naked before him, in the pose of 'The Charioteer'. It was a new situation, where Louis had acted on impulse. Usually, he had time to accustom himself and be in a stronger position. Here, he was all too aware of the limited time, and that he was indebted to Reuben for obliging. He was also too conscious of the man's admiration for him. This threatened to inhibit him. He controlled his rising anxiety, and concentrated on the figure drawing. Reuben remained very still. Louis was aware of the strong masculine power of the man as he rapidly sketched his muscular torso and firm legs. Louis did not always expect to succeed; much, he knew, depended on his confidence.

Reuben stared back at him unflinchingly through his deep brown eyes. Finishing the first sketch in record time, Louis re-positioned his model and began on the next sheet. He was increasingly aware of the man's short, muscular member, and the generous sack behind. He was sure that a fleeting smile crossed Reuben's face, and he thought that here was a man as powerful as he. He was not really sure whether there were thoughts of seduction deep in his mind, but he knew that it would not be an easy matter.

He relayed instructions and requirements to Reuben and Reuben immediately understood and complied. He was a good model, and the planes and moulding of his body were pleasing to capture. He was familiar with the poses, having studied art history. Louis thought of him as a suitable model for a perfect Greek man. Though he was content to have him now, he was also sorry that the arrangement was to be so short-lived. It would be a challenge, to render him in oils. Reuben stood obligingly for hours whilst Louis recorded him from every angle.

'Shouldn't you take a break, Louis?' Reuben asked at last as the light began to fade. He smiled as Louis looked at him, as though it was most unusual to hear a human voice, and then passed his hand across his eyes, acknowledging his weariness.

Louis smiled at him. 'Forgive me – you haven't even had a drink,' he apologised as Reuben dressed. Now released, his body surged with repressed sexual hunger.

Reuben shook his head. 'I'm okay . . .' He smiled.

Louis checked his watch. 'Shall we join them at the hotel for dinner?'

'That's fine.'

Louis gave him a can of lager from Nicky's fridge, suddenly realising how weak and hungry he was. He lit a cigarette. Inhaling made him dizzy.

'You should have asked for a break, Reuben.'

'I'm alright,' Reuben assured him, lightly placing his fist on Louis' arm in a friendly gesture.

They walked along the Arno and past the Uffizi in the same silence which had enveloped them all afternoon. In the Piazza della Signora, where people strolled or gathered, a pretty young Italian girl greeted Reuben, who caught her close and kissed her, explaining to her, in Italian that he had to meet people for dinner, and that he would see her next week. He introduced her to Louis, as Francesca, and Louis spoke to her in Italian and kissed her hand. 'Ciaow . . .' and then she ran off. Louis and Reuben exchanged grins, and Louis knew that Reuben had recently had sex with Francesca. His own cock unfurled longingly as he looked after her. 'Bellissima. . .' He laughed. They exchanged a look of complicity and masculine understanding.

They were just in time to join the others for one of Claudio's famous dinners. Amy scowled at Reuben, and ignored Louis, but she was obviously finding solace with Sarah as they whispered and touched, sitting close. Jacob had calmed her, for now, trading on her pride, to give Louis a little time. Amy was not going to let Louis know how bothered she was by his claiming

Reuben. After dinner, they went to the large room which had been transformed into a temporary studio. They were to have a go at sketching the models in some of the poses they had seen of the statues in the Bargello.

Simon posed for them naked as Michelangelo's young inebriate Bacchus, with his strong left leg firm, and his right raised onto its toes and a little behind the other, its heel raised and knee bent, so that his right hip was more curved. He held a bowl in his right hand and his face was tilted a little to one side, his mouth open, his eyes glazed. Laughingly, Louis provided Simon with a goblet and theatrical head-dress of grapes and vine-leaves, such as the god had. Amy recalled Louis' love of the original. She noticed – did Reuben? – how the artist stood very close to the youth, looking into his eyes. He had no shame. She looked to see whether Louis would touch Simon's naked penis. They all, including Louis, concentrated on their task. The atmosphere seemed purified by this devotion to art.

Sarah posed as Botticelli's graceful Venus, her right hand over her right breast, her left on her left thigh, her right knee raised a little, this stance closing her legs firmly. Though Sarah's generous sex was not covered by her long hair, as was Venus's. Louis took it upon himself to give them advice on execution, standing provocatively close to the naked models, both of whom, Amy knew, he had seduced and his hand was so close – perhaps just a touch would send them squirming. But maybe this was just her own state. She imagined arguing with Louis; challenging him on his art, continuing the attack she had made at his house. But she knew that this was sacrosanct to Louis, and even Amy could respect this, until she thought of him, alone all day with her sexy boyfriend.

They continued for hours into the night, invigorated by this unusual opportunity, and each others' enthusiasm, and drinking copious amounts of Claudio's best wine. Simon was Apollo Belvedere, maintaining his complicated pose, his torso twisted, leaning to one side, his arms raised, one across his chest, the other above his head, his legs crossed. Sarah, the Medici Venus, bent her opulent figure slightly forward, her head looking to the side, one hand hovering over her breast, the other extended lingeringly across her pubis.

Louis suggested to Jacob that Simon, and perhaps Reuben, could have a go at posing 'The Wrestlers', a Hellenistic work they had seen in the Tribuna of the Uffizi. Amy cajoled Jacob and Louis into demonstrating the complex pose. Though, frustratingly for her, the men remained clothed, they agreed. They took up their practised positions gracefully. They were very natural together. No doubt, thought Amy, they had often rehearsed and discussed poses. Challengingly, Louis took up his position on the floor. He supported himself on one knee, and with his other lower leg, which was bent double, his left arm flat on the ground. His head was turned as if he was attempting to rise, to throw off Jacob, who pinned him down, his body straddling him. Jacob's leg was under Louis' (*close to his hidden genitals*, thought Amy). His thigh was against Louis' thigh, his abdomen above Louis'; the left side of his body along Louis' back. Jacob's right arm was raised and held back in preparation to strike Louis. The wrestlers were caught in a crucial moment of dynamic force. Amy was filled with decadent enjoyment: how thrilling it would be to witness the friends naked, and in bed. Fucking.

However, Amy had to admit that their intimacy was as though they were used to sharing physical activities, rather than sex. Their approach was business-like, and they paused to discuss getting it right. Amy gained great pleasure in seeing them thus engaged. They maintained their concentration as they helped Simon and the easy-going Reuben to maintain this pose. Amy was certain that she was not alone, of the women in the group, who squirmed in delight as she watched these delicious men, with their varying good looks, together. Perhaps it was sexy, she thought, to watch men actually wrestling. Though, unlike in ancient Greece, they would not be naked . . .

At length, seemingly satisfied, Louis and Jacob withdrew. Amy was very conscious of her own body's excited response to the proximity of the men's bodies as they worked hard to maintain the complex and demanding pose. She found it difficult to draw. She also glanced frequently over to Louis, who was sketching in an aura of deep concentration. She saw that he continued to drink his wine. Jacob, taking this as another task allotted to them, wandered around, looking at their efforts. He remained behind Eleanor, chatting to her about her drawing, for a few moments, and then seemed to settle himself, with natural, though unconscious intimacy, behind Louis. He watched Louis keenly, even reaching out his elegant fingers to trace some aspect of his drawing as he spoke quietly to his friend. Louis nodded and the two men chatted quietly about the models, seeming to discuss various points and possibilities. Louis obviously respected Jacob sufficiently to listen to his advice. Whether he needed it or not, Amy could not say. She smiled at this close understanding between them, even envied, a little, the very special quality of their friendship. She decided that they would fend off any interference with the sanctity of this, and turned to imagine sleeping with Louis and Reuben. Here, she was filled with unreasonable jealousy, though she was not quite clear of whom she was jealous.

Eleanor frowned, lost in deep concentration, as she laboured to reproduce the mens' twisting, contorted bodies; the force between them as they paused mid-fight, each determined to beat the other. She was aware of the effort it took for Simon to hold the pose, and felt sympathy for him, torn between thinking that he needed a break, and apprehensive lest they should not be able to get into the exact pose after this, and her efforts so far would be wasted – no, not wasted, but she would not be able to finish this particular attempt. She shook her head in recognition of the selfishness of the artist. She would very much like to see how Louis was tackling this. This was the first time (of many, she dreamed) that they would attempt the same subject. She anticipated the usefulness of being able to study his drawing later. She was caught, as she glanced up at the invisible net holding Louis and Jacob as they conversed quietly.

From their pose, and from her angle, Eleanor was unable to see the men's private parts though naturally she had looked at

Reuben's earlier, as they had got into position. He was well-endowed, and had a lovely body. Amy was lucky. She looked across to Amy. She did not look very happy. Eleanor recalled her anger earlier at not being able to go to the studio where Louis had been sketching Reuben, and her silence during dinner. Just then Jacob turned away from Louis, happened to catch Eleanor's eye and smiled encouragingly at her. He came over to her to discuss her attempt.

The men were rising and though he caught his robe around him quickly to hide it, Amy saw that Reuben had an erection. She fumed as she saw that Louis had noticed too and had exchanged an amused smile with her lover, widening his eyes at him in mock surprise. His attention was then taken up with Simon who, trailing his gown casually, wandered over to look at Louis' sketch. She was sure that Louis kissed him briefly, and embraced him lightly just to tease Reuben. Eleanor also joined them, and Jacob turned to speak to Reuben. Amy was damned if she was going to fawn over the man.

Simon put his arm affectionately round Eleanor's shoulders as she came to look at Louis' drawing. Louis smiled at her.

'Let me see yours?' Louis said, closing his book.

Tremulously, Eleanor put her open book on Louis' table. She felt almost as naked as she had been when she had posed for him. Louis looked at her sketch in silence for some seconds, nodding, and then began to offer her some pertinent advice. Eleanor felt pleased: Louis was frank and business-like, yet she could tell he liked what she had done.

'Do you fancy a drink?' Amy asked Simon, tiring a little of the various intricacies of the group. Simon accepted.

'Come back in ten,' Louis called.

Simon turned and nodded. Amy was annoyed by Louis' bossiness.

It was with intense pleasure that Eleanor looked at last at Louis' own drawing. It was exquisite. Taking into account what he had said, and his own version, she knew how she had to continue. Wandering out to the balcony lounge for a coffee, she

192

encountered Amy charming Simon. She knew how much Simon admired the older woman. She shrugged her shoulders and returned to the main room. Reuben and Louis were now in deep conversation, standing very close. Eleanor wondered at all these unusual liaisons.

'After this,' Jacob was saying to her, 'I thought I'd go out to do a few night-time – or early morning – sketches?'

Eleanor nodded, smiling to herself. She would enjoy accompanying him. The next long session passed quickly, so immersed was she in her rendering of the naked men.

Seven

'Louis, I'll have to tell Amy where you are today. She's bound to ask,' Jacob said in their suite before breakfast the next morning. 'I managed to put her off yesterday, but she was not at all pleased, you can imagine. Maybe Reuben's told her?'

Louis smiled and then shrugged.

'Are you alright?'

'I'm shagged!' Louis smiled ruefully at him.

'We're going to the Pitti Palace this morning, and then, after lunch, to Fiesole. How can you bear not to come?' He smiled at Louis, who returned this.

'I think I'll have a day to myself tomorrow. Catch up . . .'

'Say hello?'

Louis nodded. 'I'll go to Fiesole, San Gimignano – maybe Siena . . .' He teased his friend, who groaned with envy, unable to spare time from his students.

'You should take Elli—'

Louis inclined his head to one side, as though considering this.

'She could be as good as you, Louis, one day.'

'Yes,' Louis agreed, 'she could . . .'

Eleanor loved the opulence of the Pitti Palace, and spent the entire visit alone, in the Galleria Palatina, wandering from room to room, drinking in its riches in a state of near-ecstasy. She felt that this visit to Florence was profoundly enriching her life. She spent a long time gazing in adoration at Raphael's beautiful 'Madonna of the Chair'. Mary cuddled her child lovingly to her, whilst the infant John the Baptist gazed up at her. The portrait was in the form of a circle, the colours rich and bright. The model for Mary, Eleanor knew, was Raphael's beloved mistress, La Fornarina. Eleanor was very moved by the woman's enchanting beauty, so sensitively captured by the artist, and imagined the romantic love between her and her beautiful Italian lover. The supreme artist. She moved from picture to picture of this woman, who had so loved Rafaello Sanzio, that on his premature death, she had run, distraught, after his coffin, in the street, and had thrown herself upon it. Eleanor gazed into the woman's painted eyes, gazing out so lovingly, in Raphael's 'La Donna Velata'. She could not prevent a brief indulgence of dreaming of herself with Louis . . .

For hours, Louis had painted the reclining male nude. Today, he posed Reuben as the beautiful youth, Cephalus, being awakened by Aurora, or the dawn. He worked efficiently and economically with watercolours. Quicker than oils. He had shrugged off his weariness. His brain was clear and intent. He planned to do an oil, based on this, at home and even – looking ahead – one with Reuben as live model. The man had agreed with alacrity to pose again for him at the end of the year, when he completed his course. However, he must utilise this opportunity. One never knew . . . Louis felt he had to grasp every occasion for a painting that the world and his imagination offered to him.

As the bus laboured up the hills to the hill town of Fiesole, where the Brownings had settled and had made famous, Eleanor looked out of the window to capture the repeated and varied views of Florence as the bus rose and turned. Louis was right: this was *the* most beautiful bus journey.

'It's like looking down on heaven . . .' Eleanor said dreamily as they surveyed the Tuscan city from Fiesole, with the familiar view of the Duomo and the tower of the Palazzo Vecchio. Eleanor looked over the countryside, with its cypresses, villas and olive trees. 'Being in Florence is like being in heaven,' she added impulsively, colouring as she realised how much she had given away, so enthusiastically.

Jacob smiled affectionately at her, squeezing her arm. She returned his smile.

'Complete with angels?' he asked, his grey eyes twinkling.

Eleanor nodded, and then took out her drawing-pad. Jacob watched her as she sketched rapidly. He recalled the younger Louis, and his need to capture all he saw in this way.

'You must get Louis to show you his Italian sketch-books,' he encouraged her.

'I'd like that.'

Eleanor herself had spent every minute immersed in the wonder of Florence. She went out alone when the others were resting, to fill her sketch-books with drawings of some of the Renaissance buildings, including the Duomo – the cathedral of Santa Maria del Fiore; the Baptistery (the oldest building in Florence); the Ponte Vecchio (with its ancient goldsmiths' shops); San Lorenzo; San Marco and the beautiful façades of Santa Maria Novella and Santa Trinita. It *was* like being in heaven, for the young artist, at the heart of where western art had sprung from. Perhaps one day she would visit Greece, too, the spirit of which was the fount of Renaissance glory. To do any kind of justice to the churches and palazzi would take time, and so Eleanor had to content herself with quick sketches – a taste for the future.

If, incidentally, whilst she was sketching the buildings, a group of students or a lovely child caught her eyes, then Eleanor would make a rapid sketch of these. She was used to being out and about, alone, and to the interest of passers-by who glanced at her work. It was second nature to her to make pencil-notes of anything which appealed to her. This had, since she was a child, been her way of interpreting the world around her. She felt marvellously happy, and very much at home here, she had even used a little of the Italian she had learnt from tapes. She filled book after book with her impressions. In the museums and galleries too, she wandered off from the others, taken by certain works of art. Often, when they came to leave, someone – usually Jacob – had to seek her out. Once, she noticed the glance which passed between Louis and Jacob in understanding that she was one of them, and she was warmed by their friendship. She was so engrossed that she scarcely even thought of sex, though her body was alive to the sensuality of her surroundings. This gave her an ethereal look. She thought that Louis must be aware of her sensually suggestive state, as she often caught his lingering looks. She knew that he valued her talent, and understood her sensitivity. She was not strange to him, as she had been to many young friends. Her dreams were filled with vivid images of the places they had visited. When she talked to Louis it was from the equal level of the discussion of art. Louis looked at her work, and offered valid and sensitive comments. Eleanor made notes on what he said – often in cryptic sketches. Though she was assured of her ability, she was sufficiently humble – eager – to learn from an experienced and successful artist. She gained, from this visit, verification of her calling and strength for her future. Some of the drawings she did were of the same subjects she had seen in Louis' bedroom. If she thought about it, Eleanor was aware of Louis' admiration and the seriousness with which he regarded her. She was not conscious of his sexual interest.

Eleanor therefore, for the most part, was blissfully unaware of the complexities and jealousies of the older members of the group. When she did perceive them it was from the protective prism of her own self-contained world.

Louis watched Eleanor as she sketched the Palazzo Vecchio; she was completely immersed and did not appear to be conscious of the cold at all. Her face was a little flushed, and her lips parted, the red tip of tongue between as she concentrated. It was a joy to witness such devotion in another; an approach so familiar to him. He smiled, slowly coming closer.

'It's good, Elli . . .' he said softly.

Eleanor looked up, taking a moment to emerge back into reality. Louis knew that state.

'Louis!'

'Do you think you could take a break? I've arranged with Claudio to borrow his car for the day. I thought we could go to

San Gimignano. I need a break.'

'Yes – that would be lovely.' Eleanor glanced across at the building and then at her sketch.

'You'll have time to finish it before we leave,' Louis assured her. 'And I'm sure you'll catch up with what Jake is doing today.'

'Yes.' Eleanor closed her pad.

She was filled with delight as Louis drove them through the Tuscan countryside south of Florence. Part of her pleasure was at being alone with the handsome Louis, who turned to smile at her every now and again.

'I love Italy,' she told him.

Louis nodded, 'Me too . . . I think I could live here – easily.'

'Oh, yes . . .' she agreed enthusiastically, turning to smile at him, meeting his eyes.

Eleanor was enchanted by the walled medieval town of San Gimignano. Evocative and picturesque, perched on a hilltop, its skyline was broken with towers.

'There's twelve left,' Louis told her as they strolled through the streets and squares, little changed since the time of Dante. 'Once, there were seventy. Florence too had many tower-houses – places of protection, especially in the feuds between Guelphs and Ghiberlines . . .'

'I've got lots of reading to do,' Eleanor confessed.

'There's time,' Louis assured her.

'I'll have to do a few sketches,' Eleanor told him.

Louis smiled and nodded. This was only natural to him.

'I wish we could go on to Siena, but I have to continue my painting of Reuben when we get back . . .' Louis said wistfully. 'And tomorrow . . .'

Eleanor nodded. She would have very much liked to have spent another uncomplicated day with Louis. Though they were often quiet, she felt easy with him now.

'This has been a lovely day . . .'

'Yes – it has, Elli,' said Louis, kissing her head softly.

She could understand that he would find Amy, or Sarah – or even Simon or Reuben more of a partner than she, but she felt she had his friendship.

Reuben lay, warm and relaxed, existing in the familiar pose of the languid Cephalus. He was caught in Louis' web, basking in the attention the talented artist gave him. This was added to by his previous respect for Louis Joseph. His admiration was enhanced as he was direct witness to the prodigious patience of the man, and his tireless ability to concentrate and continue painting. He lay languidly, enjoying the artist's continuous gaze as he watched Louis begin to look more and more tired.

At last, Louis nodded, let his brush drop and came towards Reuben, kneeling before him in an attitude of worship, submission or just weariness. Reuben appreciated that he was drained. He wanted to go and see his painting. Tentatively, he reached out to touch Louis' thick hair. Just then, Louis looked up at him and smiled. His eyes were heavy with weariness. He looked along the warm, now close, body towards Reuben's cock. Reuben was amazed when his prick filled under the artist's look. Louis looked back at him and grinned.

'A reflex action,' Reuben explained.

'Right,' said Louis, standing. Moving away. He went to the window, lit a cigarette and looked out. Reuben was filled with a ridiculous sense of a lost opportunity. 'You can get dressed,' Louis told them, without turning round. 'We should go and eat.'

Without rational thought, Reuben went over to him, pulling on his long T-shirt, which covered his cock, now determinedly semi-tumescent. He stood close to Louis. Louis reached out and took his penis firmly within the hand which had so recently grasped a paintbrush. Reuben shivered, though, he realised, his cock was swelling again, and his body delighting as Louis pulled familiarly on him.

'Louis, I've never . . .'

Louis placed his other hand on the back of Reuben's head and he pulled his face to his own to kiss him hard on the mouth. Reuben was not prepared for the surge of animal need which gushed through him. He put his hands on Louis' shoulders and moved closer into his experienced hold. He moved his mouth to Louis' neck, biting to alleviate his intense passion, panting as

Louis caressed him urgently. His body was against Louis'. His masculine power was very different from a woman's. Reuben felt that his unusual reaction derived merely from the special circumstances of the past few days.

Amy ran up the stairs, and, still breathless – mostly from anxiety – she burst into the room. Reuben jumped and sprang guiltily away from Louis, his long black T-shirt scarcely covering him. Louis merely narrowed his eyes at Amy and licked the fingers which had stroked her lover's penis. A smile hung about his eyes and mouth.

'Aren't you – fortunate . . . ?' he whispered to Reuben.

Amy was shouting at them, enraged and frustrated.

'Amy – nothing's happened,' Reuben said reasonably, going to her, taking her arm.

'Oh, don't disappoint her,' Louis drawled, lighting another cigarette, seeing that Amy was torn between taking Reuben and making him pay. She glared at Louis. He took a deep drag and then exhaled, leaning back against the window, regarding them challengingly.

Amy's eyes filled with strength as she made her decision and lifted Reuben's T-shirt, keeping Louis' eyes as she went down his body slowly, and took his full penis into her mouth. Louis closed his eyes, feeling his cock urge painfully at his jeans, imagining Amy's mouth taking him into its muscular warmth. He went over to Amy and stood behind her. He reached to take her breasts in his hands, and kissed her neck under her long tangled hair. He ran his hands to her belly, massaging this, and then to her sex. Amy continued to work on Reuben, jerking on him with energy. But, as Louis' fingers found her naked vulva, she released Reuben and sank into Louis' expert embrace.

Reuben met Louis' eyes as Louis pulled the ecstatic Amy to her feet. Louis smiled (as if offering Reuben unfamiliar treasures), pulling up Amy's dress to expose her breasts and sex, pressing his crotch against her bottom. Louis let Amy rest back against him, and placed his palms above her breasts, kissing her neck. As Reuben watched, Louis let his hands reach her breasts, capturing her red nipples between the edges of his fingers. He nodded once. As if released, Reuben touched Amy's deep pink clitoris. She gasped and began to writhe her body in abandonment as Louis began to massage her breasts vigorously, pinching her erect nipples hard. He sank his teeth into her neck, and she cried out as he sucked powerfully on her.

Meanwhile, Reuben was working his fingers along her exposed sex. Led by his cock, he took it into his hands and pushed the sensitive end against Amy's vulva. Amy continued to squirm in abandoned enjoyment, pressing herself back and forth between the men who ran their hands over her almost naked body. Louis looked at Reuben, who was now inserting his erect member into Amy. Louis held her in place as the other man entered her. He could feel Amy's bottom urging against his restrained prick. He released it and held it against her anus as Reuben supported her, becoming lost in his fucking. Louis witnessed the potent man's release into a state of absolute sexuality and overwhelming need. Louis worked his own cock up and down Amy's crack, holding her buttocks around it as she clung to Reuben. They continued like this for several minutes, supporting Amy as they worked her back and forth along their cocks. Louis knew that Reuben saw the hunger in his eyes. He indicated the bed and Louis nodded.

Amy's copious sexual juices covered Reuben's stiff rod as he withdrew. Amy cried out in anger and sadness. They got her to the bed and Louis undressed. Reuben took off Amy's crumpled dress and ran his hands over her body as he watched Louis take off his pants to reveal his generous prick. Drunk with pleasure and anticipation, Amy eyed Louis' sex greedily. They lay down, with her in between, and held Amy close to them as they kissed and sucked on her. Amy seemed in a rapture of libidinous abandon as her warm, lithe body tossed and squirmed between them, inciting them. Louis knew that Reuben watched as he covered his cock with lubricant. He smiled at the man lasciviously, then leaned over to kiss him, knowing that Amy was excited by this lust.

Reuben sucked greedily on her jutting nipples, and forced his aching member into her dripping hole. Amy worked her tight muscle along him energetically, and he had to help Louis hold her still as he eased his cock into her tighter passage. Then the men began to work along her, pushing her between them so that she was surrounded by masculine heat and scent. Louis held on to her breasts tightly, and Reuben had his hands on the round hemispheres of her grinding buttocks as they moved in a steady rhythm.

Through a haze of sex, Reuben gazed at Louis' full lips and dark, seductive eyes and then closed his eyes and kissed Amy deeply. Amy whimpered and moaned in pleasure as they fucked her. As if spurred on by awareness of the other's prowess, they kept up their deep penetration for a long time, moving her so that, as Reuben worked her vagina to the tip of his cock, Louis forced his prick into her anus more deeply, and when he almost released her, but held on, Reuben pushed his prick almost to her womb, until Reuben could hold out no longer and released his spunk in an agony of shuddering, crying out. Louis narrowed his lovely eyes and smiled at the man, feeling Amy's orgasm possess her trembling body.

Louis slowly withdrew his stiff member, and, as Reuben lay back, he pushed Amy onto her back and plunged his cock into her. As he took her slowly back to heaven, Louis reached out and grasped Reuben's penis, jerking it cruelly until Reuben groaned in anguish. Then, Louis released it and concentrated on making Amy come again, gazing down at the sleazy, dishevelled woman as he raised his agile body high and then rammed forcefully into her, causing her to jerk upwards at each powerful movement. Amy gripped his hot penis tightly with her vagina, sliding her clitoris along his cock, staring at him knowingly, making him reach his orgasm. Louis smiled at her, and came, as she had marvelled at him before, with stillness in his face and body, his black eyes staring deeply into hers.

Then, with a mocking smile at Amy, he took Reuben's cock into his mouth, though Reuben cried out in pain. Transfixed, Amy stared at Louis as he sucked on Reuben, squeezing his buttocks tightly. She marvelled to see that, already, Louis' big prick was stiff once more and she was filled with a mixture of amazement and overwhelming lust. Louis released Reuben and went from them. Naturally, Reuben turned to Amy, and as she took him into her arms, she was aware of his confusion and need. Louis put on his long shirt and shorts and turned to his canvas. Then, he concentrated on sketching them as they rolled and tumbled, fucking wildly, further excited by his presence and his darkness.

'Let him fuck you,' Amy whispered to Reuben, feeling her lover become suddenly still at her surprising request.

'He doesn't want me to,' Louis drawled, his tone advising Amy to stop.

'Well – let him fuck you,' Amy threw at him.

Louis shrugged, continuing to draw. He knew that Amy was deeply excited by the prospect of getting her lover to do this. Reuben, in a state of anguished lust, hesitated. And, for once seemingly in accord in their manipulative deeds, Amy and Louis regarded each other in speculation. Then, Amy released Reuben, and he lay, a lascivious victim. Louis came to the bed, took off his shirt and sat beside Reuben. Amy positioned herself at the foot of the bed, her legs parted as she fondled her swollen labia and watched. Reuben looked at her. Louis leant and kissed Reuben, and Amy felt a surge of wild, tangled emotions sweep up through her as he began to caress the man tenderly. She had not expected this: for him to make love to Reuben, and she wanted to tear him away. She had simply expected the men to perform a brief and forceful act of buggery for her. She wanted to wrest Louis' hands from the body of her lover, as Reuben lay passive, and Louis explored his body, as if enjoying the muscular feel of the anatomy he knew so well. It was as if, because he was so familiar with the clinical make-up of the body, he also knew where to touch to give pleasure. As Reuben's writhing body told of his enjoyment, Amy had to realise that Louis was not simply selfish and demanding. Her own body glowed as witness to this. He was an expert lover, and could utilise the attractiveness of his own body to charm and subdue. But, although Reuben enjoyed this manipulation of his body, he shook his head at Louis, who could choose to ignore his silent negation, but who did not. Louis smiled at Amy, flicking his glance at her own increasing stimulation of her sex as he rose.

Amy caught him and kissed him deeply, and he responded, drawing his hands over her naked flesh, and her into avid life. Then, he gestured his head at Reuben and Amy went to Reuben and Louis returned to his drawing and, as they made love, Amy wondered whether Louis had aroused them to this frenzied pitch so that he could draw them. And, although she was in wonder at his sexual prowess, a tiny edge of anger remained, to grow, at his powerful manipulation of them, and his taking of her, anally, when she had been fucking Reuben. It seemed that she was destined to remain in some kind of passionate rage with this man. Would he have fucked Reuben, had she not come along? She was sure that Reuben would not have prevented him, even this time. And how did he feel now, as he seemed lost in his drawing? Was it some kind of pornography? This she knew was unfair. Could he really sublimate his sexual appetite to art?

All this muddled her head as she showered and dressed, but then she told herself that she had enjoyed herself and was deeply satisfied – for now. The drawings were tender. She left the men, her mind occupied with devising some means to get back at Louis: to be in a position of power. It took some time for it to dawn on her that she had let Louis draw her, naked, without any discussion – a gift she had been withholding. She was filled with fury. As she sat by the river, smoking furiously and watching passers-by, a delicious thought of how she could get back at him occurred to her: she would teach Eleanor how to seduce him.

'He drives me crazy.' Amy flung at Jacob, smoking and prowling restlessly round the sitting-room he shared with Louis.

'Who?' asked Jacob, taking in her extreme agitation.

'Louis! I don't know how he does it . . . but he does!' Her green eyes were filled with wildness as she looked at him.

'Is he with Reuben?'

'Yes – but it's not what you think. I've been with them. He didn't screw Reuben – probably because I asked him to!' She stopped suddenly as if realising.

Jacob shook his head, wanting to laugh at her bossiness.

'Maybe Reuben didn't want him to?'

'He would have – for me.'

'Louis isn't going to rape your lover, just because it turns you on.'

'Tttt . . .' Amy glared at him, infuriated. 'I reckon he would have done, if I hadn't been there – even now . . .' she narrowed her eyes jealously.

'Not if Reuben doesn't want it. Louis isn't that desperate.'

'How do you know – *do* you—?' She was still, suddenly, fixing Jacob with her bright glare.

Jacob shook his head, laughing. 'Just because Louis is – flexible – doesn't mean he has to possess everyone.'

'Hhhuh!'

'He's very attractive, Amy, but you're not going to pin him down. You've got Reuben.'

'Does Louis prefer men?'

'No. I don't think so.'

'What about Simon?'

Jacob shrugged.

'You've had sex with Louis, Amy – does he prefer men?'

Amy smiled and relaxed.

'I don't think he'll be screwing Reuben now. Has Reuben ever had sex with another man?'

'No! He's not interested.'

'Well, then . . . just because Louis has a dramatic impact on you—'

'He does not – he's – he's – I hate him!' she ended furiously, unable to call to mind words adequately to describe the man.

'I rest my case.' Jacob went over to Amy and embraced her, holding her against him. His body responded to the faint odour of sex still clinging to her.

'Hi!' said Louis, coming in, smiling at them as they moved apart.

Amy merely scowled at him and went off to find Reuben.

'What have I done now?' asked Louis, mockingly, pouring himself a whisky, holding the bottle up to Jacob who deferred.

'She's upset because you screwed – or didn't screw Reuben.'

Louis shrugged his shoulder and drained his glass.

206

'I just can't win, can I?' He grinned at Jacob.

'Are you going to paint her?'

Louis shrugged. Then he smiled gloriously at Jacob.

'You're bad, Louis.'

'I know, Jake.'

'She'd make a magnificent painting.'

'I know – she's beautiful.'

Louis showed his sketches to Jacob, who, as he looked at the intimate poses, began to understand a little of Amy's anger.

'Did you screw Reuben?'

'Are you jealous?'

'Did you?'

'Can't win them all.' Louis grinned wickedly at him. 'I'm starving. Shall we leave them and go out to eat?'

Jacob nodded. He was wearied by all the talking and tours and complexities of several people continually making demands on him, and it would be very peaceful indeed to share with Louis the last night of this trip to their treasured place.

'We'll come back in summer? Well – before your next class?'

Jacob nodded.

'You look worn out,' he added in concern for his friend.

'I am, Louis.'

'Come on, old friend . . .' Louis took his arm.

Jacob smiled.

Amy and Eleanor were sitting together at the table, and turned to watch the friends as they went out. The close friendship between the men tore at Amy as they disappeared. She smiled at Eleanor, who had had several glasses of chianti.

'I think he's beautiful,' Eleanor confessed, for once allowing herself to concentrate on Louis' physical appeal, rather than his artistic talent. She thought with affection of their time together this week. She certainly felt she knew him better.

'Yes, he is,' agreed Amy, looking at the younger woman thoughtfully. 'Very beautiful.'

'You've slept with him?' Eleanor could not resist asking, playing into Amy's hands.

Amy suppressed her instinctive 'Who hasn't?' and instead, still sympathetic to Eleanor, yet intent on her idea of exacting some kind of revenge on Louis, realising that he could not be immune to Eleanor, and *was* probably saving her. 'You know, Elli – you don't have to wait for him to seduce you . . .'

Eleanor flushed and looked down at her coffee. It was, Amy thought, as if she was a virgin, but she had slept with Simon, and, probably, Jacob. She wondered how Louis felt about that.

'I don't know what you mean . . .'

So, Eleanor *was* interested . . .

'You could go to him. Make the first move. He won't throw you out. He's saving you. Be in power. Don't be under his thrall . . .'

'I value his advice. He's been really helpful. I want to be his friend – for a long time . . .'

'Yes. Yes. I'm sure you will. You have a lot in common. So – you don't really fancy him?'

'Of course I do – I *do* – but . . .' Eleanor confessed, and Amy could see in her eyes that she wanted him like crazy. And, to the young romantic, where better than here, in this wonderful city? Amy would be doing her a favour as well as foiling Louis' precious plans. She smiled, and placed her hand over Eleanor's.

'So – it's not as though you don't want to sleep with him, for the sake of preserving this platonic friendship?'

'I don't think I could manage that,' Eleanor admitted sheepishly.

'I know what you mean. He really gets to you, doesn't he?'

'And is he, is he – good?'

Amy sighed and nodded, stubbing out her cigarette in the crystal ashtray.

'I have to confess – he's a wonderful lover.'

The women's eyes met and they smiled. Amy knew that she was succeeding in convincing Eleanor. It had to be soon. She hoped that the men were not out all night on their 'walk'. She would have to get Eleanor another drink, help her to relax. Give her a few tips and help boost her confidence. She gestured to the waiter and ordered more chianti.

'So, Elli – he knows every inch of your body, so you don't have to be shy. Simply get in there . . . Go to his room. You know what to do. Drive *him* crazy. He's used to powerful women, and you aren't inexperienced yourself – you can use your experience to get him. Start as you mean to go on. Empowered. Louis will like that. He's too accustomed to people allowing him to use them.'

Eleanor looked very uncertain, though tempted.

'I've got an idea . . .' said Amy.

Jacob and Louis walked in silence, lingering to look at the glorious cathedral, and the golden doors of the Baptistery, then sauntered down Calzaiuoli, past Orsanmichelle and to the Piazza della Signora, past the Uffizi and along the river to the Ponte Vecchio. As he walked with his friend, Jacob relaxed, as if this quiet, undemanding walk with Louis was healing his spirit; suppressing the memories of noise and bustle with his students along this same way and into the darkened buildings they now passed. It was hard work responding to everyone's needs and questions. He had had little time to himself and was very weary. They crossed the river, entering the Oltrarno, and went to a bar close to Santa Maria del Carmine. There, they ordered wine and sat back, still with no need to converse, though soon they would begin to chat about the past week, about Amy, and Eleanor.

Later, they stood before the church of San Miniato ai Monte, having listened to the monks singing their Gregorian chant, and looked over Florence. A lovely and familiar view. Treasured by them both, and reiterated often. They were silent for a long time. Then Jacob turned and took Louis' cigarette from him and inhaled. He handed it back.

'You shouldn't, Louis . . .'

'Ha!' Louis laughed.

After a moment, Jacob said, 'You know, Louis, I don't ever want to get physically involved with you.'

'No more squash then?' Louis joked.

'Okay,' Jacob sighed. 'Sexually, I mean.'

'You don't have to decide right away,' Louis quipped.

Jacob shook his head. 'It would only complicate things. Our friendship is too important to me.'

'Don't be shy if you change your mind,' Louis continued, in humour, 'I'm quite easy going, really.'

'I won't, Louis.'

Louis took a few drags on his cigarette, and then nodded. He turned to meet Jacob's eyes, and then moved to kiss Jacob lightly on the forehead. Then he smiled at his friend. Jacob relaxed.

It was relatively quiet when, after dinner, and more wine, and lingering over their 'arriverderci' to Florence, they returned to the hotel. Most of the others had gone to a club, living it up on their last night. Sarah had been waiting up for Jacob, and so Louis shrugged ruefully and went up to their suite to work on his sketches. It seemed that Jacob was staying with Sarah, so after a last drink and cigarette on the balcony, and with a sense of sadness at leaving the city tomorrow, Louis showered and went to bed. He was dozing off when he heard a noise, but thought it was Jacob, returning.

'He's asleep . . .' Eleanor whispered to Amy, as though Louis would be reluctant to be awakened by two sexually eager and attractive women.

Amy pushed her into Louis' room. She was obviously regretting Amy's plan now.

'Take down the sheet and begin to caress him. Don't kiss him, use your hands to arouse him. Remember what I told you.' Not that it would take long. Perhaps they should tie him to the bed, though she didn't think Eleanor would take to that idea, somehow. Louis stirred, obligingly flinging the sheet from his body. His bed was under the window, and his body was swathed in moonlight. He looked very beautiful, with the clear light throwing the contours of his body into relief.

Eleanor gazed at his body, enraptured. His penis was full, yet relaxed, resting against his thigh. His eyes were still closed, his dark curls against the white pillow, one hand curled up by his head, the other across his chest. She was deeply stirred by his masculine beauty. She felt the same reverence as when she stood before a lovely painting.

'Go on . . . Take off your gown and sit astride him,' Amy encouraged, sounding as if she would go herself and do so, if Eleanor lingered too long.

Louis moved his head and his hand slid towards his filling cock.

'I can't . . .'

'Don't you want him?'

'*Yes* – he's lovely. But, Amy . . .'

'I'll show you – watch . . .'

Amy slipped off her black satin gown as she walked across the moon-lit room, her white body almost incandescent in its light. Confidently, she sat astride Louis' body, her sex resting lightly on his generous balls. Louis opened his eyes and, though a dark gleam crossed them as if in reflex response to her audacity and her supreme stance, he smiled and reached out his hands to her breast.

'No, I want to show – someone – what to do . . .' she told him, moving out of his grasp.

Eleanor withdrew into the shadows as Louis looked towards where she was hiding. But he could not see her, and he complied with Amy's request. Did he suspect? Eleanor thought, torn between the desire to flee from embarrassment, and intense curiosity. Amy fondled the wonderful hair and then leaned to kiss Louis' neck. He turned to allow her to, closing his eyes in pleasure as Amy began to plant kisses all over his shoulders and chest, licking at his breast, and moving her position to continue on down to his belly.

Eleanor watched as Amy kissed the sensitive area above and around his penis as she continued to massage his chest, and then moved to caress his inner thighs lingeringly. Her womb glowed as she watched Louis writhing in pleasure. Louis took Amy's breasts in his hands and kissed her. Though allowing herself a little time to enjoy this, Amy then moved deftly away to beckon to Eleanor, who was mesmerised by the size of Louis' extended cock. He looked like some wild beast, or god from Greek legend.

Tremulous, Eleanor emerged into the moonlight. She

211

continued to hold her new white gown closely around her naked body.

'Eleanor . . .' Louis smiled, smiling as she came nearer. He sounded overjoyed that it was her. She was reassured: she had irrationally assumed he would be shocked or annoyed.

It was possible that he had wanted to seduce her later, but he took this in good grace . . . he surely could not but do so, as he had imagined making love to her, so many times. Louis – any man – thus aroused would not waste time arguing with two naked women on his bed.

Eleanor was trembling as she came slowly towards him, and Louis foiled Amy by reaching out for Eleanor compassionately, and taking her in beside him, covering them with the sheet. He held her close, kissing her head. He did not question Amy, but indicated with his compelling eyes that he would also welcome her, next to him.

Amy cursed Louis once again, and turned to leave. Though she had used Eleanor, she could not really come between them now. It was all too obvious what they felt for each other that she had merely done them a favour, hastening the inevitable. And perhaps Louis was only being kind to her. Knowing that she would not remain.

'Amy . . .' called Eleanor sympathetically.

'It's okay . . .' Louis assured her, kissing her, 'Jacob is back . . . unless you want her to stay too?'

No fear. Eleanor wanted Louis all to herself, especially as she knew of the older woman's passion and skills.

Coming in, Jacob caught Amy as she reached the door, tying her robe around her naked body.

'What's this? Has Louis upset you again?'

'No!' said Amy vehemently, though Jacob could feel her emotion, trembling through her as he held her. 'He's with Elli . . .'

'Oh, I see. Then, since Reuben's gone, will I do?' he asked softly, pulling her close and kissing her passionately.

Louis pulled back the coverlet and knelt by her feet. Eleanor looked up at his warm body, moulded by the white light. She wanted to smooth her palms over his muscular arms, and bury her fingers in the thick mass of curls. She wanted to spend all night awake in Florence, getting to know Louis' body.

'Have I ever told you,' he asked, his voice a little husky, and looking over her naked body as if allowed to see it, at last, for the first time, 'how very beautiful you are, Elli?'

Eleanor thrilled at this affirmation of her desirability to this man. She thought of their day in San Gimignano. Though soon, she could think of nothing but his eager hands on her body. He ran his hand from her ankles to her inner thigh, parting her legs to enable him to drink in the glory of her spread sex. He smiled beautifully at her, and began to kiss the sensitive inner part of her ankle, and then trailed his hot mouth up her calf and up to her quivering thighs, kissing and nibbling as he went. Eleanor gasped as he came to her vulva and began to lick delicately at it, his eyes closing in pleasure as though he tasted particularly rare and delicious fruit. Then he lay beside her, leaving her vagina throbbing – as erratically as her heartbeat. He pulled her closer, his fingers burning into her skin as he kissed her tenderly. Eleanor could taste her own scent on his tongue as he flicked it across her mouth.

She could feel his sex hot and large against her leg. She opened her mouth to him as he sought entrance. As he urged his seeking tongue inside to explore the hot depths of her mouth, she felt his hand on her breast, which swelled as he caressed, very gently. His touch, so gentle, caused her body to leap into life, and she forgot her awkwardness. Louis' tongue was encircling hers, and his fingers were stimulating her nipple. And now his mouth was on one breast and his hand on the other as she writhed in delight under his exquisite touch. It was as though she was breathing in pure oxygen as she became intoxicated with his love-making. His closeness and affection were extremely life-affirming. And mingled in with this was the knowledge of their similarities, and how well they could understand each other intellectually.

Louis let his hand caress her belly and then his fingers feathered down to her pubis, and he traced the sensitive flesh of her inner thigh, only incidentally brushing against her labia with his knuckles. Suddenly, he lay on his back and lifted her to lie on him, her belly against his, his cock pressed against her sex and belly. She looked down into his face and returned his glorious smile. She felt one hand now on her bottom, gently stroking it, and the other on her breast. She could not help but begin to move urgently against his cock. It seemed that all sensation was concentrated there between them as she pressed her clitoris against Louis' erection. Eleanor felt the force of her fantasies of this exquisite man invade her mind. Whilst she was still capable of coherent thought . . . Louis kissed her, and held her very close to him as he moved in time with her. Eleanor cried out as spasms of sexual feeling were suddenly released from her clitoris, to echo in her vagina and womb. She felt the sweet wetness come from her passage and onto Louis' penis.

Louis stimulated her nipples as she came and then held her close as she relaxed. He kissed her and smiled up at her. It was good to be in such a position of power with this powerful man. Eleanor returned his smile and traced the angular perfection of his face with her hand, lingering on his full lips, appreciating with touch, as well as eyes, his absolute beauty. As she lay against him, she felt her body surge with renewed desire for him. Louis urged his penis between her legs, and continued to caress her, with easy access to her small, sensitive breasts.

Eleanor had not yet experienced sex in this superior position, and there was a special quality in Louis' giving her this, as if he urged her to recognise her own power. More than anything she had ever wanted, she wanted Louis to allow his penis to penetrate her. Now. It felt so very natural. She saw his lovely eyes become hooded as his cock naturally found the entrance to her vagina, but he gazed up at her, meeting her clear eyes as it slid gradually into her, filling her up completely. They held each other's dark eyes at this moment of consummation. And Eleanor found that she was able to press her clitoris against Louis, her vagina stimulating his cock as she pleasured herself. It was lovely. Louis kissed her. Louis held on to her waist as she slipped up and down him, filled with passion for this glorious male, and the realisation of how he revered and treasured her. As they became lost in the consciousness of each other's sweating, toiling body, each concentrated on that supreme seat of pleasure. She was very very happy and assured.

Eleanor nurtured the growing feeling in her womb and sex, becoming more frenzied. This was the first time she had been so absorbed in the sexual act. For the first time, she was completely lost in a man's body, feeling that they were as one as Louis responded so naturally to her. After all her trepidation, she felt very much at ease with him. When she came she felt Louis throbbing within her as they clung to each other in ecstasy. Then she collapsed on Louis and he held her close, kissing her and massaging her breasts gently as he ebbed away. Then, they kissed and kissed as though not really wanting to release each other, before enfolding each other in their embraces and lapsing into a languorous, contented sleep.

It was light when Louis opened his eyes to smile at Jacob, who had brought them coffee. He still held Eleanor close to him, and his smile broadened when he saw Jacob. Jacob shook his head and smiled, wondering whether his wild friend had been caught at last. Was Louis actually in love with this young artist, who had so very much in common with him? That would explain his earlier reticence. Eleanor refused to wake and snuggled down deeper, against Louis' evocatively masculine body. She reached out to stroke the member that had given her so much pleasure, smiling as it swelled proudly at her acknowledgement.

'We've got to get the plane, Elli . . .' Louis whispered.

'Oh, no . . . I don't want to go. Let's stay here, Louis, in Florence . . .' said Eleanor sleepily.

For a beguiling moment, Louis considered this, and then said:

'You've got to get to Art School, Elli . . .'

Elli laughed and emerged, her short hair tousled. How sensible he sounded. She struggled to sit, exchanging a wonderful smile with Jacob before he left.

'Can I come back with you – to go into the Uffizi stores?' she asked.

215

Louis nodded his head seriously and handed her coffee.

Eleanor put her mouth to his ear and whispered:

'Have we got time to make love again, Louis?'

'Oh, there's always time for that, Elli . . .' He smiled at her, and kissed her. 'I'll just go to the bathroom.'

Eleanor drank coffee and looked out of the window at the dome of the cathedral. Her womb ached from Louis' ministrations, but her vagina ached for more. She had never felt so good.

Amy looked at the unashamedly naked Louis as he paused, as if for admiration, at the end of Jacob's bed, waiting for Jacob to come out of the bathroom. Amy obliged and let her look travel over his bronzed body, lingering on his glistening cock, which would, at any moment become fully erect. Louis smiled warmly at her.

'So, Amy . . .' he asked, '*Are* you going to let me paint you when we get home?'

Amy smiled slowly. Their exchanged smile was friendly at last.

'I might,' she teased, glancing at his cock, and then letting her gaze travel up his body to meet his dark eyes. Their eyes remained locked for seconds before Jacob returned and Louis went into the bathroom. Amy enjoyed perusing them as their naked bodies passed familiarly.

'He's going to paint me!' she could not help blurting out to Jacob.

'Well, there's a surprise,' said Jacob, smiling at her evident happiness. Louis!

'He doesn't sleep with his models . . .' he reminded Amy.

Amy smiled. 'I think Elli's cottoned on, at last . . .'

'Yes . . . So, anyway – you'll be at our place quite a lot?'

Amy nodded. 'I look forward to seeing you there, Jake . . .'

Jacob met her smile, and nodded.

'Likewise, Amy,' he agreed as he took her back into his arms and kissed her.

Returning, Louis met his friend's grey eyes, shaking his head affectionately at Jacob, who returned the laughter in his own.

216

Adult Fiction for Lovers from Headline LIAISON

PLEASE TEASE ME	Rebecca Ambrose	£5.99
A PRIVATE EDUCATION	Carol Anderson	£5.99
IMPULSE	Kay Cavendish	£5.99
TRUE COLOURS	Lucinda Chester	£5.99
CHANGE PARTNERS	Cathryn Cooper	£5.99
SEDUCTION	Cathryn Cooper	£5.99
THE WAYS OF A WOMAN	J J Duke	£5.99
FORTUNE'S TIDE	Cheryl Mildenhall	£5.99
INTIMATE DISCLOSURES	Cheryl Mildenhall	£5.99
ISLAND IN THE SUN	Susan Sebastian	£5.99

All (*Group Division*) books are available at your local bookshop, or can be ordered direct from the publisher. Just tick the titles you would like and complete the details below. Prices and availability are subject to change without prior notice.

Please enclose a cheque or postal order made payable to *Bookpoint Ltd*, and send to: (*Group Division*) 39 Milton Park, Abingdon, OXON, OX14 4TD, UK. Email Address: orders@bookpoint.co.uk

If you would prefer to pay by credit card, our call centre team would be delighted to take your order by telephone. Our direct line *01235 400414* (lines open 9.00 am–6.00 pm Monday to Saturday, 24 hour message answering service). Alternatively you can send a fax on *01235 400454*.

TITLE		FIRST NAME		SURNAME	

ADDRESS	
DAYTIME TEL:		POST CODE	

If you would prefer to pay by credit card, please complete:
Please debit my Visa/Access/Diner's Card/American Express (delete as applicable) card number:

Signature .... Expiry Date ....

If you would *NOT* like to receive further information on our products please tick the box. ☐